Vengeful Lies

JANE BLYTHE

Acknowledgments

I'd like to thank everyone who played a part in bringing this story to life. Particularly my mom who is always there to share her thoughts and opinions with me. My wonderful cover designer Letitia who did an amazing job with this stunning cover. My fabulous editor Lisa for all the hard work she puts into polishing my work. My awesome team, Sophie, Robyn, and Clayr, without your help I'd never be able to run my street team. And my fantastic street team members who help share my books with every share, comment, and like!

And of course a big thank you to all of you, my readers! Without you I wouldn't be living my dreams of sharing the stories in my head with the world!

CHAPTER
One

September 1st
8:51 A.M.

This felt wrong.

Cade Charleston sensed it down to his bones.

He shouldn't have come.

Knowing they had no other options right now, that the danger surrounding their family was only growing, and if they didn't find some answers soon things were only going to get worse, meant he'd had no choice but didn't make it any better. He should have found another way. Would have if he'd had more time.

So far, he and his family had been lucky. His younger brother, Cooper, and his now girlfriend, Willow, had been lucky to survive what happened to them in Egypt, and without the intel they'd managed to gather they'd be no closer to proving their mother was innocent. That she was no traitor who had betrayed her husband and her country.

But the price of those answers had almost been Cooper and Willow's lives.

Now, the men behind the conspiracy to frame his mother and stepfather had made attacks on his brother Cole's neighbor, who they mistakenly believed was Cole's girlfriend, and his brother Connor's ex-girlfriend. Luckily, both Susanna and Becca had survived, and each time they gained a tiny piece of intel they hadn't had before.

Not enough though.

Never enough.

Which was why he was there even though every cell in his body screamed at him that this was wrong. That he was making a mistake, one that might not be easily rectifiable.

What choice did he have though?

Allow Becca, whose family had lived across the street from his when they were children and who had practically been part of their family, to come?

Alone at that?

Because those were the instructions she'd been given in the phone call she received last night.

A man who had briefly worked at her charity while living and working in a small village in Cambodia had called her out of the blue. She'd told them that the man had replaced someone else at the last minute and she'd never had a good feeling from him.

That alone would have put them all on edge.

But it wasn't all the man had told her.

He'd claimed he was the half-brother of Cade's baby sister, Cassandra, and he had information on their father that he wanted to pass along to her.

Only a few weeks ago, they'd learned that Cassandra had a different father. Their mother had been gang raped on what would have been her last CIA mission. That one of her assailants had impregnated her and the men responsible for that rape were determined to cover up their crimes by whatever means necessary.

Including having their victim's husband's Delta Force team ambushed and slaughtered then setting her, and the only survivor of that attack, up to take the fall to silence them. Then going after his family when it became clear they were starting to get close enough to find the proof they needed to exonerate their deceased mother's name.

They couldn't pass up the opportunity to meet with him just

because they had no way to corroborate whether this man, who called himself John Jones, was telling them the truth . If he really was Cassandra's half-brother, they'd either have the name of her father or, at least, in the event that John was another product of rape, more intel to put together with what they had.

If the man was lying, then hopefully, Cade could interrogate him and find out who he really was and who had sent him to Cambodia to watch Becca and told him to call her.

Answers.

They were desperate for them.

Desperate enough for him to sit in his car watching the busy parking lot of a local mall where John Jones had told Becca to meet him.

Although Becca had been willing to meet with the man she'd known in Cambodia, even though he'd asked her out several times and made her uncomfortable, the entire family had vetoed it. She was only just recovering from her and Connor's ordeal a week ago, no way were they throwing her right back into the line of fire.

Connor couldn't handle putting the woman he loved, who he'd been missing for twelve long years, in danger again, and honestly, she wasn't the best person to interrogate this John Jones guy anyway. Even if she wore a comms unit and they were in her ear telling her what to say and how to respond, it was much easier for one of them to do it.

Since he was the only single guy left of his four biological brothers he'd volunteered.

Watching Cooper, then Cole, then Connor fall in love had been painful. It dragged-up memories of his beautiful wife. The woman who had seen past his gruff exterior and loved him even when he wasn't all that lovable.

There was a lot of anger inside him, but Gretel hadn't seen any of that.

All she'd seen was him.

She was the best thing to ever happen to him and losing her had almost crushed him.

If he hadn't had a tiny baby girl, not even a year old yet, who was depending on him for literally everything, he very well may have given in to the grief and anger raging inside him.

But Esther was his world, and he had to go on for her.

Right now, what Essie needed the most from him was to clear this threat hanging over the entire family's head. He didn't want his tiny little tornado of energy to grow up under lock and key, kept separate from the rest of the world for her own safety.

He wanted his baby girl to be able to spread those big wings of hers and fly high.

So, he had to sit there, had to fight through the anxiety gnawing at his gut and wait.

There had been no sign of John Jones at the point where Becca had arranged to meet him. Since they had all agreed Becca couldn't go and he would meet with the man who claimed to be Cassandra's brother himself, he had a photo of him so he could recognize him and he was sitting in his car with a clear view of the front doors of the mall where the meeting was supposed to take place.

Minutes ticked by.

His tension mounted.

Nine passed with no signs of the man who was supposed to meet with Becca.

Was John Jones sitting in one of the many cars waiting to catch a glimpse of Becca? Was he unwilling to get out before he saw her in case they played the exact switch-up they had, sending someone else in her place?

Debating whether it was worth it to call Connor and Becca, asking them to go down there, and have Becca pretend she was going to be the one to meet with John long enough to lure him in, he decided it was worth the risk. After all, it wasn't like John could try much of anything with so many people about anyway. Cade pulled out his cell phone and was just about to bring up his brother's number and call it when his phone dinged with a message.

The number was the same one that had called Becca last night.

They'd used their Prey Security resources—one of the benefits of working for the world-renowned company as part of Charlie Team—to try to trace the number. While they'd been able to ping the location as close to this mall where John Jones had asked Becca to meet with him, they hadn't been able to get anything else from the phone. It was one of those prepaid throwaway things that only hinted further that whoever this John guy was he was somehow involved in this whole mess.

How had the man gotten his number?

He'd had Becca's because they'd worked together in Cambodia, and as an employee of her charity he'd had access to her number, but why was John texting him now? Did he somehow know that Becca hadn't come but he'd come in her place?

The sense of foreboding that followed him since Becca got the call last night suddenly surged until he could barely breathe.

Something was wrong.

This was a trap of some sort.

Whether to get their hands on Becca, which they'd been trying to do for the last couple of weeks or because they'd decided to move on to a new target, he had no idea.

Nor did it matter.

Because the words running across his screen as his eyes scanned the message shattered his entire world.

> You should have backed off when you
>
> had the chance
>
> Now it's too late
>
> You'll never see her again
>
> What happens next is up to you
>
> Your daughter can either be killed
>
> quickly and painlessly if you stop looking
>
> for answers, or she can be sold and you'll
>
> wish you stopped while you had the chance

A second after the message came through there was a photo of Essie's nanny Gabriella Sadler's vehicle. It was sitting at a red light, surrounded on all sides by other vehicles.

Cade didn't need to see what was about to happen next, he already knew.

Essie was about to be abducted, Gabriella would likely be killed, and there was nothing he could do to stop it from happening.

~

September 1st
    9:00 A.M.

Gabriella Sadler hesitated as she left the house where she lived with her boss, Cade Charleston, and his four-year-old daughter, Esther.

Something felt wrong.

Only she couldn't put her finger on what exactly it was.

Some might find the choices she'd made for her life unusual, given her age and the vast resources at her disposal. Growing up in the foster system after being taken away from her biological mom, who was an abusive druggie, she'd always wanted a family of her own. While foster care was tough and she'd been bounced around a lot, only adding to her desire to find a place to belong, she had an advantage a lot of other kids in her situation didn't have.

An IQ that tested off the charts.

Something she'd used to her advantage because she firmly believed that in life you had to take what you were given and find a way to work with it.

So she had.

After graduating high school at thirteen, she jumped into college and wound up designing a program that was now part of every major cell phone company in the world. Her program allowed anyone, whether they were the owner of the phone or not, in the vicinity of a phone to call out for help, and her voice-activated program would allow the phone, so long as it was turned on, to automatically send an alert along with a location to the closest emergency services dispatcher.

Of course, some people had abused the system, shouting for help just to see if it would work, but that was to be expected. Her system had also saved thousands of lives, and she was proud of it.

The millions she made selling it had also helped.

Well, helped her financially, but it hadn't given her what she really wanted. Her ex-husband had dumped her after several miscarriages when it started to become clear she probably couldn't give him the heir he so desperately craved.

Alone, still longing for a place to belong, she'd decided to do something completely different with her life and, at twenty-one, had answered an ad to become a nanny for a one-year-old girl whose mom had died from cancer and whose dad needed someone to care for her full-time.

Finally, there she'd found her place.

With Cade and Essie, and the entire Charleston Holloway family. Their fights, struggles, and goals had become her own, and she would always support them any way she could.

Just because her feelings for Cade weren't reciprocated didn't mean she didn't love him, gruff and standoffish though he could be. He loved his baby girl fiercely, and his love for his wife hadn't diminished in the four years since she'd been gone.

She hesitated because she loved this family like they were her own.

If there was one thing she'd learned from being part of this family it was to always trust your gut. Right now, her gut was telling her she should go back inside, lock the doors, and skip the visit to the indoor pool that she'd had to work to convince Cade to let her take Essie to so the little girl didn't have to skip the swimming lesson that she loved.

"Come on, Gabby," Essie complained, tugging at her hand.

"Hold on a minute, cuddle bug," she said, scanning the street.

There didn't appear to be anything out of the ordinary. It looked like it always did, the older couple across the street were out working in their spectacular front yard, there were a couple of kids riding bikes, and a few cars driving up and down the road.

Nothing out of the ordinary.

"It's fine, Gabby, you're just being paranoid," she muttered to herself, a bad habit of hers.

"What's pamanod?" Essie asked, looking up at her with wide gray eyes.

"Not a word for little girls," she replied as she hurried them both down the street, anxious now to be within the relative safety of the car. It was silly, but she didn't want to be out in the open any longer than she had to be, it wasn't safe.

Although she supposed nowhere was really safe for anyone in this family right now and she was part of this family. All the guys were like brothers to her, and she had quickly accepted Willow, Susanna, and Becca as sisters. While the little girl holding her hand might not be her daughter by blood, she'd helped to raise her since she was a year old, and she couldn't have loved Essie more if she'd given birth to her.

"Morning, Ms. Sadler," Gavin greeted her as he opened the back-door for her and Essie to climb in.

Gavin was one of the bodyguards assigned to her and Essie. They had four who worked in pairs for twelve-hour shifts before clocking out. Since Gavin and Dave did the day shifts, she was better acquainted with them and liked them both, although Dave was rather quiet and didn't say much.

"Good morning, Gavin," she returned with a smile as she helped buckle Essie into her car seat. "And I've told you at least a hundred times to call me Gabriella or Gabby."

"Sorry, ma'am," he said with a grin that told her he wasn't going to do that any time soon.

She was chuckling to herself as she sat down and did up her own seatbelt. It was weird having bodyguards. It did make her feel safer as she tried to keep Essie's life as normal as possible while also being sensible and keeping her little charge safe. The threat continued to escalate, and she was sure it wouldn't be long before Cade decided to send them both away somewhere no one could get to them. Most likely that would be to the Delta Team guys where Cade's little sister Cassandra was currently hiding out. Those Delta guys were scary, but they could also be sweet, she'd witnessed that herself with how they treated Essie the handful of times they'd met her.

"Gabby, what game we playin' today?" Essie asked, looking at her expectantly.

Usually, they passed away car trips, even short ones, playing games since she preferred to limit screen time as much as possible. There was a whole wide world out there to explore, so driving in the car was always a time to talk and play games.

"How about we count how many red cars we can spot," she suggested.

"Okay!" Essie enthusiastically agreed.

So that's what they spent the next ten minutes doing. They were up to six when they stopped at a red light. There were only another five minutes to go until they reached the pool, and she could relax a little. It was too busy a place for the men after Cade's family to try anything, and she'd be in the water with Essie while Gavin and Dave watched over them.

"Look, Gabby! Right next to us is a red car," Essie squealed in delight.

"How many does that make now?" she asked.

The four-year-old scrunched up her nose as she thought. "Umm ... nine?"

"Not quite. Let's try again, we'll use our fingers." When she held up both hands Essie copied her. "Okay, so we already had, one, two, three, four, five, six," she said, putting up one finger for each number. "Now let's add one more. How many does that make? Count them again if you're not sure."

Looking at her little fingers, Essie counted. "One, two, three, four, five, six, seven. Seven. Seven red cars," she said excitedly.

"That's right, you're getting so good at addition," she encouraged. While she had no formal degree in childcare and no idea what had prompted Cade to hire her when she was sure there were more qualified candidates, she'd worked hard to learn about child development and ensure she was the best nanny Essie could have.

Leaning over to tickle the little girl's tummy, she caught sight of a car stopping in the middle of the street crossing theirs that currently had the green light.

"What a terrible place to break down," she said absently.

"Stay in the car, Ms. Sadler," Gavin instructed, his tone hard and unyielding.

Before she could ask what he meant, he climbed out and pulled out his weapon.

Four men spilled out of the large SUV she thought had broken down. They were all dressed in black, their faces were covered with ski masks, and they held weapons.

A kidnapping attempt.

The people after Cade's family had decided to come for little Essie.

In a panic, she realized there was nowhere for them to go as she looked around. They were in the middle lane, three cars were ahead of them and at least a few behind them. They were trapped and outnumbered.

Gunfire erupted around them, car horns honked, people screamed, cars took off, some hitting each other as drivers panicked and tried to get away.

Outside the car Gavin dropped, blood covering his body and spreading, his eyes already wide and vacant in death.

Dave cursed as he got out of the car, returning fire.

It did no good.

He dropped too.

Leaving her and Essie all alone.

Gabriella reached over and unbuckled Essie, wondering if she could slip away with the little girl in the chaos around them.

"Stay with me, don't make a sound, and do what I say," she told the little girl staring in shock at the carnage around them. The poor child was going to be traumatized for life.

Opening her door, Gabriella climbed out, taking Essie with her. Eyeing up their options, she decided they would head back down the line of cars behind them and then head into the nearest store.

They made it three cars down before the men in black were there, surrounding them. Grabbing Essie and ripping the child from her arms.

She screamed and fought.

She couldn't let them take the girl.

Essie was only four, so young, so small, so vulnerable.

A blow to the side of her head stunned her, but Gabriella shoved aside the pain and dizziness and kept fighting with everything she had.

"Bring her with us," a voice ordered, and she was snatched off her feet and both she and Essie were carried back to the SUV.

Inside, she was shoved down in the space behind the passenger seat. With the man who had grabbed her sitting on the back seat, it left her barely any room, even less when the door was slammed closed beside her. On her other side, a sobbing Essie had been shoved down between the backseat and the driver's seat, two other large men sitting side by side on the backseat as the last jumped into the passenger seat and the SUV sped off, tires squealing.

In less than two minutes her entire life had changed.

Had ended.

Because she feared neither she nor Essie were getting out of this alive.

But if there was a chance, even a small one, that she could save the little girl she loved, she would take it. Cade had already lost his wife, and she would do everything within her power to make sure he didn't lose his daughter as well.

No matter the cost to herself.

CHAPTER *Two*

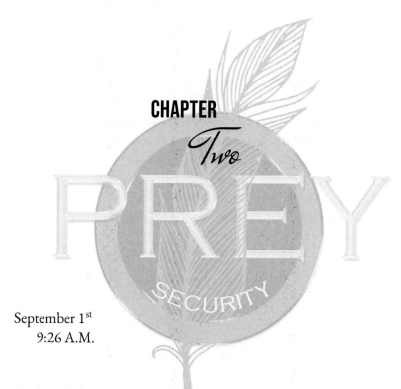

September 1st
9:26 A.M.

As though his presence could change the outcome, Cade screeched his car to a stop outside where cops were rolling out crime scene tape to keep people out of what looked like the set of an action movie.

There were crashed cars littered about.

Blood was smeared on the asphalt.

And he could see white sheets covering bodies.

Whose bodies?

Essie?

Gabriella?

The bodyguards?

Innocent bystanders?

Panic coursed through him as he shoved open his car door and jumped out. Not bothering to waste time closing it, he ran to the closest officer.

Thankfully he knew the man who seemed surprised to see him there. "Cade, is this related to Prey?"

"No. Personal," he muttered. Much too personal. As personal as it got.

He knew he should have said no when Gabriella asked if she could take Essie to her swimming lesson. It wasn't safe. Nowhere was safe, but he hadn't wanted to send his little girl away to live with people she barely knew.

That desire to keep Essie close and keep her life as normal as possible could have wound up costing his daughter her life.

If she died, he'd never forgive himself.

Never forgive Gabriella.

There was no way he should have allowed himself to be talked into letting Essie go to the pool. She could miss a few weeks of swimming lessons, and he was sure Gabriella could have kept her distracted and she never would have even thought about the pool.

Dragging his hand down his face he knew it wasn't Gabriella's fault.

It was his.

He was the dad.

Giving him a sympathetic nod, the cop lifted the tape to allow him to pass under it and now that he was this close to the carnage, Cade found that he could barely force his feet to move.

His steps slowed until he moved so slowly that he may as well be going backward. If it was his daughter's body under that sheet he was going to lose it.

The only reason he had survived losing Gretel was because of Essie. His sweet little daughter was his reason for living. In so many ways she reminded him of her mom, and he loved seeing her grow and learn new skills. She was so confident, bright, warm, loving, and caring. She was funny and silly and rarely threw tantrums.

Essie was perfect.

There was no way she could be gone.

The cops standing near the bodies looked over at him as he approached, one he knew, one he didn't. The one he didn't started toward him, his hand hovering by his weapon, but his voice was calm and confident when he spoke.

"You can't be here, sir," the man said in a tone that brokered no argument.

"It's okay, we know him," the woman said, stepping up beside her partner. "I didn't know Prey was going to be here."

"Personal," he said, hating that word more each time he had to speak it aloud. "How many dead?"

"Just two," the woman officer replied. "There were a few minor injuries, but all witnesses are saying that the shooters were targeting this vehicle specifically. I'm guessing you know why."

Unfortunately, he did.

Two dead gave him hope though.

The bodies under the sheets seemed too large to belong to either his little daughter or Gabriella, and the text he'd received had said they intended to kidnap Essie not kill her, but he couldn't allow himself to believe it until he had confirmation.

Kneeling beside the closest body, he reached out a hand that trembled slightly and pulled back the sheet.

Relief rushed out of him in a harsh breath.

It wasn't his little girl.

Not that Dave deserved a death like this.

Knowing he had to do it, he covered the man's body back up and rounded the car to the other side.

This time he was able to pull back the sheet without shaking. Gavin's body lay beneath it, riddled with bullets just like his partner's had been. These were two good men, men who didn't deserve to be gunned down in the street just because three rich, powerful men thought they got to play God with other people's lives and do whatever they wanted.

Rage clogged his throat making it almost impossible to breathe.

"You know them?" the female cop asked gently.

"Yeah. They were hired to watch my daughter and her nanny."

"Witnesses said an SUV pulled up, blocking traffic. Four men got out and fired at this vehicle. A woman and a little girl tried to run but they were grabbed and taken by the men in the SUV," the male cop informed him.

Did it make him the most horrible human being ever to be glad that Gabriella had been abducted too?

Cade knew it did. Gabriella was everything he could have hoped for in a nanny for his daughter. Given the nature of his job, he needed someone he could trust to step in and be a parent to his child when he was traveling. Not only did Gabriella parent Essie, but she actually loved his daughter every bit as much as he did.

He was lucky to have her, but he never went out of his way to make sure she knew that.

If anyone was going to do everything within their power to protect his daughter it was Gabriella, but it was a lot to ask of her. She was young, almost a decade younger than him, and she didn't need the job, he knew she was worth millions. Yet she stayed, worked hard, gave Essie everything she had to give, baked, did crafts, and got down on the floor and played with Lego and dolls. They made puppets and put on shows, went to the park, and made frequent trips to the beach. They went to swimming lessons, ballet classes, and gymnastics. Gabriella even coached a soccer team for Essie and her friends.

Now because of him and his family and their quest for answers, she'd been abducted. Her life was on the line, and unlike with Essie, their kidnappers had no reason to keep her alive.

She was expendable.

"Cade!"

Shoving to his feet he saw Cole and Jax running toward him. As soon as he'd gotten the message telling him they were going after his daughter, he'd sent out a text in the group chat to let his brothers know that not only had the meeting with John Jones been a bust, but that Essie was being targeted.

"She's not here," he told his brothers as he walked toward them.

"Gabriella?" Cole asked.

"Gone as well," he replied as guilt surged inside him. Guilt for blaming Gabriella even for a second, guilt for not firing her the second he realized these people were ruthless and would go after anyone, guilt for not sending both Essie and Gabriella away someplace safe, guilt for being glad she was still with his daughter.

"This was pretty ballsy," Jax said, looking around the scene. "Taking a woman and child in broad daylight like this, right out in the open, with a whole ton of witnesses. Takes a whole lot of guts to do that."

"Whole lot of determination and a whole lot of money," Cole added.

"We're going to need security footage," Cade said, turning around and noting that three of the four businesses on the corners of the intersections appeared to have cameras. He needed to contact Prey's Cyber Team and get them tracking the vehicle on every camera they could find. They needed to track where Essie and Gabriella had been taken before anyone laid a hand on his precious little girl.

"We need to talk to the witnesses as well, get everything out of them that we can," Jax said.

A couple of dozen people were hanging about, another half dozen police officers working their way through questioning them all. It would take hours to interview all of them and hours for Prey to access all cameras in the area in an attempt to follow the SUV that had been used in the abduction.

Too long.

Longer than Essie and Gabriella had.

For six weeks, the men who had raped his mom and set her up as a traitor to try to silence her and get her out of the way had been trying to get to them. For six weeks they kept failing. Cole and Susanna had survived being targeted, as had Connor and Becca. These men were getting desperate. They knew his family was doubling down on safety and that trying something risky like this was the only way to get to them.

Now they had an innocent little girl at their disposal.

What better way to manipulate him and his family into backing off than causing injury to a helpless child.

If they hurt his daughter, would he be able to keep up this hunt for answers?

Cade loved his mother, and he harbored a lot of guilt over how he'd treated her those last few months when she remarried Jake and Jax's dad. Because of his anger, his younger brothers had also treated their mom badly. That was on him, and he'd vowed after her death to be a better role model.

As much as he loved his mother, Essie was his daughter, and she was only a little girl, virtually nothing more than a baby. Nothing was more important than her, and he would do anything to protect her.

Including backing off and leaving his mother's name forever tarnished.

~

September 1st
11:58 A.M.

They'd been driving in circles for so long, switching vehicles multiple times, that Gabriella was completely turned around and could no longer figure out where they were or where they might be going.

It didn't help that with each vehicle change, she'd been shoved down into the same cramped position between the front passenger seat and the back seat, crammed in between the legs of the man occupying the back seat.

Forced to sit as she was, she was painfully aware of the fact that the man's legs were spread and there was a bulge in his pants. One she was sure that sooner or later she was going to be made to address.

From the smirk on the man's face, he knew it too.

And he couldn't wait.

At some point, maybe after the third vehicle change but she couldn't quite remember anymore, all the men had removed their ski masks.

That wasn't a good thing.

Gabriella knew enough to know that.

If they were okay with her and Essie seeing their faces, it meant they weren't worried about either of them being able to give the cops details on their descriptions.

Because they weren't going to be talking to any cops.

They wouldn't be able to.

They'd be dead.

Still, if there was a chance, however miniscule, that she could save Essie's life, or at least buy enough time for Cade and the others to find them, she was going to take it. Nothing was more important to her than that little girl's life.

If she didn't make it out of this alive, she wouldn't be leaving behind anyone important. Just a biological father who probably didn't know she existed, a biological mom who cared more about drugs and alcohol than her child and could have already put herself in an early grave, foster parents who had been ambivalent toward her, and an ex-husband who didn't think she was good enough because she couldn't produce him a child.

The closest thing she'd ever had to a family was Cade's family. They'd accepted her immediately and without reservation. Watching them, she'd learned what unconditional love looked like, and for that, she would be forever grateful.

In return, she had to repay them by doing everything in her power to save Essie.

"Gabby, I have to pee," Essie wailed in desperation. It wasn't the first time the little girl had asked, but both previous times, the men had refused to stop the vehicle and let her find a bathroom for the child.

Since she'd been Essie's nanny for almost four years, she knew what that tone meant.

It meant they had about five minutes at the most before she was going regardless of whether she was sitting on a toilet or not.

"Okay, cuddle bug," she soothed, mustering calm she definitely did not feel in an effort to keep the little girl's terror to a minimum. Then she mustered a little courage and looked at the man whose legs she was sitting between. "She's desperate. If you don't let her go, she won't be able to hold it more than a couple more minutes."

"I'm not sitting in a car filled with urine," the man in the passenger seat snapped in irritation. "Let the kid go to the bathroom."

"I'm not stopping now," the driver snapped back. "It's three minutes tops until we get to our location. The kid can hold it. The kid *better* hold it," he added, and she heard the threat in his voice even if it passed over Essie's head.

If Essie didn't hold it, she was going to be punished.

"Baby, can you hold on just three more minutes?" Gabriella looked over at the terrified little girl, wishing she could pull her into her arms.

But the couple of times she'd tried she'd been rewarded with a hard slap to the face. Not that she minded being struck, she'd take anything to protect her little charge, but each time she got hit, Essie got progressively more agitated. Now she reached out a hand to the girl. "That's not even as long as it takes to count to two hundred. Can you wait that long, baby?"

"Not a baby." Essie huffed. If there was one thing the little girl hated above all else, it was being treated like she wasn't the big girl she believed herself to be.

"I know you're not, cuddle bug. That's how I know you can wait just a few more minutes. How about we count together?" Essie was so smart and she loved numbers and words. Even though she wasn't supposed to start kindergarten for another couple of days, she could already write several words by herself and knew all her letters. She could count all the way to one hundred with hardly any help, and she knew some simple addition and subtraction.

"O-okay," Essie agreed.

"There's my good little cuddle bug. We'll count together, you ready?" When Essie nodded, they began.

They reached one hundred and thirty-two before the vehicle finally stopped outside a large warehouse. There was nothing else around other than another three warehouses that looked exactly the same as this one, and she was pretty sure that whoever had organized their abduction owned them all.

Running in broad daylight with five armed men in the car, and another who knew how many more inside would be pointless.

But she wasn't giving up.

She'd find a way to protect Essie no matter what she had to do.

As soon as the man sitting before her got out of the vehicle, she scrambled out so he didn't get a chance to reach in and grab her, then hurried around to Essie's side of the car. The man who had been sitting with her had picked the little girl up, but Gabriella didn't hesitate to reach out and snatch the child into her arms.

"Where's the bathroom?" she asked.

"Follow me," the man who had been holding Essie ordered, and she did.

He led them inside, past a couple of closed doors that likely led to offices or smaller storage rooms, and then to a bathroom.

With no time to waste, she set the girl on her feet and lifted the lid. "Do you have to stay in the room with us?" she asked the man still standing in the open doorway.

In response, he merely smirked, leaned his shoulder against the door jamb, and crossed his arms over his chest.

Gabriella would love nothing more than to smack that smirk right off his face, but because she knew that would be stupid, angering these men was only going to make things worse for Essie, she turned her back on him and stood so she was blocking his view of the little girl.

Essie had already stripped off the dress she'd put on over the little girl's swimsuit, so she leaned over and helped Essie pull the swimsuit down so she could climb up onto the toilet. The child sighed in relief as she did her business, and Gabriella was so proud of her. Essie had inherited her dad's strength, and it was the only thing that was going to get her through this mess and out the other side.

"You did so good, cuddle bug," she told the child.

"I never helded it so long afore," Essie told her.

"You haven't. That's because you're almost five," she said, brushing a wisp of baby-fine hair from Essie's face. The little girl's skin was warm and blotchy, her eyes red from crying, but so far, she'd done everything Gabriella had asked of her. She prayed that continued.

"I don't want to stay here, Gabby," Essie said in a loud whisper she was sure the man watching them could overhear. "I wants to go to my swimming lesson, and then I wants to have milkshakes likes we always does. Then I want to go home, and I want to finish choosing my cake for my birthday. I don't want to miss my unicorn party."

"Oh, cuddle bug, you won't," she lied. Essie's fifth birthday was only three weeks away, but she could not ensure they would be found and rescued—or even still alive—by the time Essie's birthday rolled around. "I promise you, I will do everything I have to do to make sure you don't miss spending your birthday with your daddy, at your unicorn party, with all of your friends."

Because she was only four and so very trusting, Essie nodded, and she helped the girl off the toilet, then helped her get her swimsuit and dress back on after she'd wiped herself. Then she flushed the toilet, washed their hands, and lifted the little girl into her arms, wanting Essie as safe as she could make her.

As she walked back over to the man in the doorway, he straightened and reached out to palm the bulge in his pants. Keeping Essie's head tucked against her shoulder so she didn't have to explain any grown-up things to the four-year-old, she met the man's dark eyes with a fearful gaze.

"You want to protect the kid, I'm sure we can all come to some sort of arrangement," the man told her with another smirk.

Gabriella gulped. Knowing exactly what arrangement he wanted to make with her and praying she was strong enough to hold up her end of the bargain.

She had to be.

For Essie.

For Cade.

CHAPTER
Three

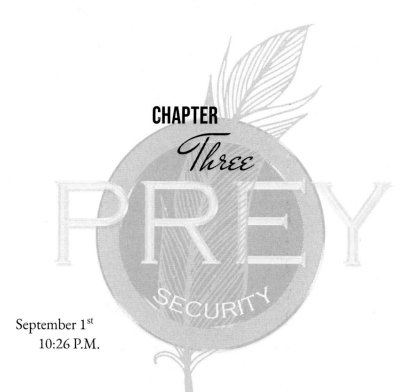

September 1st
10:26 P.M.

Never in his life had thirteen hours felt like a lifetime.

There had been times when Cade had thought he was going to die. Being a pararescueman was not a job for the faint-hearted, and his life had been on the line many more times than he'd admitted to his wife.

There had also been a time when he'd been forced to sit beside his ill wife's bedside as he watched her fade away a little more each day.

In all those instances, it felt as though time was dragging, that seconds felt like hours, hours felt like days, and days felt like weeks.

But it had never felt like this.

Putting his life on the line had been his choice. Knowing the dangers his job would entail he'd taken them on because he believed what he was doing was important. Same thing when he'd gone to work for Prey. What he did saved lives, and it was worth the risk.

As hard as watching Gretel waste away from cancer had been, they had decided together when they found out she had cancer just three weeks after learning she was pregnant, that she would put off treatment and try to carry their baby to term. It wasn't a decision he would force on other people, but it had been right for them. Even though they had known that with an aggressive form of cancer, it was unlikely Gretel would survive, he would never regret having his daughter, even as he missed his wife with a pain that had dulled over the years but would never leave him.

Now, with his precious little girl in the hands of men who wouldn't hesitate to hurt her even though she was only four years old and was completely innocent, every second felt like an eternity.

One eternity on top of another until it felt like he was losing his mind.

Cade sat in his empty house, alone, staring into space, with barely enough energy to breathe let alone do anything. While his family had been worried about him and hadn't wanted to leave him alone, he'd insisted that he needed some time to himself to try to decompress, get his head on straight, and figure out how to get his daughter back alive.

In the thirteen hours since the abduction, he and his brothers had talked to every witness who had been there at the time. They'd gone through every piece of security footage they could recover. No matter how horrific it had been watching his tiny daughter being kidnapped and stuffed into the back of an SUV, he'd watched it over and over again, trying to see something that would tell him the identities of the men who had taken Essie from him.

They had a detailed picture of what had happened, but in the end, they didn't know anything that mattered.

There were no names and no location.

This meant his daughter was lost out there, scared, and he wasn't there to comfort her, to make everything better.

That was his job, and he was failing at it.

Already he'd failed his wife and hadn't been able to save her even though his logical mind knew her cancer was just too aggressive and that even if she hadn't carried her pregnancy to term, it was unlikely she would have survived. Now he was failing their daughter. His final words to Gretel had been telling her how much he loved her and promising to raise a daughter she would be proud of.

Anger, grief, and fear warred inside him.

The grief was the worst because he felt like it was a betrayal of Essie. Thinking about her being gone when she was still alive, imagining how empty his life would be without her when there was still a chance he could get her back.

The fear was almost paralyzing. All he wanted to do was scream and rage at the universe for taking from him all he had left.

The anger wound up adding shame to the list. It wasn't Gabriella's fault that Essie had been in the car. Just because she'd convinced him to let her take Essie to the pool didn't negate the fact that he'd agreed. Blaming her in any way was unfair especially given he'd seen how she'd tried to protect his child.

Feeling like he was moments away from spinning out of control, Cade threw the glass in his hand across the room, getting a tiny sliver of release when it exploded and shattered into hundreds of pieces, littering the floor of the room that was too full of Essie. While Gabriella always kept their home clean and tidy, there were signs of his almost kinder-gartener everywhere. Her toys were packed neatly away in her toy box and on the shelves that lined one living room wall. Her artwork covered the refrigerator, a pile of her clean laundry sat on the kitchen table, waiting to be taken upstairs and put away, a half-started craft project sat on the counter, ready to be finished after lunch.

It was too much.

He couldn't be in this room a second longer.

Snatching up Essie's favorite teddy bear, one he and Gretel had picked out when they found out she was expecting but before the diag-nosis, he headed for the stairs. Despite being five years old, the toy was in good condition, its light brown fur still soft, its eyes and nose still intact, Essie loved Winkie-Bear and took such good care of it.

If it had been any other day other than swimming lesson day, the stuffed animal would have been with Essie. She rarely went anywhere without it, but Gabriella had convinced her that pool days were days Winkie-Bear would be happier at home.

Clutching the teddy in his hands, Cade fought against the idea that this might be all he would have left of his daughter. This teddy bear and a bunch of other toys and clothes that all smelled like his child and reminded him of her and the times they'd shared together, but were such a pale comparison to the real thing.

When he reached the second floor, heading for Essie's bedroom, he found himself pausing in the open doorway to Gabriella's room. Because he could be gone for days or weeks at a time it had made sense for the nanny to live with them to make it easier and less disruptive for Essie. This room was smaller than the master, but it had its own bathroom which meant Gabriella had her own space. Now as he stood in the doorway looking around it, he was overcome with the sweet honey scent that was so intrinsically Gabby.

Like how she kept the house, her room was neat and tidy, a huge four poster bed piled high with fluffy pillows and a lacy white bedspread that matched the curtains. There was an antique roll-top desk and a bookcase with a rocking chair beside it. Butter yellow was her favorite color, and accents of it around the room made it seem even more like her.

Sitting in the middle of the bed was an old ragdoll. She'd told him once that it was the only thing she still had left from her biological mom, and she'd taken that doll with her to every foster home she'd lived in, then to college, and then to the home she'd shared with her ex. Now, it sat alone on the bed, and he was struck for the first time by how truly lonely Gabriella's childhood must have been.

No matter what had gone on in his life, he'd always had an amazing family at his back.

Gabriella had no one.

Well, she used to have no one. But now she had him and his family.

Before he even realized what he was doing, his feet carried him over to the bed and he snatched up the ragdoll and held it and Essie's teddy against his chest as he headed back into the hall.

There were so many things he wished he'd said to Gabriella when he had the chance. Had he ever made sure she knew how much he valued her and what she brought to Essie's life? Had he ever actually said the words to her rather than assuming she knew? Had he made sure that she understood she wasn't just his employee, she was a part of his family, and his daughter loved her like a mother?

Had he ever let on that the feelings he knew she had for him but never let on that he was aware of weren't as unreciprocated as he allowed her to believe?

That one he knew the answer to.

He hadn't.

He'd always been content to let her think that it was one-sided, that he wasn't even aware that she was infatuated with him, because if he acknowledged it aloud, he might have to give into his feelings.

That was something he couldn't allow himself to do.

He'd already lost one woman he loved, and he had a little girl, letting himself get involved with someone else wasn't on the table.

Not even the woman he'd fallen asleep thinking about more nights than he should, who'd starred in more dreams than he could count, who loved his daughter like her own.

It made him a jerk, but it also kept him safe.

Safe, but as he held Gabriella's doll beside his daughter's teddy, he knew he'd also cost both of them a chance at happiness.

~

September 2nd
    5:06 A.M.

Literally, the only reason she wasn't panicking was because of the little girl sleeping restlessly in her arms.

Without Essie's presence and her desire to do her best to keep the child as calm as possible, Gabriella was under no doubt that she would be a sobbing, hysterical mess.

But she couldn't fall apart.

Because if she fell apart then Essie would follow.

Yesterday, after Essie's trip to the bathroom, they'd been locked up in an empty room. There were no windows, no furniture, nothing for them to do but sit and wait. For what she wasn't sure yet. They'd been taken for a reason. Well, Essie had, she'd been taken more than likely to provide a little entertainment for the men who had abducted them, but so far, no one had asked anything of her.

No food had been delivered, and she would have been tempted to think they'd been left alone and all the men had gone, only when Essie next decided she needed the bathroom, she'd hammered on the door and called out, just to see what would happen. Her calls had been answered, and she'd been allowed to take the little girl to the toilet again.

This time, she'd gone as well, and they'd both drunk some water from the sink because she wasn't sure if the men were going to feed them. It turned out to be a good idea because no one had dropped off any food or water for them.

Since she was wearing her watch, Gabriella knew they were approaching the twenty-hour mark of when they'd been taken. Honestly, she'd expected something more to have happened by now.

Wasn't the point of kidnapping his daughter supposed to send Cade crazy and make him compliable?

Cade.

Her heart ached for him.

He'd already lost so much and now his little girl was in danger.

It was her fault. She should have listened when he said it was too dangerous for Essie to be out and about. She'd been too focused on trying to make sure Essie didn't realize what was going on and didn't develop fears and anxieties because of being locked away.

What she should have done was trust Cade.

This was what he did, and it was his daughter.

"I'm sorry, cuddle bug," she whispered as she smoothed a sleeping Essie's braids.

Because there was no furniture, nowhere comfortable for them to sleep, and no coverings in the chilled room, she'd stripped off the light jacket she'd been wearing, and the sundress she'd thrown on over her swimsuit, and used them as bedding for the child. It left her chilled but at least she had Essie's warm body snuggled in her arms.

Safe.

"I'll try to keep her safe for you, Cade. I promise I'll do my best."

While she did her best not to make it obvious, she was hopelessly in love with Cade Charleston. Watching how he was with his daughter was like watching the sunshine come out on a cloudy day. That gruff expression he usually wore disappeared, and he wasn't embarrassed to get dressed up like a fairy princess, have makeup parties, or pretend to be a unicorn that Essie could ride.

He was loyal and protective of those he loved. The way he'd stepped up to help care for his younger siblings after their parents' deaths, the way he fought to get justice for his mom, even how he was with her. Although he could be a grumpypants, he paid her well, didn't treat her like the help, and was respectful even when all she wanted him to do was haul her into his arms and kiss her like she'd dreamed about so many times.

But he could never be hers.

Not really.

And one day he wouldn't need help with Essie anymore.

Already the little girl would be starting school, and soon, she would be old enough to take care of herself. Cade would still travel sometimes for Prey and Essie would need to be looked after during that time, but three of Cade's brothers had fallen in love and would no doubt be looking to start families. That meant there would be plenty of people who could take her in when her dad was away.

No matter how badly she wished it wasn't true, the reality was that she wasn't a part of the Charleston Holloway family.

Time was running out for her as much as she'd been pretending it wasn't, and she didn't know what her life was going to look like without Essie and Cade in it.

"Gabby?" Essie's sleepy voice focused her thoughts on the little girl depending on her.

"Right here, cuddle bug," she said, touching a kiss to Essie's forehead, so very glad the men had taken her, too, so this little girl wasn't all alone.

"I'm hungry," Essie complained, opening her big, gray eyes. "And I miss Daddy, and Winkie-Bear."

"I know you do." She wished so desperately that there was something she could do, but unfortunately, she couldn't fix any of those problems. She had no food and no way of getting the child back home where she belonged.

"Maybe we can play a game, distract you from that grumbly tumbly," she teased, pasting on a smile, and tickling Essie's tummy, managing to get a giggle out of her. At least she'd been able to keep the little girl occupied the day before by playing game after game. They also sang songs, and Gabriella had weaved stories for the child. When it reached Essie's bedtime, she'd sung the girl to sleep just like she usually did.

Sometimes, when she was sitting on the edge of Essie's bed, singing to her Cade would come and stand in the doorway, listening. When they put her to bed together, he'd always sit back after he'd read his daughter a story and waited for her to sing.

At first, she used to get self-conscious. She was an okay singer but nothing special, still the way he looked at her ... she could have sworn the love she felt for him wasn't quite as unrequited as she believed.

"Can we do thumb wars?" Essie asked, perking up, her rumbling tummy forgotten as she held out her hand.

"Course we can." Gabriella sat up, too, crossing her legs as she faced the little girl, but before they could start, the door to their room was opened, and two of the men she recognized from the abduction stood there eyeing her up like she was a piece of meat.

"Morning," one of them drawled, his heated gaze roaming her barely covered body. Since she was dressed in only her swimsuit and it was cold in there, she knew her nipples were pebbled. Both men stared at her chest, and the one who hadn't spoken ran his tongue along his bottom lip.

"Thought you might want to come and get some breakfast," tongue man spoke.

While his words sounded innocent enough, his expression had nausea churning in her stomach. But she had to get food for Essie and take care of the child. It was her job, but more than that, she loved the little girl.

Slowly she stood, fighting against the fear that urged her to grab Essie and run. That wasn't going to work though, so she locked her knees together, forced a smile to her lips, and faced Essie. "I'll be right back, okay?"

"I don't want you to go," Essie said, her fear evident.

"It's going to be okay, cuddle bug. I'm just going to get us some breakfast." Infusing confidence and calm into her tone worked, and Essie gave her a nod, her fingers clutching at the jacket she'd used as a blanket.

"Pinkie swear?" Essie asked.

Leaning down she held up her pinkie. "Pinkie swear."

Following the men out of the room, they locked the door behind them and led her into a larger room where the rest were waiting for them, plus a sixth who hadn't been in the car the day before. There were piles of food strewn about, not anything she'd usually make for breakfast, but there was some fruit, and a couple of loaves of bread, enough for her to feed her little charge.

"Bet the kid is hungry," one said, shooting her a smarmy smile.

"What are you willing to do to feed her?" another asked, grabbing his crotch and squeezing.

Gabriella gulped, and her voice shook when she answered. "Anything."

"Down on your knees," the man who had sat before her in the vehicles yesterday said as he stalked toward her.

Her entire body shook and she wanted to scream at these disgusting men that she wasn't going to do what they wanted. But she couldn't. Because the little girl she loved was sitting in a room waiting for her to bring back food for her. It had been almost twenty-four hours since they'd last eaten, and her stomach was cramping badly, she knew Essie's would be the same.

There was no other choice.

No way out.

Fighting back a sob she dropped down to her knees. Chuckles and hollers sounded around her, but she couldn't look at the men or she'd lose her nerve. Instead, she stared at the floor.

Watched as a pair of boots appeared before her.

The sound of a zipper opening had her lifting her head to find a penis right in front of her.

Try as she might, she couldn't make her lips part to take it inside.

When she didn't move, rough hands tangled in her long red hair, and gripped her face hard enough to squeeze her cheeks and her mouth popped open.

As he stuffed his length inside it, making her gag, tears trickled down her cheeks. Gabriella felt like she was selling her soul to the devil but so long as what she was buying was food and protection for Essie, she would pay whatever price was asked.

CHAPTER

Four

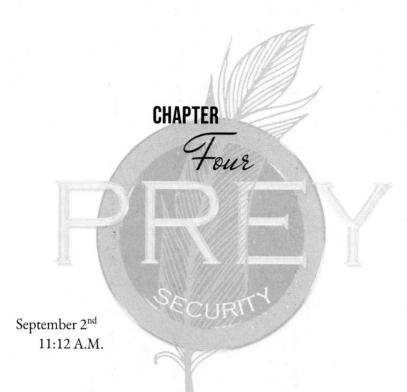

September 2nd
11:12 A.M.

"How is that possible?" Cade roared into the phone.

Only one thing had kept him going the last twenty-six hours, and that was that he believed in Prey. Believed in their skills and resources, believed in the men and women who worked for the world-renowned company, believed they were the best of the best, and believed that if anyone could locate his daughter and bring her home, it was them.

Now those beliefs were being smashed to smithereens.

"I'm sorry, Cade," Olivia Oswald said on the other end of the line.

"I don't want you to be sorry," he snapped at Olivia, the wife of Prey's founder and CEO, legendary former SEAL, Eagle.

Part of his brain registered that he was being harsh with the wrong people, that Olivia and the rest of the team working for Prey's cyber division were doing their best. If he got Olivia offside then he got Eagle offside, since the man adored his wife. Getting on the wrong side of Eagle Oswald was like getting on the wrong side of the President. The man had connections everywhere and had billions of dollars at his disposal, money he wasn't afraid to use to get what he wanted.

It wasn't keeping his job Cade was worried about. He would gladly give up anything in the world if he had to. It was fear that if he alienated Olivia and thus Eagle, he was cutting off what he still thought was his best chance at getting Essie back.

"I want you to find where my daughter is," he said into the phone, a thread of desperation in his tone. Not that there was any point in hiding it. Olivia was a mother. She and Eagle had a four-year-old daughter, Luna, and a one-year-old son, Apollo. If anyone could empathize with his feelings right now, he knew it was her.

"I'm doing everything I can, I promise you I am. I can't imagine how hard this is for you, Cade, if I'm being perfectly honest, I don't even want to. Essie is the same age as Luna, and if someone took my daughter from me, I don't think I'd be able to breathe." Olivia paused and he could hear her dragging in a ragged breath. "I'm sorry. I know I let you down, but I can't find them."

Not what he wanted to hear.

If Olivia and Raven Oswald and the rest of their team couldn't find his daughter, who could?

The answer to that question hung heavily over him, slowly smothering him to death in the worst possible way.

"I don't understand," he snapped, the fear and anger inside him too big to contain. "How could you lose them? You already followed them to three other vehicles, there is no way they could have just disappeared."

Even though she'd already been over this with him several times, Olivia's voice was completely patient when she spoke. "They had this well planned. The first vehicle change was just around the corner from the abduction site. They didn't want to spend long in that SUV because they knew the cops would be looking for it almost immediately. They basically drove in circles around the city and changed two more times over the course of almost three hours before they went into an underground parking lot at a mall. They obviously did another vehicle change there, but it wasn't caught on camera. I'm so sorry, Cade, but my team and I can't track every single vehicle that entered and left the mall yesterday—"

"You can and you will," he bellowed into the phone.

"Enough," a voice barked in his ear.

No longer was he speaking to Olivia, it seemed Eagle had taken over, and he wasn't going to stand by and let anyone talk to his wife disrespectfully.

"I'm cutting you some slack, Cade, because of what you're going through, but nobody talks to my wife like that. My wife who didn't come home last night and tuck her children into bed and kiss them goodnight because she stayed at the office working on finding your child," Eagle said, making him feel bad. Olivia must have been aching to hold her children close, the reminder of how precarious life could be fresh in her mind. But she hadn't done that because she was determined to help Essie and Gabriella.

"It's okay, Eagle," he could hear Olivia's faint voice in the background. "Give me back the phone."

Eagle grumbled something but must have handed the phone back to his wife because her voice was louder and clearer when she spoke.

"If you'd let me finish, I was saying we can't track every single vehicle that entered and left the mall yesterday in only a few hours. I have everyone working overtime, and we will find which car they left in, and we'll keep tracking it until we find where they took your daughter. No one is giving up on Essie or on Gabriella. I know I have no right to say this when my babies are safe at home, but the best thing you can do for your daughter right now is do your best to hold it together. I can only imagine how hard that must be, but only clear heads are going to be able to figure this out."

Somehow, her words seemed to penetrate the blanket of fear surrounding him and he drew in a deep breath.

Olivia was right.

If he didn't hold it together, he might lose his chance at getting his daughter and Gabriella back.

No way was he going to fail either of them.

"Thank you. I know you're doing everything you can," he told Olivia because it was true. Losing faith in Prey now would be the same as throwing out his parachute right before jumping out of a plane. There was no way to guarantee he'd land safely even if he had the parachute, but without it, all he would be facing was certain death.

Somehow, he had to find a way to hold onto hope.

No matter how impossible it seemed.

"I promise I'll call you the second I know anything, and if I can't then Raven will, or one of the others," Olivia vowed.

"I appreciate that."

"You're not in this alone, Cade. Prey is a family, and you have all of us at your back. Essie and Gabriella aren't alone either. We're all fighting for them, and you know no one on this Earth besides yourself would fight harder for your little girl than Gabriella. She adores Essie."

What Olivia didn't say, wouldn't under these circumstances, was that Gabriella didn't only adore Essie. For some reason, she seemed to see beneath his often-harsh exterior to the man underneath. The man he might have been if he hadn't been consumed by guilt over how he'd treated his mother in the months leading up to her death, if he hadn't lost his wife, if his world wasn't filled with darkness.

Cade had no idea why or how she did it, but Gabriella just saw him.

It was refreshing and he'd selfishly indulged in the way she made him feel when he knew he had nothing to offer her in return.

Now, because of him, she'd been kidnapped, and while he knew she would absolutely do exactly what Olivia had just said and fight as hard as she could to protect his daughter in any way she could, he wondered what exactly the cost to her would be.

Uneasiness settled inside him.

Selfish as it was, Essie was his daughter, and she was only four years old, barely anything more than a baby, he wanted Gabriella to do what she could to help his daughter. Wanted Essie to be safe and unharmed, to return to him as the same sweet, confident, caring, intelligent, sassy little girl she was.

But he didn't want Gabriella hurt.

Thinking about what she might put herself through to fulfill her role as Essie's nanny made him nauseous.

"We'll find them, Cade. Sooner or later, we will find the men who raped your mom, who sacrificed your dad and his team, who set up your mom and stepdad. Who hurt Cole and Susanna, and Connor and Becca. Who took Essie and Gabriella. We'll find them, and when we do, they will face the entire weight and might of Prey Security. We're going to make them wish they'd never been born. I'll call when I know something," Olivia said before disconnecting the call.

It was a long time before Cade could move, Olivia's words echoing through his mind on a loop.

These men were going to pay.

That was something he was going to see to.

If they hurt a hair on his daughter's head, or that of Essie's nanny, then he was going to make sure they suffered before they died.

Taking Essie was a mistake. It wasn't going to make him back off, it was going to make him come at them harder than he ever had before.

He wasn't going to be content just making sure these men regretted ever being born, he was going to do whatever he could to make sure their souls would suffer for all eternity.

~

September 2nd
    12:23 P.M.

"Gabby, I have to go to the bathroom."

The whimpered plea tugged at her heart. Essie was being so brave, doing everything she'd asked of her. She hadn't whined or complained, she'd cried a few times but had rallied every time Gabriella had suggested a new game.

But the little girl didn't belong there.

Essie should be at home, with the daddy she adored, preparing for her first day of kindergarten.

Instead, she was trapped in a windowless room, with no toys, change of clothes, bathroom, fresh air, and only what food Gabriella could pay for with ...

Nope.

Not going there.

If she allowed herself to think about what had happened in the room that morning, she was going to lose it. And if she lost it then Essie would lose it, too.

The important thing was she'd walked away with as much food as she could fit in her arms. There were two loaves of bread, several apples, a jar of peanut butter, some granola bars, and a huge bottle of water they would ration out for as long as they could.

While she hadn't been able to stomach eating anything, Essie had quickly devoured the breakfast Gabriella had made, and for a while that had perked up the little girl's energy level. They'd chased each other around the room playing tag, then practiced some steps Essie had been learning at dance and gymnastics.

Tumbling around the room, it had been so easy to forget for a moment that they weren't in the family room at home. Sometimes they'd push all the furniture out of the way so they had an open space in the center of the family room and tumble and twirl around until they were both giggling. If he was home, sometimes Cade would join in, and seeing the huge, muscled man trying to do ballet turns, and cartwheels was hilarious.

Were those times gone for good?

She was doing her best, but she didn't have the skills or the knowledge of how to get Essie out of there.

"Gabby?" Essie tugged on her hand, and she wearily pushed to her feet, giving the girl a reassuring smile.

"I'll go knock on the door and ask," she replied. Since it had been well over twenty-four hours since she last ate, and she hadn't slept at all the previous night, her resources were depleted, and she was feeling it today.

"I don't want you to leave me 'gain," Essie said, pressing close against her leg and clinging to her in a most unlike Esther Charleston kind of way. The little girl brimmed with confidence, she was the kind of kid who went to the park and left having made friends with every child and adult there. She always put her hand up to participate in the classes she took, was always happy to play teacher's demonstrator, and excelled at everything she did.

This clingy little girl wasn't the child she knew, and her heart broke knowing that even if she survived this ordeal, Essie would never be the same again.

"I'll do my best to stay right by your side," she promised, not wanting to outright lie because she knew those men were going to want more from her if she wanted to protect Essie and she didn't want the child to see that.

Already they knew her weakness, knew she could be manipulated, and she had no doubt they would exploit that weakness.

"'Kay," Essie mumbled, clutching at her hand as she walked over to the door and knocked.

When no one immediately answered, she knocked again, louder this time, and called out. "Hello? We need to use the bathroom."

Since they'd been allowed to go every other time she'd asked, she suspected mainly because one of the men seemed totally turned off by bodily fluids and didn't want them stinking the room up, she had no doubt they'd be allowed this time.

But this time would they want a payment?

How far were they going to go?

Last time they'd made her suck off every single one of them before allowing her access to the food. More than once she'd thought she was going to pass out when they refused to let her take a breath, shoving into her much more roughly than she'd ever had a man treat her. They'd made her swallow everything, and honestly, she wasn't sure she'd ever be able to get the taste out of her mouth no matter how long she lived.

Just as she was about to knock a third time, she heard someone on the other side of the door unlocking it.

"So, you need to use the facilities, huh?" the man who had opened the door said as he lounged against it. "How much are you willing to pay for the privilege?"

"Please, she's only four, she needs to go," Gabriella begged. She would pay whatever price they asked because Essie came first, but she didn't want the little girl to see.

"Nothing in life is free, darling," the man drawled, reaching out to grasp her breast and squeezing painfully tight.

Biting her lip was the only way to keep her moan of pain in, and she was eternally grateful for the fact that she'd gone shopping for this one-piece suit when Essie took up swimming. Normally, she'd wear a bikini to the pool, but knowing she was going to be in the water with a toddler, with a bunch of other toddlers and their parents, she'd decided a sensible one-piece was much more appropriate. While it was still skintight, and showed off everything, at least the pale-yellow material was more modest than one of her bikinis would have been.

"I have to go real bad, Gabby," Essie cried.

Lifting pleading eyes to the man she asked. "Please, let me take her, then ... then you can do whatever you want."

Offering her body like this felt more like offering up her soul on a platter to the devil. But what choice did she have? Let Essie starve? Let these men lay their filthy, disgusting hands on a little girl?

Leaning in so she could feel his breath, which reeked of cigarette smoke, against her cheeks, he whispered, "So long as you're prepared to pay double, for yourself and the kid."

Giving him a nod of acceptance, she gripped Essie's hand, edged around the man, taking care not to touch him, and hurried for the bathroom. The sound of his laugh crawled over her skin like a million fire ants, and she wondered for the millionth time how she was supposed to do this.

Where are you Cade?

Why haven't you found us?

Please, we need you.

Essie needs you, and ... I need you, too.

In the bathroom, she hurried the little girl through doing her business, then had Essie look the other way while she did her own. Once they had both washed their hands she guided the child back into the hall.

Where, of course, the man was waiting for her.

"Essie, go back in the room for me, sweetie," she said, releasing her hold on the little girl's hand and nudging her toward the door.

"But you promised you wouldn't leave me," Essie said with a pout.

Don't be stubborn now, cuddle bug.

Getting the child out of the room was her top priority, so Gabriella used the tone she usually only reserved for when Essie was in trouble, and she meant business. "Now, Esther. Why don't you make us some lunch like a big girl," she suggested, softening her tone for that last suggestion.

Eyes lighting up a bit, any hint of being treated like a big girl was always a winner with Essie, and she nodded. "I can make it all by myself?"

"Yep, you sure can," Gabriella quickly agreed.

"'Kay, but don't be long," Essie said as she entered the room.

As soon as the little girl was out of sight, a hand circled her neck and she was shoved up against the wall hard enough that her head snapped back, slamming into it. Stars danced before her eyes for a moment, but she quickly willed them away.

Expecting things to take a sexual turn, Gabriella was caught off-guard when instead a fist rammed into her stomach, shoving all the air out of her lungs.

Choking and spluttering, barely able to breathe, she would have been helpless even without the hand locked around her neck, holding her in place but not cutting off her air supply. Another blow caught her in the ribs, then in the shoulder. One to her face had her seeing stars all over again.

When instinct had her trying to fight off her much bigger attacker, the hand around her neck moved to instead clamp around both of her wrists, pinning them above her head and leaving her stretched out and vulnerable before this man.

"The plan was just to take the kid, but I'm glad we took you, too." He sneered as his free hand moved to one of her breasts, tugging away the material of her swimsuit to bare it. Then he leaned down and clamped his teeth around it, cutting through her flesh with a vicious bite.

She didn't want to scare Essie, didn't want to give this man the satisfaction, but Gabriella couldn't help letting out a scream as reality set in.

She wasn't walking out of this alive.

CHAPTER *Five*

September 3rd
8:05 A.M.

The unicorn lunch box and backpack sitting on the kitchen counter mocked him.

Today was supposed to be a special day, a milestone in his daughter's life.

Her first day of kindergarten.

Essie should be there, wearing the cute pink and yellow sundress she and Gabriella had gone shopping for back at the beginning of summer after Essie finished preschool. His daughter had been too excited to wait until it was closer to school starting and the two girls had gone on a huge shopping spree, buying everything any child could possibly need at school.

Last week, it had all been packed up into Essie's brand-new unicorn backpack, and because Essie liked looking at it Gabriella had left it out in the kitchen.

Now it mocked him.

Because Essie wasn't there getting dressed and having her hair done in the cute style she'd picked out because his daughter liked to have everything perfect. She wouldn't be holding up a cute chalkboard with her name, the date, and what she wanted to be when she grew up on it. There would be no first day of school pictures, no driving her in and dropping her off, and watching with pride as she took the next step in life.

For as long as Cade could remember, Essie had been excited to start school. His daughter was smart and curious, and she loved learning new things. At least a few times a day she'd ask some random question, and if he or Gabriella didn't know the answer, they'd grab Essie's iPad and look it up.

Essie should be there.

Rage at the people who had taken her from him was so all-consuming that he could barely do anything else. It pulsed inside him like a red-hot beast, desperate for an outlet. It howled out its pain inside his skull until he had a constant throbbing headache. Every one of his muscles ached because he was so tense, wound so tight that when he finally snapped, it would be epic.

Now, though, he had no outlet.

Nothing to do but sift through intel that didn't appear to be leading him anywhere and battle his fear for his daughter and Gabriella.

Cade couldn't get Olivia's words out of his mind.

What had been said to comfort him only made his fear worse the longer he pondered it.

It was true, Gabriella was going to do whatever it took to protect his daughter because she truly loved Essie. It was why he'd hired her. From the moment they met, it was clear that Gabriella and Essie were going to get along. It hadn't mattered to him that she had no training, he didn't either when he became a dad, all that mattered was that whoever cared for his child would treat her the same way he would.

If he were the one abducted with his daughter there wasn't anything he wouldn't do to protect her.

Anything.

Gabriella would do the same.

What horrors was she enduring on his daughter's behalf?

It made him physically sick to think about it. In fact, when he'd gotten home last night he'd gone straight to the bathroom and thrown up, unable to stomach the fear any longer.

How was he going to survive if he couldn't bring his child and her nanny home?

"Cade?" The front door to his house opened and he heard Cooper call out his name.

Company was the last thing he wanted. All he wanted was to be alone to wallow in a pit of anger and terror without any witnesses. There was nothing anyone could say that would change or fix this situation and he wasn't able to summon enough energy to be even vaguely hospitable.

Knowing his family meant well didn't help, he just wanted them to leave him alone.

"Cade?" Cooper said again as he entered the family room. Not alone. Almost the entire family was there, everyone except Connor and Becca. Ironically, they were the only two who could even come close to understanding what he was going through. Becca had miscarried their baby boy twelve years ago. Connor had just found out about it and the two of them were now grieving the loss together.

"Sorry to show up when you said you needed time alone, it's just that ... you shouldn't have to be alone. It never helps," Susanna said softly. While she was the newest addition to their family, even though they'd known her in passing for the last three years since she was Cole's neighbor, she'd fitted in seamlessly. The woman had major trust issues, and he respected the hell out of her for working on them, making an effort to change the patterns of a lifetime now that she finally had a place she felt safe and people she felt safe with.

Maybe he needed to learn a lesson or two about taking on his fears rather than ignoring them. If he had, maybe he would have let Gabriella know that he thought she was gorgeous, smart, funny, caring, kind, compassionate, loyal, and the kind of woman you could build a life with.

How could he argue with Susanna's words?

They knew her story, how she'd been hurt and called a liar, how she'd built a life all on her own and yet still had such a big heart and cared for others so deeply.

"You're right," he reluctantly agreed. Raking his fingers through his hair, he forced himself to accept that sitting alone in his home was just a way to punish himself. Essie and Gabriella were alone right now so he should be too. But his suffering didn't alleviate theirs. If anything, it made theirs worse because the deeper into this hole he dug himself, the harder it would be to get out of.

His girls were counting on him, and he couldn't fail them.

Wouldn't.

"I am?" Susanna asked, her green eyes widening in surprise, drawing a chuckle from him.

"You are," he told her.

"See, I'm not the only one who thinks you're always right," Cole teased, drawing his girlfriend against his chest and touching a kiss to her temple. Despite their relationship being new, they'd fallen into such ease with one another. Cade remembered what those early days were like, you couldn't get enough of the person who had captured your heart. You wanted to touch them all the time and spend every second with them. He wished Cole and Susanna, and Cooper and Willow, weren't having what should be such a special time tainted by the fact that they were all in danger.

Shoving to his feet, Cade headed into the kitchen. "Who wants coffee?"

After a round of affirmatives, they all bustled around his kitchen, making coffee and raiding his pantry for snacks. By the time they were all set up at his table, he was already feeling a little better. Susanna had been right, and he'd been wrong. What he needed was to be reminded that he wasn't fighting for his girls alone. An entire team was at his back, and together, they were more powerful than the men they were up against.

"Where are Con and Bec?" he asked.

"They went to the cemetery," Jax replied.

"They've wanted to go ever since the ordeal at the cabin, but they haven't had a chance yet," Willow added. "They didn't want to go today, they wanted to be here for you, but we told them they should go. They need that time together to say goodbye to their son."

He didn't disagree.

The whole mess of the pregnancy twelve years ago had driven Connor and Becca apart. Now that they were getting their second chance, they needed to be able to lay the past to rest, and part of that meant having a real chance to grieve their son together.

"They're going to come by after," Jake said.

"When did Essie get the ragdoll?" Cooper asked, glancing at the doll and teddy bear sitting side by side on the kitchen table.

"It's not Essie's," he replied. Since he'd found the doll in Gabriella's room, he hadn't been able to go anywhere without it and Essie's teddy. Having them close felt like maintaining a link to the missing girls and he needed to cling to it right now. "It's Gabriella's. The only thing she had from her biological mom."

Gabriella had been open with all of them about how she'd grown up, so he wasn't breaking any confidence. In fact, given that he'd worked hard to maintain distance between them, he wouldn't be surprised to know that his brothers knew more about her and her past than he did.

"It was in her room," he said softly, reaching out a hand to brush a fingertip across the worn pink material of the doll's dress. How many times had he had to curl his fingers into fists to stop himself from reaching out and touching Gabriella over the last four years? To stop himself from caressing her freckle-dusted cheek? From running his fingers through her wild red curls? From dragging her into his arms and kissing her until neither of them could breathe?

From telling her that she was more than just his daughter's nanny, but he was afraid of losing her if he let her in?

Only he'd lost her anyway.

All that keeping distance, pretending he didn't catch the longing and heated glances she threw his way, pretending that they were just friends, pretending that he didn't crave more, hadn't protected Gabriella or him.

In the end, he'd lost her anyway.

And there might never be a chance to make things right.

September 3rd

3:29 P.M.

"Truck!" Essie announced triumphantly, beaming with pride.

"That's right!" Gabriella encouraged her little student. "T-R-U-C-K spells truck, that's awesome! You're going to be reading in no time."

"Then I can read *you* books at bedtime," the little girl said, preening with enthusiasm and pride in herself.

Since they'd been there for over two days, she had to get creative in what she could do to keep a young and active child occupied. Since Essie loved learning and was always enthusiastic about learning her letters and numbers, Gabriella had decided to start trying to teach her some more words. So she was sounding them out, and letting Essie think which letter made each sound and how the letters went together to form a word.

It was a poor substitute for spending what should be her first day of kindergarten at school with her teacher, making new friends, and embarking on a new adventure, but at least she was learning something and having fun while doing it.

So far, no one had made any move to do anything to the little girl, nor had they made any move to contact Cade. At least as far as she knew. Obviously, since she'd been stuck in there, she couldn't know for sure that they hadn't, but she wasn't stupid, she knew the reason they had been taken was to put pressure on Cade and his family to get them to back off. The best way to do that was to hurt them and send the Charleston Holloway family proof.

While she may not be a part of that family by blood, she knew they cared about her enough that they weren't just hunting for Essie but for them both. They'd do whatever they could to get them out of there alive and she hoped they found them sooner rather than later.

"You sure can. You can read me one every night and then I'll read you one," she agreed. Keeping up a positive attitude was wearing on her, especially since she'd barely slept again the previous night and still had pretty much no appetite. Since Essie had been so proud of the lunch she'd made yesterday, Gabriella had nibbled on a bit of it and done the same at dinner when Essie had excitedly proclaimed she'd cook again.

Now they were basically out of food, and she dreaded what she'd have to do to get them more.

The door to their room suddenly swung open, and even before anyone said anything Gabriella's stomach dropped.

Something bad was happening.

Other than yesterday morning at breakfast, no one had come for them. She knew someone was always out there because whenever she knocked and asked if they could use the bathroom someone answered, but it was always only one man.

Now four of them strolled into the room.

If the number of them hadn't set off her alarm bells, then the smarmy looks on their faces would have.

They were excited about what was coming next.

She, on the other hand, was terrified.

Picking Essie up, she stood and clutched the child against her chest. Whatever was happening they weren't hurting this little girl.

Any sacrifice she had to make to ensure that, she was prepared to do.

"Who's ready for a little photoshoot?" one of the men asked as he prowled toward them.

"I think we've let daddy stew for long enough, don't you little one?" another asked.

When he reached out a hand to touch Essie, Gabriella quickly stepped back. "Don't touch her," she snapped. Her inner mama bear was coming out. Just because she wasn't Essie's mother didn't mean she didn't love this child as though she was. Anyone who tried to hurt her would have to go through her first.

The man chuckled like she was hilarious. The hand that had been going to touch the little girl instead grabbed a handful of Gabriella's red curls and yanked her closer. "You want to be the star of the movie, I think we can make that happen. Don't you, guys?" he asked his friends who all snickered and whooped in response.

"Let's go," one of the other men said, and with his hand still tangled in her hair, the man who had grabbed her threw her forward, almost causing her to lose her balance and fall.

Somehow, she managed to remain upright, and with no choice but to follow the men, she clutched Essie tighter in her arms and walked where she was led.

"It's okay, cuddle bug, I won't let them hurt you," she whispered in the girl's ear.

"I don't want them to hurt you neither, Gabby." Essie whimpered, her little face wet with tears.

"I don't want you to worry about that, Essie. I'm a grown-up and it's my job to protect you. Okay?" How could she explain to such a little girl the love she felt for her and how it precluded anything else?

"Put the kid down," one of the men ordered when they walked into another small room like the one they'd been kept locked up in. Only this one wasn't completely empty, there were two chairs in the middle of the room, and a camera had been set up facing them.

Even if she had zero imagination and zero idea of what to expect when they'd been kidnapped, she could have figured out what they had planned in less than a second.

"On one of the chairs," another added.

As badly as she wanted to refuse, Gabriella was afraid of what would happen if she did. These men could quite easily force the little girl out of her arms, and if they did, they wouldn't be gentle about it. Essie would wind up hurt and she couldn't allow that.

So feeling backed into a corner, she slowly crossed the room and deposited the child on one of the chairs.

Essie whimpered and clung to her when she tried to straighten.

"Shh, cuddle bug, I'm still right here," she soothed, fighting the urge to snatch the child right back up again.

"Sit beside her," one ordered her.

That was a much easier direction to follow. Taking the other chair, she wrapped an arm around the little girl's shoulders and tucked her in against her side.

The men all pulled on ski masks, and she noted they were all dressed in black today, including black gloves. There was nothing that would help Cade and the others to identify them.

Nothing in this room to identify where they were being held either.

In front of them, the camera switched on, and one of the men strolled in front of it. "Missing something?" he sneered as he circled around to stand behind them, running a hand down her hair and then doing the same to Essie.

"Unless you want your kid getting a real up close and personal lesson in the birds and the bees, I suggest you back off, stop looking for answers about topics that don't concern you," one of the other men said as he walked over to her chair and shoved her legs apart.

"Close your eyes, Essie," Gabriella quickly whispered. She had no idea how far these men were going to take things, but she certainly didn't want Essie getting a lesson in the birds and the bees from watching her be raped. "Keep them closed, okay? Until I tell you to open them."

The man groping her chuckled and lifted a hand to wrap around her neck, holding her still as he crushed his mouth to hers. The kiss was harsh and forceful, and with his body pressed against hers and his hand squeezing her neck just tight enough to begin impeding her ability to breathe there was nowhere for her to go.

From behind her the other man roughly grabbed her breasts, kneading them painfully. The bite mark, which had torn through her skin and left behind horrible red welts as well as dark black and blue bruises, stung horribly as his large hand squeezed her flesh.

Gabriella whimpered at the violation of his tongue forcing its way between her lips, and she was so very aware both of the little girl still tucked against her side, and the fact that this video was going to be sent to Cade.

When he saw it, he was going to lose it.

His fear for his daughter and what was going to happen to her would be off the charts, maybe even bad enough for him to agree to stop searching for answers about who hurt his mom.

That wasn't what she wanted for him or his family, they deserved to be able to clear their mom's name after all these years, but she didn't want to die in the process. Nor did she want Essie to have to pay the ultimate price.

The facts were, there was no good outcome.

And even if Cade agreed to back off it didn't guarantee that she and Essie would be returned alive.

Hopelessness drowned her, and a single tear trailed down her cheek as she lifted her gaze to look square into the camera.

CHAPTER Six

September 3rd
6:43 P.M.

"There has to be a connection," Cade growled in frustration.

He couldn't believe there wasn't.

And yet, after hours—days—of going through the lives of the ten men who had attacked Connor and Becca at the cabin a couple of weeks ago, they weren't able to identify anyone who was related to them in any way who might be involved in Essie and Gabriella's abductions.

They'd gone through their lives with a fine-tooth comb.

A finer than fine-tooth comb.

They'd checked into every relative, friend, neighbor, acquaintance, and person the men had served with in any way, and still nothing.

No one had turned out to be a credible lead.

If the only survivor of the attack hadn't taken his life while he was in the hospital under police guard, he would have gone down to the hospital and done whatever it took to get answers out of him.

A name.

A location.

He needed something if he was going to bring his girls home.

"I don't think there is, Cade," Jake said, uncharacteristically gently for a man who was so much like him. Both of them didn't bother to waste time mincing words, and while he would never outright say anything to upset somebody, he also didn't sugarcoat things. He wasn't the one who dealt with victims, wasn't the one who could handle their tears and fears. But he loved his family with everything he had and would sacrifice anything for them.

Anything.

But without answers he was stuck.

His hands were tied.

He could not make a move when he didn't know what direction he should be moving in.

Which left his girls trapped.

Helpless at the hands of people who would enjoy tormenting them, who would take pleasure from their terror, who wouldn't hesitate to use them as pawns as though they were no more important than an inanimate object.

Only his daughter and Gabriella were important.

They held more value than anything else in his world.

"Uh, Cade," Cooper said somewhat hesitantly.

That tone immediately set him on edge.

Something had happened.

Something bad.

Had a body been found?

It had to be Gabriella's if there was. Essie was his daughter and thus held higher value. He was surprised they'd even taken Gabriella. As an adult, she would be harder to manage than a small child. Then again, Gabriella was a gorgeous young woman, and it didn't take a lot of imagination to see why five men might find kidnapping her and having her as their helpless plaything an appealing prospect.

While he certainly didn't want his daughter to die, he didn't want to lose Gabriella either.

Even if he could never make her his, her presence in his life grounded him, soothed him, and brought him a peace he'd thought he'd never be able to find again in the days after Gretel died.

It should be an easy choice.

Essie over Gabriella.

And it wasn't that he was saying it was the other way around, it was that he couldn't imagine losing either of them.

"What?" he demanded, much harsher than he'd intended. If there was intel, he wanted it. No matter how bad it was. Like ripping off a Band-Aid it was better to just do it and get it over with.

Saying it gently wasn't going to change whatever horror he was about to learn.

"You just got an email. With a video attachment," Cooper informed him.

Even if he hadn't grown up in a military family, and even if he hadn't dedicated his entire adult life to his career as a PJ and then working at Prey, he would know what that meant.

This was the reason they'd taken his daughter.

They wanted to show him what they would do to her if he didn't convince his family to back off and stop trying to find the men who had raped their mother.

It wasn't even a question, whatever he saw on that video would kill a part of him.

"Do you want us to watch it for you?" Connor asked softly.

"No," he shot back adamantly. This was his daughter, his ... whatever the hell Gabriella was to him. He had to watch. They were both innocent and they'd been taken because of him. Hurt because of him. The least he owed them was to watch whatever horror they had to endure.

"It won't serve any purpose to put yourself through that," Jax spoke up.

"We won't miss anything. Swear," Cole added. "Any detail in there that will help us we'll pick up on."

"Don't put yourself through this," Jake said, a slight air of authority to his tone.

Only Cade was the big brother, a year older than his stepbrother, two years older than the twins, three years older than his other step-brother, and four years older than his baby brother. Perhaps not a huge age gap, especially now that they were all in their thirties, but he was the oldest, and besides, this was his family that had been taken.

"I have to watch," he told them. "And don't say it doesn't serve any purpose. It does. Essie and Gabriella were taken because of me. I owe them this."

Before one of his brothers could argue the point, he grabbed the laptop on his kitchen table where they'd set themselves up that morning and turned it to face him.

With sighs and understanding looks, his brothers all moved to stand around him so they could watch with him. Offer the only support they could, their presence.

The email came from what was clearly an email address created exactly for this purpose. Since it had been titled lessonsforcade, he wasn't sure if Olivia and the others would be able to trace where it had been sent from, but as soon as he watched the video, he'd forward the email to her.

While he hoped the others wouldn't notice, but sure they would, his hand was shaking as he moved it to click on the video link. There was no text in the email and there didn't need to be. The email address said it all. As did the subject line, which simply read, this was fun.

When he opened the video, Essie and Gabriella appeared on the screen.

His momentary relief at seeing them alive was quickly eaten up by fury at the terrified looks on both their faces. Essie was wearing the same dress he'd seen her in that morning before he left to meet with the man who claimed to be Cassandra's half-brother, but Gabriella was wearing only her swimsuit. It left her long, lean legs on display for these men, and he could see bruises peeking out from underneath the skin-tight material.

There were bruises on Gabriella's face as well, but Essie's seemed clear. Cade didn't need to guess why. The protective way she kept Essie tucked to her side and the glint of defiance in her green eyes said that Gabriella had been doing what they all had expected her to do and protecting his daughter as best she could.

And it had cost her.

"Missing something?" a man dressed in black and wearing a ski mask asked as he strolled into view. The man walked until he was behind the girls and ran a hand down both of their hair, making Cade see red.

Nobody touched his daughter without her permission.

"Unless you want your kid getting a real up close and personal lesson in the birds and the bees, I suggest you back off, stop looking for answers about topics that don't concern you," another man said as he walked over to the chairs and shoved Gabriella's legs apart.

"Close your eyes, Essie. Keep them closed, okay? Until I tell you to open them," Gabriella's soft voice whispered urgently, and his daughter obeyed without hesitation.

Even in the face of groping, Gabriella couldn't stop putting his child first.

The man between her legs laughed and then clamped a hand around her neck. When he leaned in and crushed his mouth against hers, Cade thought he was going to explode with rage. The other man palmed her breasts and began to squeeze them, and even on the video, he could hear Gabriella's small whimper.

It was the single tear that trailed down her cheek that broke him.

Of course, he wanted his four-year-old daughter safe and protected, but the cost was so high. His Gabriella was being broken in the process.

When Gabriella's eyes lifted and looked directly at the camera, Cade was unable to bear watching this horrific travesty a second longer. He didn't care if there was more to the video, he didn't want to see it if there was, Cade picked up the laptop and hurled it with all his might across the room.

It spun as it flew through the air, then connected with the glass sliding doors leading out onto the back deck with a satisfying crash as both the door and the laptop shattered.

Then he shoved to his feet, ran blindly toward the downstairs bathroom, dropped to his knees in front of the toilet, and threw up.

∼

September 4th

7:34 A.M.

Gabriella was unsettled this morning, but she couldn't tell why.

They were almost seventy-two hours into their ordeal, and while things had been terrible and she'd been forced to allow men to touch her and to touch them, things hadn't been as bad as she'd thought.

Yesterday, after the man kissed her while filming that video for Cade, he'd stopped, they'd delivered a final message to the Charleston Holloway family that if they didn't back off immediately Essie was going to be next, then returned them to their room.

She should be glad it had stopped at that.

Should be glad that she hadn't been forced to do anything to get more food for herself and Essie. When they'd been returned to their room, someone had left behind a huge pile of food for them, enough to last a couple of days.

As usual, they'd been allowed bathroom breaks when needed, and she and Essie had played games until bedtime. Once again, she'd struggled to sleep. Her body cried out for a break, she knew she was teetering on the edge of exhaustion, and she badly needed sleep if she wanted to be able to function, but she just couldn't seem to let her mind shut off.

Any time she did drift off to sleep, she'd startle awake at the teeniest sound or movement.

Half the time she was sure she was reacting to nothing.

Fear for the little girl who sat before her, happily munching on a candy bar the men had left for them occupied her every second. Candy for breakfast wasn't something she usually allowed, but what did it matter right now? They were prisoners, they were pawns, pain and suffering were in their future, if eating candy for breakfast helped Essie in any small way, she wasn't going to deny the child some comfort and enjoyment.

"Gabby?"

"Yeah, cuddle bug?"

"I'm bored," Essie whined.

"I know you are, sweetie."

"I want to go outside."

"If I could take you I would, but I don't think we're going to be allowed." Maybe it was worth asking, just in case. She was sure nobody was close to where they were being held so they may agree to it. There would be a price to pay if they did say yes, Gabriella was well aware of that, and maybe it was why she held back.

Or maybe it was the oppressive sense of foreboding.

Something bad was going to happen and she didn't want to rock the boat.

This calm before the storm wouldn't last, and she was so afraid that she knew what the sense of foreboding was about, and that she wouldn't be able to stop it from happening.

Essie.

Next they were coming for the little girl.

Maybe they wouldn't rape her, maybe they wouldn't do anything sexual to her at all, but they'd do something. Hit her, break her tiny, fragile bones, cut her, maim her, something that would show Cade the extent of the consequences of him not doing what they wanted.

What if she couldn't stop it?

Or what if she tried and they killed her to get her out of the way?

How would Essie survive there alone without anyone looking out for her?

"I want to go outside," Essie said again, pouting. Normally, she was an easy-going little girl, she didn't lose her temper very often, she rarely threw tantrums, and she was good at listening and doing as she was told although she loved to try to negotiate to get her way. But they'd both been under a lot of stress and it was no wonder it was starting to get to Essie and affecting her attitude. She was lucky the girl had kept her attitude for three days.

"I can ask, but I can't make any promises," she warned the child.

Pushing to her feet, Gabriella shook off a wave of dizziness as she stood. Besides the lack of sleep, she still hadn't been able to force herself to eat much, her stomach was constantly churning with nausea, and she had no appetite. She was eating only because she had to, but it wasn't anywhere near enough.

Knowing the rules Gabriella had put into place, Essie shifted into the corner, the one furthest from the door. While it wasn't going to protect the child, she always felt a little better when she knocked on the door knowing there was the maximum distance between the little girl and whoever would answer.

Just as she lifted a hand to knock on the door it swung open, startling her.

She stumbled back a step but managed to catch herself before she landed on her backside before them.

The thought of being on the ground in front of these men brought back memories of that first morning when they'd made her suck them all off in return for food. A wave of terror crashed down upon her, almost stealing her ability to breathe as tears flooded her eyes.

Managing to wrangle control of her emotions before they rendered her useless, she saw three men standing in the now open doorway.

That sense of foreboding hovering over her all morning suddenly seemed to fill the room like a thick fog.

Whatever bad thing she'd been anticipating was about to happen.

How was she going to stop it?

Everything in her screamed at her to snatch up Essie into her arms and make a run for it. Logic told her that would never work. There were too many men there and they were all armed. Running would be giving herself a death sentence, maybe handing Essie one, too.

Since running wasn't an option, she stood there, waiting to see what her fate held.

Behind her, she could feel Essie's terror joining with her own.

Never in her life had Gabriella felt so inadequate. She was doing her best, but she didn't have what it took to protect this sweet, vibrant little girl. There was nothing she would be able to do to stop it when these men decided to shift their attention from her to Essie.

Helplessness buffeted her like a raging storm, and she took a desperate step toward the three men. "Don't touch her," she pleaded. While she would have loved to say her voice had come out strong and authoritative, it didn't. The opposite. She sounded as terrified as she felt.

"Boss wants to send a stronger message," one of the men said, taking a menacing step into the room.

No.

She couldn't let that happen.

"Please, she's just a baby. Whatever message you need to send, use me. Please." It probably wasn't wise to beg these men because it only left her reeking of the desperation she felt. But she *was* desperate and would beg and plead if it got her what she wanted.

"You really think they care more about you than the kid?" another of the men asked, a chuckle accompanying his words like she was delusional.

Those words shouldn't hurt her because, of course, Cade and his family would care more about their daughter and niece than someone who was merely the child's nanny. But they did cut into her heart. Because they reminded her that no one in the world loved her the way Essie's family loved her.

But this child *did* have a family who loved her, and she had to do whatever she could to make sure the little girl got home to them.

"No. They don't," she said, riding a sudden wave of confidence and bravado. "But I'm prepared to stand in her place."

More chuckles met her words, and one of the men was suddenly right up in her personal space. A hand circled her already tender neck, and before she knew it, she was shoved up against the wall, her back pressed so tightly against it that her shoulder blades ached.

The first strike to her stomach had her crying out.

"Essie, close your eyes," she managed to call out before another blow stole her ability to even think let alone speak.

The blows kept coming, raining down on her body like a bevy of hailstones, hitting her over and over again until she couldn't even tell where they were striking because her entire body ached and throbbed.

It was only because the men were holding her up as they hit her that was keeping her on her feet. If they released her, she'd crumple to the floor, might not even have what it took to curl into a ball to protect her vital organs.

As it was, she couldn't protect anything, and they weren't stopping.

Above the roaring of her pulse thudding in her ears, she could hear the men laughing and Essie sobbing.

There wasn't much more of this she could take.

Please, Cade, where are you?
Why haven't you come?
Essie needs you.
I need you.
Please come.
Before it's too late.

CHAPTER
Seven

September 4th
12:33 P.M.

A growl rumbled through his chest as he looked at the phone.

Cade had never heard himself make a sound like this.

It was a cross between a howl of pain and the rumbling roar of a grizzly bear.

Definitely more animal than human.

And it didn't even come close to letting out any of the swirling mix of emotions raging inside him.

"What's wrong?" Cole asked, immediately concerned.

Concern had been the dominant emotion rolling off all three of his brothers and both his stepbrothers ever since they got the video yesterday. He couldn't say he blamed them. It was evident to anyone with eyes that he was dangerously close to losing it.

It was why all his brothers were watching him like a hawk, prepared for him to get pushed over the edge and do something stupid.

They weren't wrong.

And this photo had shoved him a whole lot closer to that edge.

"He got another email," Jax replied from the kitchen table where he hammered away at a laptop's keyboard.

"From them?" Jake asked what had to be a rhetorical question because what else would have him growling like he'd lost his mind?

"Photo," he snapped, grabbing the nearest chair and sinking into it because he absolutely did not want to embarrass himself by passing out in front of his brothers. As if them seeing him throwing up wasn't bad enough, if he fainted, he'd never have their respect again.

"Not a video this time?" Connor asked, moving to stand behind Jax, who if the changing expression on Connor's face was anything to go by had the email open on the screen.

"Does it matter?" he snapped. Video or photo, both were hell when the two most important girls in his life were in danger. Well two of the three. Cade thanked God they'd moved Cassandra out to live with Delta Team until this was over, although he cursed himself for not sending Essie and Gabriella as well. He'd wanted to but he'd stupidly thought that he could keep them safe himself.

Fail.

"It's Gabriella," Jax said tightly, anger etched into his features.

Whatever the others were feeling was nothing compared to the pure fury inside him. He'd never felt anything like it before. Of course, he hated to see innocent people hurt and abused, and of course there was anger when the people he loved had been in danger. When Cooper and Willow had been caught in Egypt, when Cole and Susanna were lost in the mountains, when Connor and Becca were captured in Cambodia, all those times he'd been angry his family was being hurt.

But not like this.

This felt like a volcano was getting ready to erupt, he just didn't know when exactly he was going to start spewing boiling lava and molten rock.

"What the hell?" Cooper said, taking the phone from his hand and glancing at the picture. "Look at what they did to her."

Cade didn't fight his brother taking the phone, honestly, he wasn't sure how much longer he could have sat there and looked at the photo of a bruised and battered Gabriella slumped on the floor of an empty room like the one the video had been filmed in. He didn't know if it was the same room or a different one and it didn't matter. That room wasn't a hospital, and he wasn't sitting by her side, holding her hand, and telling her everything was going to be okay.

And where was Essie?

Had they put their filthy hands on his daughter?

Was she also beaten and barely conscious?

"If they'd hit Essie too there'd be a photo," Connor said as though reading his mind.

"Text says, how many more do you think she can take before her heart gives out?" Jake said, having moved to stand beside Cooper, as had Cole.

Given how bad Gabriella looked in the photo his guess was not many.

While she was fierce and brave and strong, had survived a childhood mostly on her own without the love, support, and guidance of parents, and she'd built a fortune with nothing more than her brain, she was no trained operative. She hadn't been taught how to withstand torture, and even if she had there was no cheating death. In the end it came for everyone.

But not Gabriella and not Essie.

Not now and not this way.

There had to be a way to determine where they were being held.

When his phone began to ring, Cooper held it out to him. "Olivia," his brother told him.

Unless Olivia was calling to tell him she had an address or a name he wasn't really interested. Still, he reached out and took the phone, hitting accept.

"Cade, I got something," she said immediately.

The excitement in her tone was infectious and he relaxed a smidgen. "What?"

"It's not an address exactly but it is an area," Olivia explained. "I was able to trace the basic location from where the email was sent. Then I went back to the footage we've been going through of all the vehicles that left the underground parking lot at the mall the day Essie and Gabriella were taken, and I think I put a few pieces together."

Relief and hope edged their way inside him, cooling the simmering volcano, but Cade clamped them down. It was too soon to get his hopes up.

"One of the vehicles that left was a work van, for a stationary company," Olivia continued. "Only when I started looking into the company it went under almost twelve months ago. So I wondered why someone would be driving a white van with the company logo on it. I did a little more digging and the company owned a huge plot of land with four warehouses. After the business closed, they were never sold or rented to anyone else. And they fall within the area that the email was sent from."

"Olivia," he gasped, realizing she'd just given him his only chance at getting his girls back alive. How could he ever repay her for that? She was quite literally giving him life saving information, and he wasn't just talking about Essie and Gabriella's lives. Without them, he would die. There was no doubt in his mind about that. Without any will to live he'd be a liability to his team, and sooner or later, wind up doing something reckless that would get him killed. "Thank you."

"Psshh," she said, and he could imagine her waving off his gratitude. "We're family, we don't thank each other for having one another's backs. Now there are no guarantees I'm right and I'll keep going through footage so we're not behind if I'm wrong, but at least you have a lead. Let me know if you need anything at all, and we'll ensure you and your team have it."

"I will."

"And, Cade, be careful. I know you want to run in and grab your girls, but don't forget that one wrong move will get them both killed," Olivia warned before she disconnected the call.

A warning he needed.

Because his instincts screamed at him to jump in his car, drive to the address, shoot anything that moved, and rush inside to get Essie and Gabriella.

But Olivia was right.

If he showed up there, chances were the first thing those men would do was kill his girls. There was no way they could risk them identifying any of them, and they were loose ends.

Smart.

His only chance at saving their lives was to play this smart and not fast.

"What did she say?" Cole asked as Cade lowered the phone from his ear, his mind already putting together a plan that he thought might work.

"She has a potential address," he told the others.

After getting the email yesterday, of course he and his brothers had tried sending numerous replies, but none of them had been answered.

These men had one goal.

To get his family to back off from trying to get the names of the men who had hired them to abduct his daughter.

Knowing how ruthless and powerful these men were, there was no chance they were going to let go of the only leverage they'd managed to get without a fight. It was the only way they could ensure they kept their freedom.

Prey was a mighty opponent, one that had to at least equal whatever power they had. These men thought they'd found the weak link in taking his daughter, but they were about to find out what happened when you messed with a man's child.

There was one way he could think of that. At least for now, everybody got what they wanted, but it might be a hard sell to convince his brothers that this was their best move.

"I have a plan, but I don't think any of you are going to like it," he announced.

~

September 4th
4:59 P.M.

It hurt to breathe, it hurt to lie down, it hurt to sit up, it hurt to move, it hurt to be still, it just plain hurt.

Gabriella had been one throbbing mess of pain ever since those men beat her, then let her drop to the ground like a discarded piece of trash.

She remembered them taking a picture of her before they left the room, and she hadn't heard from them since.

The worst part about the whole thing was seeing Essie's terrified little face, hearing her petrified screams, and knowing there was no longer much she could do to protect the child from their captors.

While she might not have stood much of a chance fighting those men off before, now whatever chance she might have had was gone. Wiped away. She could barely push herself up to her feet and had, in fact, only managed it the one time Essie said she needed to go to the bathroom.

If those men came after Essie next, she'd be powerless to protect the little girl.

Which would make her a failure.

It was literally her job, one that she was paid well for even though she didn't need the money since she was already worth millions in her own right, to protect and care for Essie.

Knowing she couldn't do that killed her.

And that served to remind her that eventually these men would in fact end up killing her.

Could her body survive another beating like that?

Another two? Three? Four?

Sooner or later, it would be too much, the damage done to her internal organs would be too great, and she'd simply die. There in the small room with only a bunch of evil men and a little girl she loved to witness it.

"Gabby?" Essie's little voice called out, and she forced open her heavy eyes to see the little girl on her knees beside her.

"Yeah, cuddle bug?" After she'd been beaten and the two of them had been left alone again, she hadn't had the energy to entertain the child like she had been. All her efforts went into not sobbing in pain and further traumatizing the little girl.

Not that it seemed to matter.

Essie seemed to have lost all enthusiasm for anything, and simply stayed curled up against Gabriella's side, staring into space, or softly humming to herself.

The beating seemed to have broken both of them even if she'd been the only one they put their hands on.

"Are you cold?" Essie asked, her little face worried.

"I'm okay, baby," she assured the child. She was cold, and now that the little girl had drawn her attention to it, she could see that her body was shaking, although she wasn't sure if it was because she was cold or in shock. Or if she was cold because she was in shock.

Either way it didn't matter.

She'd already put her sundress back on over her swimsuit earlier and her jacket was staying on Essie. It wasn't much, but a little layer of protection for the child, covering her almost completely from wrist, to neck, to ankle, and shielding her from the men's vile stares.

They weren't going to feel bad when the time came to hurt an innocent child.

And that infuriated her.

If they were going to use a four-year-old as a bargaining chip, as leverage to control her father, then the very least they could do was feel conflicted about it. How could they beat on something so small, or do sexual things to a tiny child, and not feel bad about it? Didn't they have consciences?

"But you're all shaky," Essie protested.

"Yeah, sweetie, I am, but I'll be okay," she lied through her teeth, anything to prevent this little girl more pain.

"The bad men shouldn't hit. It's wrong to hit people," Essie said like she was highly offended that these men would forget such a simple rule.

"It is," she agreed. Using what strength she had left, Gabriella reached out and wrapped an arm around the little girl's shoulders, urging her to lie down and snuggle close. Regardless of what she'd endured these last few days, she was grateful that the men hadn't killed her outright on the street when they'd abducted Essie. At least she'd been able to protect the child a little bit, and she prayed she could hold out long enough for Cade to find them so Essie never experienced what she had at the hands of their captors.

"I wouldn't hit people," Essie said as she stretched out on the ground and tucked herself close.

"I know you wouldn't, because you're a good girl."

"My daddy ... does he hit people?"

Reaching out to grasp the child's chin, Gabriella tilted it up until they looked in each other's eyes. "Your daddy doesn't hit people, cuddle bug. Sometimes when someone hits you first it's okay to hit back to protect yourself. That's like what your daddy does. He protects people who are being hurt."

"Like you gotted hurt."

"Yeah, sweetie."

"Then why doesn't Daddy come?" Essie asked, sounding frustrated.

"He will, baby."

"I want him to come now."

"Me too, Es, me too."

Together they lay side by side, and Gabriella, although she did her best to stay awake and keep watch over the little girl, succumbed to exhaustion and dozed in fitful slumber until she heard someone unlocking the door to their room.

When the men came in uninvited it meant only one thing.

Something bad was coming.

Rolling Essie up and over her body, Gabriella grunted in pain but didn't stop until she had the little girl between herself and the wall. It was the only protection she could offer right now, and it wasn't much but she was ready to accept another beating rather than watch Essie get hurt.

The door opened and she blinked.

Positive she was hallucinating.

Had to be.

Because there was no way this was real.

Only the figure in the door didn't shimmer out of sight.

Instead, he ran toward her and dropped onto his knees at her side.

There was so much fear, regret, anger, and guilt swirling in the brown eyes that looked down at her.

Tenderness too.

And affection.

A hand palmed her cheek, fingertips caressed her skin for the briefest of seconds before he reached behind her and snatched up the little girl.

"Daddy!" Essie shrieked in delight as she wrapped her arms around her father's neck.

Cade sank to his backside beside her, holding his daughter on his lap, rocking her from side to side as the little girl clung to him. Gabriella could have sworn she saw a couple of tears tumble down her gruff boss' cheeks.

"You came," Essie babbled. "I wanted you to come. You took too long though, Daddy. The bad men hurted Gabby. Did you hit them? Hitting is wrong but Gabby said that if someone hurts you then you got to protects yourself. She said that you only hits bad people who hitted other people firsts and that's okay."

Barking out a laugh at his daughter's rambled monologue, Cade buried his face in her hair and held her tight a moment longer. Then he surprised her by shifting Essie to balance on one leg, then with his other arm he very carefully tucked it around her shoulders and eased her up. Once she was sitting, he dragged her onto his lap and locked both arms around her and his daughter.

"I did what I had to do to come for you, my little princess," he told Essie cryptically, and Gabriella couldn't make out what he meant.

But he had to mean that he'd killed the men who abducted them, right?

If he hadn't how could he be there?

And he was there.

Warm and solid and strong beneath her.

Knowing it was inappropriate given he was her boss but way too exhausted to care, Gabriella relaxed against Cade and rested her cheek on his broad shoulder.

For a moment they all just sat like that, her and Essie on Cade's lap, his arms around them, and for the first time in days Gabriella finally felt safe.

Far too soon he sighed and shifted, shooting her a look that she knew meant don't even think about lying. "Can you walk?" he asked.

"I ... could try ..." she said, not entirely sure she could, but there was no way he was going to let Essie walk and carry her, so she had to figure out a way to do it.

"Essie, I need you to go on my back, okay?"

"A piggyback ride?" Essie asked, brightening at the suggestion.

"No, Cade, you need to hold her," she protested.

"You can't walk," he said simply. There was a hint of possessiveness in his tone she was sure she imagined, but he didn't give her another chance to argue. Simply helped his daughter onto his back, then moved his arms so one was around her back and the other under her knees. "Hold on tight, okay, Essie?"

"'Kay, Daddy," the child agreed.

Standing like their added weight was nothing, he quickly carried them out of the building. While she expected to see dead bodies and blood everywhere, there was no sign of a shootout or anything, so how had Cade gotten to them?

In the four days they'd been there, the men had never all left at the same time she was sure of it. Even if they had, what were the chances none of them would be there when Cade happened to track them to their location?

Expecting bullets to start flying at any second, none came and soon they were met with a blast of fresh air. It was mild and the feel of the sun and the breeze against her skin revitalized her a little.

Not far away, Cade's brothers stood around a large black SUV. They all seemed anxious but none of them were shooting and no bodies were lying about.

What the heck was going on?

And why didn't she feel more relieved about being rescued?

"Hey, Messy Essie," Cole said, his voice falsely bright as he took hold of the child.

"I'm not messy, Uncle Cole," Essie protested like she always did when he used the silly nickname.

"Here, I got her," Jake said, holding out his arms and she was deposited in his hold.

Not what she wanted.

Gabriella wanted to stay with Cade who was standing there looking at her with an expression she couldn't figure out.

Once again that rough palm cradled her cheek, calloused fingertips brushing over her skin. "Take care of my daughter."

Then he was gone.

Walking away from them.

That's when it hit her.

They hadn't been rescued, not really, Cade had somehow managed to convince the men to make a trade.

Him for them.

"No! Cade!" she screamed, fighting against Jake's strong arms that kept her tight against his chest.

He didn't stop.

"Come back! Cade!" she yelled again, doubling her efforts and almost managing to knock them both over.

"Stop, Gabs, he knows what he's doing," Connor told her, trying to move to block her view of Cade who was almost back to the building he'd just carried her and Essie out of.

"No! Why are you letting him do this? Stop him!" she begged as tears rushed down her cheeks. Cade didn't think he was coming back alive. That's why he told her to take care of his daughter. She knew it. Could feel it. Even if he could never love her like she loved him she didn't want to lose him. She'd rather have him in her life as her boss than not at all.

Suddenly, Cade dropped to the ground.

Gabriella screamed, fought, but it didn't change anything. She was shoved inside the vehicle and Cade's brothers drove away leaving him behind.

CHAPTER *Eight*

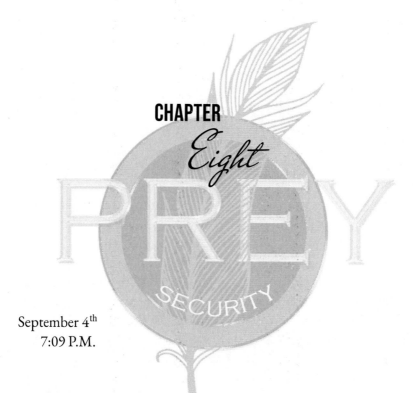

September 4th
7:09 P.M.

Satisfaction was the first thing to hit him when he swam slowly back to consciousness.

Cade woke up with a grin.

It didn't matter to him how bad a situation he was in, or if he was going to survive, or whatever torture might be in store for him.

His girls were safe.

That was the only thing he cared about.

Of course, he didn't want to die. Essie had already lost her mother, and he didn't want her to lose her father as well. She'd been through a traumatic ordeal, and she needed her family around her as she healed. She still needed to reach so many milestones in her life, and he wanted to be there to support her through them and watch how high she soared.

But she was alive and safe.

When it all boiled down to it, that was all he wanted.

His daughter was safe and loved with Gabriella and the rest of his family, and if he didn't make it home to her, he knew they would love her every bit as much as he could.

Blinking open his eyes, he found himself in what looked like a basement. There were no windows in the large open space and the walls were rough concrete with an old coat of white paint that had mostly peeled off. Likewise, the floor was concrete, although it had been smoothed out better than the walls had been.

There wasn't much in the space. He'd been chained up in a corner, the one furthest from a set of rather rickety-looking wooden steps that led up to a door he was positive was locked. They knew he was dangerous, and he was sure that even though he was shackled they would have wanted a double layer of security.

Smart of them.

Just because he'd come up with this risky plan didn't mean that he wanted to die there.

On the contrary, he wanted to use this situation to his advantage, finally flip the script and give himself and his family an edge. For the last couple of months—hell, for the last couple of decades—they'd been at a disadvantage, walking blind through this maze in an attempt to find answers to clear their mom's name.

No more.

It was time to get ahead, stop playing defense, and go on the offense.

Because even if he didn't survive this, his brothers weren't giving up. It didn't matter what they'd said in that email, those were lies he'd been more than happy to tell if it meant getting his girls out alive.

Doing a mental examination of his body, Cade found he had no injuries that he could detect. After hitting him with the tranquilizer, they must have just bundled him into a vehicle and driven him there, wherever there was. They'd chained him up, wrists were locked into metal cuffs, as were his ankles, and both were attached to metal rings embedded in the concrete wall and floor.

So, these men weren't just afraid of what he might do to them if they weren't careful, they were terrified. The chains weren't overkill, even with his wrists and ankles bound, he would have made a move when the time presented itself. But even restrained as he was, he would wait and watch, and when that moment did present itself, and there was always that one moment when people let their guard down, he wouldn't hesitate to strike.

There was still a lot of rage boiling inside him. Now that Essie and Gabriella were safe with his brothers, he was more than ready to find an outlet for it.

What better outlet than the men who had taken them from him?

For now, there was still too much of whatever drug they'd given him to knock him out in his system. He might be awake, but his limbs were still heavy and there was a foggy feeling in his head. That would fade and his strength would return.

Besides, he had to make sure they believed he intended to follow through on the bargain he'd made.

His life for Essie and Gabriella's.

The picture of Gabriella's beaten and battered body had been the final straw, and he'd known if he didn't tell them what they wanted to hear, he was going to lose her. After that, he'd lose his daughter, and without Essie he was nothing. Without Gabriella he was ... drifting in the wind. He needed her to ground him, and he didn't want to imagine his life without either of them in it.

So, he emailed back and said that he would make a trade. Him for them. He said he was the one who knew what they'd learned about the men who had raped his mom so far, so having him as leverage was better than holding onto Essie and Gabriella. It served the same purpose, someone to threaten to keep his brothers in line, and had the added bonus of them being able to interrogate him.

He hadn't let on that they'd already hit on a location. That tidbit about the stationary company might lead somewhere, and he didn't want to let on that they knew because it might lead to whoever was pulling the strings cleaning house, wiping away evidence Olivia and the rest of Prey's cyber team might find. Instead, he'd pretended the address he'd been given was all new information.

The agreement was he had five minutes to get Essie and Gabriella out. If any of his brothers moved from the vehicle they'd be shot. If he didn't hand them over and head back inside, they'd all be shot.

Cade knew that whoever was working so hard to prevent them from finding proof he was involved in raping their mom and then setting her up didn't really want to kill off his whole family. That would draw a whole lot of attention to them and could get them found out anyway. It was why they kept trying to be sneaky, going after weak links.

Well, this time they didn't have a weak link in their presence.

As the oldest, he'd taken on the role of looking out for his family. Every time these men had targeted one of his siblings or someone they cared about, he'd taken that personally. Then they'd made the mistake of daring to touch his daughter and her nanny.

For that, they would die.

When the door at the top of the step swung open, he shot a cocky grin at whoever was stupid enough to go down there and attempt to taunt him.

They thought they had the upper hand, but his family had the entire might of Prey Security at their backs, he'd like to see anyone go up against Prey and win. It had never happened before, and he didn't plan on it happening this time.

"You're awake," the man said, stating the obvious.

"I am," he agreed amicably. These idiots didn't know they'd taken a powder keg into their presence. Sooner rather than later, he was going to explode, and when he did, they weren't going to know what hit them.

"You have to know our boss isn't going to be making any more deals if that's what you're hoping for," the man said, strolling down the stairs but wisely not coming too close.

"Didn't think they would," he replied as he lounged back against the wall, giving the air of calm and control while at the same time allowing his rage to slowly invigorate him and return his strength.

"You know you're going to die here," the man told him.

If that happened, he would die happy that he'd given life to Essie and Gabriella by making this trade. But he was going to do everything in his power to make sure he got home to them.

He didn't know what was going to happen with him and Gabriella, but he did know that he had to make her understand that it wasn't her that had him keeping his distance but his own fears.

Giving a disinterested shrug, he cataloged everything he could about the man. All that information would be stored until he reached the time he had to use it.

"You should know we had a lot of fun with the nanny," the man said, giving him a smirk.

The words were meant to set him off and ignite his rage. And they did. But he had a long fuse and wasn't about to set himself off when he was in no position to do anything about the anger surging inside him.

Instead, he locked his gaze onto the man's and allowed every bit of the fury inside him to seep out. "You should know that I have no intention of dying until every single one of you who touched what was mine suffers a long, slow death."

∼

September 4th
7:19 P.M.

She wanted to scream, she wanted to cry, she wanted to beg and plead for someone to do something.

Cade wasn't there, and Gabriella was terrified for him.

Why had he done it?

Why had he made a deal for both of them?

All he needed to do was get Essie out. He could have left her behind, it would have been better than him giving his life for her.

He had a family, and she had no one.

Only as Gabriella looked around the hospital room, she knew that was only her fear and deep sense of inadequacy talking.

Knowing that her mom couldn't get clean even though she had a child who was depending on her was the first blow to her self-esteem she'd suffered and that was before she even knew what self-esteem was. Never having a family of her own as she drifted through the foster system was the second. Why wasn't she good enough for someone to adopt? For someone to want to keep her?

It always seemed too easy for foster families to pack up her things and tell her goodbye when she was moved to another home.

Then, losing so many babies one after the other, wanting so desperately to have a child of her own, someone who would love her and never leave her, had torn to shreds anything that was left of her self-esteem. Even her babies didn't want to stay with her, and her husband had dumped her because he didn't love her if she couldn't give him what he really wanted.

Now Cade had left her, too.

Leaving her alone once again.

Take care of my daughter.

His last words to her echoed through her mind. She wasn't alone. She had Essie curled up in her arms asleep, and the Charleston Holloway family sitting around her hospital room.

They were there and it was her that Cade had asked to look after his child.

Not his siblings.

Now wasn't the time to let her deepest fears and insecurities shove their way to the surface. While she was vulnerable and hurting, they would decimate any last dregs of strength she had left. Just because most people thought she was confident and outgoing, it didn't change the fact that inside she often felt lacking.

Unwanted.

Unlovable.

Unneeded.

Only now she had two people who needed her desperately. The small child who had refused to leave her side when they'd reached the hospital, and the man who had selflessly bought her freedom at the cost of his own.

"I'll tell you everything I know but I don't think it's enough to help," she said softly, unable to look at the men and women surrounding her bed any longer.

They were watching over her and Essie, but if Essie wasn't there would they be?

She'd like to think they would. That four years of being part of this family meant they would support her even if their little niece hadn't insisted on remaining in her arms, and her father had told her to take care of her.

But she couldn't help but doubt.

That strength that had sustained her through the last three days had shriveled up and died.

Now she was so afraid to see judgment, anger, or resentment in their faces that she couldn't even look at Cade's brothers.

Maybe they thought she should have been stronger or fought harder.

Could she have?

Doubt assuaged her, and she probably would have sat there in silence forever, even after making her offer, if someone hadn't reached out and closed a hand around her shoulder, squeezing just hard enough to get her attention.

"You should rest, sweetheart," Cooper told her. His grip on her shoulder shifted slightly and he gently kneaded her tight muscles.

Rest is probably exactly what she should be doing. After the hysterical car ride from where she and Essie had been held captive to the hospital, she was surprised someone hadn't sedated them both the second they got there.

Other than being bruised all over, suffering from some dehydration, and the effects of not eating properly for the last few days, she was okay. Thankfully, Essie had no injuries at all. They were both exhausted, though, and while Essie had promptly fallen asleep once they'd been settled in a room to be kept overnight for observation, sleep wouldn't come for her.

She should have followed the child's lead, but she couldn't.

Gabriella was wired with fear just like she'd been since they were kidnapped, and she couldn't make her brain shut off.

"There were five of them," she said as though Cooper hadn't spoken.

"And we'll get you to work with a sketch artist after you get the rest you need," Jake said, pushing off the wall by the door where he'd been standing.

Shooting him a look like he was crazy, she shook his head. "No. It can't wait. Cade is in danger. I don't understand why you left him," she said, carefully lifting a hand and rubbing her temple, trying not to disturb Essie in the process. They'd filled her in on only the barest amount of intel on what had gone down, basically just assuring her that Cade wasn't dead and that they had a plan.

"Because saving Essie and you was his priority," Connor told her from the seat he was perched in beside her bed.

"Of course, his daughter was his priority," she said.

"Didn't say that, honey," Connor shot back.

"I know, but you meant—"

"I meant exactly what I said," Connor said, gently but firmly. "He's been walking around with both toys since you guys were taken. Doesn't let them out of his sight. Specifically said we should have both with us when we rescued you guys."

It was hard to argue with that.

While she had no idea why Cade had been in her room, she knew he'd been in there because the ragdoll her mom had given her before she was put in foster care had been in the car when Connor and the others put her in it, along with Essie's teddy. It smelled like Cade, and she hadn't been able to let it go, much the same way Essie was clinging to Winkie-Bear.

"Look, sweetheart," Cole said, moving so he was standing beside the bed, Susanna moving with him, empathy on her pretty face. "You've been through hell and protected that little girl with everything you had. Every single one of us is so proud of you. You fought as hard as you could, but now you're safe. You're with your family, your team, the people who care about you. It's time to rest and heal."

Tears filled her eyes at Cole's simple words.

Calling them her family meant everything to her, more than he would ever realize because he'd never been all alone in the world.

"But Cade isn't safe," she whispered. Fear for her grumpy boss, who had won her heart with every sweet second he spent with his little girl consumed her.

"They're not going to kill him, Gabs," Jax told her, shooting her a reassuring smile only it went little way toward reassuring her.

Maybe they wouldn't kill him right away, but they'd hurt him.

Memories of what those same men had done to her shoved their way into her mind, and she trembled even though she was tucked under half a dozen blankets and had Essie's warm weight snuggled in her arms.

She knew what Cade and his family had seen in the video, so she knew they knew about the unwanted kiss and touching. But they didn't know about her being made to get down on her knees and suck off all those men, and they didn't know about the touching and the bite on her breast from that morning in the hall.

They didn't have to know either.

If she didn't tell them then they never could know.

It wasn't really relevant, so it could remain her dirty little secret forever. They wouldn't even know she was keeping anything from them.

"Sweetheart, you're overthinking everything, I promise you you are," Willow said. "I know how scared you are, trust me, I get it. I know how terrified for Cade you are as well. But right now, the best thing you can do for him is to rest, recover a little, then in the morning you can tell us everything."

"Then when you feel up to it, maybe you might want to talk to me," Susanna added. The woman was a psychologist, and while she'd specialized in helping addicts, after being raped when the men who were after the family thought she was Cole's girlfriend, she'd decided to accept the job offer from Eagle Oswald and join the Prey Team.

The offer was tempting, but it didn't seem right. Susanna had been through so much worse than she had. Susanna had been raped, and she'd only been made to do some things she wasn't comfortable with.

It wasn't the same.

Wasn't as bad.

And even if it was, complaining about what happened to her wouldn't help Cade.

That was what she had to focus on. There was a lot she didn't understand. Why Cade included her in the trade, why he'd been in her room, why he had her doll, why he'd told her to take care of his daughter, what it all meant, and her jumbled brain couldn't seem to put it all together.

"Go to sleep, Gabriella," Jake ordered in a voice that reminded her so much of the bossy tone Cade was prone to using that tears trickled down her cheeks.

Knowing they were right, that she badly needed sleep, that she'd have more intel to give them after her brain and body rested a little, she closed her eyes. Surrounded by big, strong, highly trained men didn't make her feel any safer than she'd felt alone in that small room with Essie. The only thing that might make her feel safe was Cade, but he'd traded his life for hers and his daughters, and in doing so he'd left a gaping hole in her heart.

CHAPTER
Nine

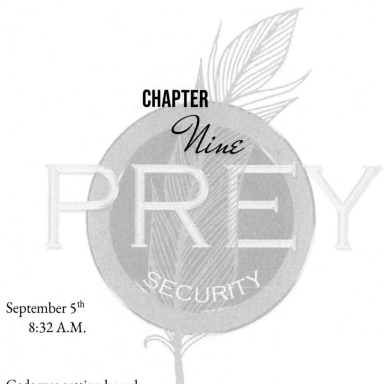

September 5th
8:32 A.M.

Cade was getting bored.

He was ready to do something.

Ready to start working on a way to get some intel that he would hopefully be able to take home to his family so they could end this mess once and for all.

Sitting around in this basement for hours had given him plenty of time to hone the anger that had raged inside him since these men took his daughter from him. Straightening it out so it was no longer a tangled and useless mess, and turning it into something productive, something that would power him through.

Knowing it likely wasn't going to make it through a screening process, his watch, which had a tracking device inside it, had been taken when he'd been hit with the tranquilizer dart and knocked out. So he also had to assume there was a good possibility that the small tracking device he'd had taped to his skin had also been found.

That meant there was virtually zero chance that his brothers were coming for him, but right now, he was way too wired to give that thought a chance to fester. This had always been a risk and one he'd been willing and fully prepared to take.

These men were trained and paid well to do their boss' bidding. This wasn't the same as just abducting him, he'd made a trade which meant they would know to be careful that he wasn't trying to double cross them.

But double crossing them was what he had every intention of doing as soon as an opportunity presented itself.

When the door at the top of the stairs finally opened, energy surged through his bloodstream.

This was it.

The chance he'd been waiting for.

A chance to actually do something other than just sitting there and conjuring up in his mind all the ways he'd loved to punish the men for abducting his girls and for hurting Gabriella. Thinking about the bruises littering her body added fuel to the fires of his fury, and he had to work to ensure he channeled that fury the right way. It had to be helpful and not a hindrance if he wanted to stand a real shot at getting home to his girls.

"Morning," he drawled lazily before any of the five men who had entered the basement could say anything.

From the way they faltered slightly, he could tell his nonchalant attitude had gotten to them. They expected him to be afraid and cowering, begging and pleading for his life. It wasn't only the rigorous training he'd gone through to become a pararescueman that had him feeling calm and in control, it was that there was nothing in the world more terrifying than knowing your helpless child and the woman who did things to you that you believed you were no longer capable of feeling were in the hands of psychopaths.

In comparison to that fear, this was nothing.

Each strike he took, any blood he shed, it was all in the place of Essie and Gabriella and that would dull any pain.

"Boss wants some answers," one of the men informed him as the five of them made their way down the stairs.

Cade studied the man carefully, paying attention to the way he moved, analyzing his body size and shape.

"You're the one who kissed her," he growled, causing the man to stumble. He would have been sure of it even without the man's shocked expression. One thing he was good at was paying attention to the details other people didn't take the time to notice.

"How could you know that? We were all wearing masks, could have been any one of us," the man said with false bravado, but Cade just grinned back, enjoying throwing them off their game.

"Your gait is slightly off, like an old injury shortened one of your legs marginally. And you keep your left shoulder higher than your right. You should work on that if you want to put your hands on women without their permission while you have an audience." Cade smirked when the man frowned at him.

Another of the men laughed and punched the guy in the shoulder. "Dude, he's got you."

"No, he doesn't," the other snapped like they were bickering preschoolers. "And even if he does, so what? What's he going to do about it? Not like he's in any position to do anything about it, and even if he was, it was only his kid's nanny, not like it was his girlfriend or anything."

Those words might be true, but they hurt.

Stuck into him like a thousand tiny darts.

The only reason Gabriella was nothing more than Essie's nanny was because he'd been too stuck in the past to do anything about what was right in front of him.

If there was one thing he knew for certain it was that Gretel would have wanted him to move on and would have loved Gabriella. The fact that Gabby could love Essie like she was her own child would have forever earned her a place in Gretel's heart. His wife had been open, outgoing, and full of love for everybody, and she loved both him and their daughter wholeheartedly.

Before her death, when she knew she wasn't going to survive, Gretel had told him she wanted him to grab hold of happiness if a second chance at love presented itself. She'd wanted him to be happy, to still experience all the things that they wouldn't get to share together, and Gabriella might have given him that chance.

But he hadn't taken it.

Because despite her words and assurances that it was what she wanted, moving on felt like cheating on his wife.

"You kissed her?" one of the men asked, strolling over somewhat cautiously like they still believed he might be a threat even though they had him chained up. "She more than the nanny?"

Deciding to get a little of his power back, the man who he'd identified as the kisser in the video also strolled over. "She's hot, man, it wasn't like we didn't get a perfect view of her body with her in that swimsuit. And she tasted sweet, like honey or something. Maybe we should have taken her for a ride before we handed her back."

Knowing they were only trying to get a rise out of him, Cade kept his face impassive. Better for them to believe that Gabriella was nothing more than the nanny, it would keep her safer. Just because they'd made this deal didn't mean that the men he and his family were hunting wouldn't make another attempt to go after her or Essie, or any of the others.

"If your boss wants answers," Cade said, directing the conversation back where he wanted it. This was an intel-gathering op, and he couldn't afford to let these men mess with his head by talking crudely about Gabriella. "Then maybe he should come down here himself and get some."

"Don't think he likes to get his hands dirty," one of the other men said.

"Doesn't need to, he's got us," the kisser said.

"Your boss is a coward, that's what he is. Raping an innocent woman, and then when he found out she had his child trying to take her out so she couldn't turn on him. Then instead of being a man about it and coming after me and my brothers, he targets innocent women and then a helpless child. Working for a man like him tells me everything I need to know about your character."

One shrugged. "The money's good."

"Now, we can do this the easy way or the hard way," kisser said as he cracked his knuckles. Everything about him screamed that he wanted

Cade to pick the hard way, and lucky for him this time they were on the same page.

"Boss needs to know if you have a name," another said, stepping closer and somewhat cautiously bending down to unlock the chains that kept him attached to the floor.

Even though a part of him wanted to pounce on these me, teach them a lesson for touching Essie and Gabriella, kill as many of them as he could before they took him down, he couldn't do that.

Well, not yet.

If he held out long enough, he hoped the boss would eventually show up in person. There were still three of his mom's rapists they needed to identify, and if he could get the name of this one, then hopefully, that would be the domino that sent the others tumbling.

When he gave no response, two of them grabbed his arms and hauled him to his feet.

"You choosing the hard way?" kisser asked, excitement dancing in his dark eyes.

Keeping silent gave them the answer they needed.

And their return answer was to start raining down blows on him.

Every one he wore like a badge of honor. Standing in the place of Essie and Gabriella made the pain of each strike more than worth it.

∼

September 5th
1:33 P.M.

"I don't understand," Gabriella said to the middle-aged woman sitting across the table from her.

None of this made any sense.

Why?

Why would Cade do all of this?

When he'd told her to take care of his daughter, she hadn't truly comprehended what exactly that meant.

Continue to love and look after Essie, sure. Make sure she stayed part of her life, absolutely. Be there for her until he came home, yes.

But not this.

It seemed in the few hours between getting a lead on where she and Essie were being held and rescuing them, he'd done more than just come up with a plan.

A lot more.

Including calling a lawyer.

The woman standing in front of her in the living room of Cade's house had just spoken words that had rocked her world, yet none of Cade's brothers or their partners seemed to be the least bit surprised.

They'd all known.

She got that.

What she didn't get was why they weren't more upset about Cade's decisions.

While they'd all treated her with nothing but the utmost respect, embracing her into their family and easing the loneliness inside her, that didn't change the fact that she was an outsider. It was one thing to be nice to her, to include her, to make her feel welcome, because she worked for their brother caring for their niece.

This was a whole other thing.

One that she couldn't believe they were okay with.

Maybe they were just pretending, and they were going to tell her they would challenge it in court if Cade didn't come home.

No.

That couldn't be it.

They'd known this was coming, which meant Cade had told them, and they obviously hadn't issued any challenge to him. Could that be just because they didn't want to add to his stress when he was so worried about his daughter?

"It's very simple, Ms. Sadler," the lawyer said patiently. They'd already gone through this several times, but it wasn't sinking in. "Mr. Charleston has named you the legal guardian of his daughter, Esther Charleston. He's also transferred the title of his house into your name. All you need to do is sign these papers and everything is official."

His daughter?

His house?

The home he'd shared with his wife, the only woman she knew he would ever truly love.

Why had he given her both?

He had three biological brothers standing right there in the living room with her, and all three were in serious relationships. He could have given custody of Essie to any of them. Or if he hadn't wanted to put on them such a heavy responsibility while they were in the beginnings of a relationship, he could have given guardianship to either of his step-brothers.

They were family.

She wasn't.

"Sign the papers, Gabs," Cooper said gently.

"But—"

"No, buts," Connor told her when she tried to protest. "This is what Cade wanted."

"I don't understand why," she said, fighting back a wave of tears. She was physically and mentally exhausted, she still hadn't been able to sleep well in the hospital last night, and her brain was not quite able to comprehend the fact that she was safe. Trying to figure out what Cade had been thinking when he'd made this decision was too hard. All she wanted was for him to come home. To be safe. To not die in her place. Essie needed him and ... she did too.

Even if he could never really be hers, she still wanted him in her life. Wanted things to go back to how they'd been before. Before he confused her by going to her room, finding her doll, carrying it around with him, and then dropping the bombshell that she was his daughter's guardian and the new owner of his house.

"Because he knows you love Essie more than anyone else and that the best place for her is with you," Cole said gently.

"Better than with all of you?" she protested.

"We love that kid with every fiber of our beings. She's family, blood, part of us. But this doesn't change anything," Connor said. "We still get to love her, and we were all in agreement when Cade told us he wanted to do this before we made the exchange. You love Essie like your own and you're the only mom figure she's ever had. She belongs with you."

"But I'm an outsider, not really one of you." Gabriella hated saying the words, but they were true. They were always true. She was always on the outside looking in. No matter how hard she tried she couldn't seem to find her place in the world. "Like you said, you're Essie's blood, her family. I'm just the nanny."

"You're not just the nanny, and you know it," Jake barked at her, startling her from her decline into a deep pit of self-pity.

"You're part of this family," Jax reminded her.

"You know that, don't you?" Cooper asked.

When she shrugged in response, she got five glares from the guys, and three sympathetic smiles from the girls.

Taking a seat at the table, Susanna reached over and placed a hand over one of hers. "I get it, Gabriella. I really do. I've always felt alone like I never had anyone at my back. Until Cole it was true. I know we haven't known each other for very long but you and Essie were the first people to make me feel like I was important, like I was part of something. That note and the donuts you left outside my apartment after I was raped, they meant everything to me."

"How can you go out of your way to make sure Susanna felt included, and not know that every single one of us consider you a part of this family?" Cole asked, then dragged his fingers through his dark hair.

"I know you all care about me, I do. You're the first people to make me feel like I was a part of a family, but the reality is I'm not. I'm just Essie's nanny, I work for Cade, I'm an employee not a relative." It wasn't that she was ungrateful for everything they'd done for her, making her feel like one of them, but she felt emotionally drained and completely raw right now.

This was just too much to handle.

Too much potential for failure.

What if she failed Essie like she had all the babies she'd lost?

The universe had decided for her that she shouldn't be a mother, yet Cade was trying to thrust it on her and she was so overwhelmed.

"I don't want to hear you say that again," Jake snapped.

"Honey, I think there's something you're missing. Something important," Willow said as she took a seat on Gabriella's other side.

"What?" she asked, desperately, but she needed someone to help her make sense of this.

"Everything the guys said is true. You are a part of this family, everyone cares about you. You are the only mother figure Essie knows, and you absolutely should be the one to have guardianship of her. But none of that is why Cade chose you when he could have picked one of his brothers if that was what he wanted."

"Then why?" she whispered.

"Because he cares about you," Willow answered.

"Cade ... doesn't see me as anything other than the nanny," she said the words, had one hundred percent believed them up until yesterday.

Only it was the doll that changed everything.

By all accounts, he had been clinging to it like a security blanket since she and Essie were abducted along with his daughter's teddy bear.

Why would he do that if he didn't care?

"Cade sees you as everything he's afraid to have in case he loses it all over again," Jax corrected.

The tears that had been building burst free and tumbled in earnest down her cheeks. Having Cade return her feelings was everything she'd wanted after about the first six months of working for him.

But she didn't want it like this.

Didn't want to find out that maybe he cared about her when he was gone, and she might never get him back. Didn't want his house or custody of his daughter. She wanted to share those things with him as a family, but she didn't want them because she'd lost Cade in the process.

"I just want him back." She wept softly. "I want him to be home, to be safe, I hate that he's in danger because of me, but it makes me love him so much more that he would willingly put his life on the line to save his daughter."

"And you," Becca added.

"Sign, honey," Cooper told her. "Sign the papers and make official what Cade wanted. None of us are giving up on him. He has a plan, and we have a lead that they don't know about. Don't give up hope just yet."

With a shaking hand she reached out and picked up the pen.

Her tears dotted the papers as she signed the documents, transferring the house's title into her name and giving her custody of Cade's daughter.

Come home, Cade. Please. We need you.

CHAPTER *Ten*

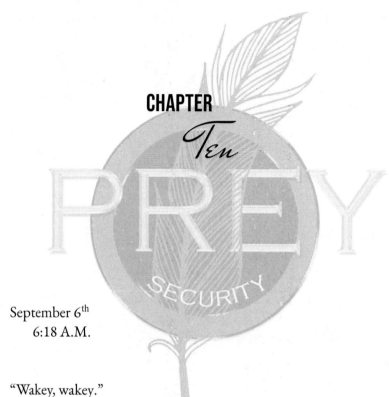

September 6th
6:18 A.M.

"Wakey, wakey."

The words had Cade lifting his head. He'd already been awake when the door to the basement was opened, but he hadn't bothered looking to see who was coming.

After delivering a fairly easy beating yesterday, they'd chained him back up and left, returning what he estimated to be a couple of hours later with some food. Since he wasn't just a prisoner but one they had reason to keep alive, they couldn't just lock him up and leave him. They had to make sure they fed and watered to keep him in good enough shape to keep interrogating him until he told them what they wanted to know.

The thing was, he didn't really have a whole lot of valuable intel.

He knew there had been four men who raped his mother and that Tarek Mahmoud, a world-renowned Egyptologist, had been one of them. Other than that, he knew nothing even close to being able to name the men and bring them down.

But he intended to find out.

Holding out and enduring these beatings for long enough was his best bet at getting whoever had hired these men to come after his family to pay him a visit.

The only piece of intel he had was the link to the stationary company, and that might not pan out to be anything at all. Still, it was something and he knew Prey would look into it and find out if it was anything that would lead them to one of the three remaining men they were looking for.

Now, as he watched two men clamber down the stairs with an urgency he hadn't seen in them before he wondered what was going on. Were they planning on moving him somewhere else? Had something happened?

With him switching places with Essie and Gabriella, his brothers were going to pretend to be holding off on their search for answers for a while. They needed these men to believe his family was going to honor the deal they'd made even if they had no intention of doing so. Quietly looking into the stationary company, hopefully wouldn't raise any heads, and as long as they thought his family had backed off because they didn't want to endanger him the longer it would keep him alive.

"You wanted to meet our boss, well, you got lucky," one of the men said as he reached down to unlock the chains binding him to the ground.

That perked him up.

Not what he'd been expecting to hear.

He'd only been their prisoner for less than forty-eight hours, he would have thought it would be days at least before the boss would make an appearance.

"He was in the area and wanted to find out for himself what you know. I suggest you decide to be more cooperative," the other man told him like that suggestion was going to bear any weight.

Even if he had the names of the other three men involved in his mom's rape and subsequent arrest for treason and fake suicide, nothing these men could do to him would make him cough up that intel.

Nothing.

He'd been trained to withstand torture, and while these men knew how to deliver pain, they knew nothing about the real art of inflicting the kind of agony needed to get a man to start talking.

Once he was unchained from the floor, his wrists still bound and his ankles still bound, he was shoved into a chair and secured to it.

No sooner had they finished locking in chains than voices sounded just outside the door at the top of the stairs, and a moment after that he saw the other three of his captors appear along with a man dressed in an expensive black suit.

It only took one look at the man in the suit for him to recognize him.

"John Jones," he said. While his face was a little thinner and his eyes brown not blue, his hair starting to go salt and pepper, this was the man who had worked with Becca in Cambodia. The man he'd been supposed to meet with when he got the text to say that Essie and Gabriella were about to be targeted. Of course, he'd known that the man was almost definitely involved in the abduction, they'd believed that even before the meeting that never happened, but he hadn't expected the man to be the boss who was orchestrating everything.

Only a little older than his own thirty-four years, maybe late thirties, no more than early forties, there was no way the man could have been involved in his mother's rape. Back then, John Jones would have only been a teenager. He'd claimed that he was the son of one of the men, Cassandra's half-brother, given his age, that was definitely a possibility.

They hadn't been able to learn a lot about the man which told them one thing.

John Jones didn't exist.

Not really.

Not in any real and meaningful sense of the word.

His cover had been passable, enough to get him the job working for Becca's charity, which provided medical aid and education to people in remote villages across Asia. But even though his background had been sufficient to get him the job, it hadn't been enough to convince Becca or her team that he was truly an aid worker. She'd known something was off about him, she just hadn't known anything about the threat to Connor's family.

Knowing this man, who may or may not be Cassandra's half-brother had been hitting on Connor's ex-girlfriend, who was now his current girlfriend again since they'd reconciled a couple of weeks ago, made him feel sick.

"I'm sorry for standing you up the other morning," John—or at least the man going by the name of John—said, when he came down to stand before him.

"Sure you are," Cade said, giving the man a scrutinizing once over. There was something familiar about him, but at the moment, he couldn't place what it was. It was like he'd seen the man before but not him exactly. His father maybe? Had he met the man who raped his mother at some point in his life? Or had he seen the man because he was some public figure? The possibilities were endless, all they knew was that the rapists had all been in Egypt twenty-five years ago when Cassandra had been conceived via rape.

"As you can imagine, I was a little preoccupied," John said, snickering at his own joke.

At least he was amusing someone.

Personally, Cade saw nothing at all amusing about his four-year-old daughter being abducted.

But since he knew that John was only trying to get a rise out of him, he didn't bother reacting to the comment. Merely continued to stare at the man trying to figure out who he really was.

"I must admit I was not surprised to find that you were willing to offer a trade. Yourself for the child. Although not just the child," John said, tilting his head to the side and examining him like he was an interesting experiment he was longing to figure out. "I believe you were almost equally as invested in protecting the woman. My investigations into your family showed only that she was hired to be the nanny to your daughter. I was unaware that there was a more personal connection. Had I known this, I might have made some different decisions."

Again, all John was trying to do was work him up and make him angry enough that he would spill information he otherwise wouldn't.

Lucky for him he didn't have any intel to spill.

Unlucky for John Jones.

"Was any of it true?" he asked, his voice perfectly calm and controlled. "Do you really believe you are Cassandra's brother?"

Something crossed over John's face. "I'm not sure. I do believe it is a possibility."

Interesting. He'd thought it was all just a lie. But if this man was the one running things, who'd sent people after Susanna, then Becca, why had he bothered to go to Cambodia himself and pretend to be an aid worker?

What was he missing here?

"You have what you want now, so there's no reason to keep going after my family," he told the other man.

"Unfortunately, it's not that easy and you know it. You understand that I cannot let you live now that you've seen me and know I'm involved."

"Yet you let my daughter and her nanny go," he reminded John. He didn't like pretending that Gabriella was nothing but the nanny, but for her safety it was the wisest choice.

"I don't like hurting women and children," John said a little too vehemently, giving away a little about who he was and what motivated him. Even though he knew Gabriella had indeed been hurt at his men's hands, there was an element of truth in his statement.

"And yet, if you're the one behind the attacks against my family, you've targeted the women almost exclusively," he reminded John.

Anger burned in the other man's dark eyes. He didn't like being called out no matter how true what Cade had just said was.

"This doesn't have to be terrible," John said. "You can just tell me what you and your family have already learned so I know what damage control I need to do, and then we can just stick you away somewhere as insurance."

Like that was going to happen.

For the first time in a long time, he had a spark of hope for more in his future, a second chance at happiness with a woman who adored his daughter and seemed to see something in him.

Now that he'd met John Jones, he was determined to figure out why the man looked familiar.

Game on.

~

September 6th
12:40 P.M.

"Did you eat enough? Are you still hungry?" Gabriella asked Essie as the little girl climbed off her chair.

"Can I have a cookie?" Essie asked hopefully. With her big gray eyes opened wide in her typical begging expression, and her dark hair hanging loose around her shoulders, she looked so much like her daddy that it almost hurt to look at her.

They'd been home for two days, and Essie was doing as well as you could hope for. She'd already had an appointment with a child psychologist who specialized in helping children who had been through trauma. So far, she hadn't had any nightmares, but Gabriella wouldn't be surprised if they came for the child at some point. While she'd done her best to shield Essie as much as she could, they'd both still been abducted and held captive for four long days.

When Essie had asked to sleep in her daddy's bed last night, Gabriella could see no reason to say no. When Essie had cried and begged her to sleep in the bed beside her, she could see no reason to say no.

So, they'd both slept in Cade's big bed, surrounded by his scent, and she couldn't help spending most of the night wondering what it would be like to be in this bed with him, his large body curled around hers. His presence would comfort her in a way nothing else could right now, and the longing for it was a physical ache in her chest she couldn't seem to get rid of.

The best thing she could do for Essie was make things as normal as possible and support her in every way she needed.

Cookies for lunch weren't necessary, and they weren't something she would usually allow.

"No, you know the rules. If you're hungry there's plenty of fruit," she told the little girl, refusing to let herself glance around the room to see if the others were judging her decisions.

Maybe they thought she should spoil the little girl and give her everything she wanted, but if she did, she was training Essie that she could always have her own way. When would be the right time to stop? To go back to their simple rules?

"Hey," she said, stopping Essie who had turned to head back to the couch to curl up with her iPad. "How about after I finish up here, we bake some cookies?"

Essie's eyes lit up. "Yes! And can we make our own ice cream? There are tons of sprinkles in the pantry."

"We can, but remember we won't be able to have it until tomorrow because it has to set in the freezer overnight."

"Okay."

"After we finish baking, we'll get your craft stuff out and get creative, okay?" Gabriella felt guilty about being unable to dedicate every second of her time to the little girl, but this was important. Cade had given his life for them, and she was going to do everything she could to help his brothers find him and bring him home.

Once Essie was settled, she turned back to where the others were seated around the table. It looked like they'd been using Cade's house as a base while she and Essie were missing, and everyone continued to congregate there. She'd be lying if she said that she wasn't grateful. The last thing she wanted was to be alone, and she'd made no argument when both Jake and Jax had insisted on staying overnight to watch over them.

If she couldn't have Cade with her then his brothers were the next best thing.

"Maybe I should have let her have the cookie," she said softly, awaiting the judgment she was sure was coming. Just because they were all okay with her having guardianship of their niece didn't mean they would approve of her rules or parenting techniques.

"If she hadn't been abducted, would you have let her have a cookie for lunch?" Connor asked.

"No. Treat foods are only for dessert and sometimes an afternoon snack if we've baked something," she replied. All the rules she had for being Essie's nanny she'd run by Cade, wanting to make sure they were on the same page. Just because she spent more time with his daughter than he did didn't mean he wasn't still the father and the one in charge.

"Then you made the right decision," Cole said simply.

"Honey, we all know what an amazing job you do with Essie, nothing has changed," Cooper assured her.

Giving him a nod because she didn't want him, or any of them, to think she wasn't so appreciative of their support, she turned to face the newcomer. It was a sketch artist, a friend of Eagle Oswald, who Prey's founder and CEO had sent out specifically to work with her and Essie.

This morning she'd stayed in a different room while Essie worked with the artist so that no one could claim that they'd shared ideas or influenced each other in any way. Being away from the little girl, even though she was just in the next room, had left her so jittery and anxious that she'd thought she was going to lose her mind.

Now that Essie was finished it was her turn. This wasn't something she was looking forward to doing even as she wanted to get it done so that they were one step closer to finding Cade and bringing him home.

Having to think of the faces of the men who had hurt her had nausea churning in her stomach and she knew the fact that she was still unable to eat much of anything hadn't gone unnoticed by any of Cade's brothers or their girlfriends.

After explaining the process to her, she spent the next couple of hours forcing herself to confront memories she'd rather pretend didn't exist as she studied the faces of the men who had abducted her and gave every piece of detail to the sketch artist that she could. The woman made adjustments on her computer for each new description Gabriella gave, only stopping when the picture looked as close to each man she remembered as possible.

All five of their abductors were done and she had run out of time.

It was time to confess what had happened in the room the first morning after they were taken. As badly as she didn't want them to know what had happened to her, they at least had to know that there had been an extra man that morning. One she hadn't seen again.

"There was one more," she admitted, ignoring all the eyes on her. "I only saw him once. The morning after we were kidnapped."

Sensing all the questions the guys wanted to toss at her, thankfully, they held back as the sketch artist brought up another face, and once again, they adjusted it until it was as close as they could get to the real thing.

"That's him," Gabriella said with shudder. There was something about that man in particular that had freaked her out. Something darker and more sinister than the others, although they were all terrifying.

"Essie didn't mention him," Jake said.

"She wasn't in the room at the time, so she didn't see him," she explained.

When the sketch artist turned her laptop around so that everyone else could see the image she'd just helped create they all gasped, but it was Becca who spoke first.

"That's John. He looks a little thinner, and John had blue eyes, and darker hair, no graying at his temples, but that's definitely John."

"John?" Gabriella asked. None of the men had given her their name, so to her, they were all just one group of despicable human beings who had tortured her and threatened Essie.

"The man who called the other night, who wanted to meet with Becca, and claimed to be Cassandra's half-brother," Jax explained.

While she knew the basics of what was going on with the Charleston Holloway family, they never hid any of it from her, she didn't always push for details because the whole thing had terrified her. As badly as she wanted them all to get the answers they needed, she'd been so afraid of losing any of them.

"That's who Cade was supposed to meet with when you and Essie were grabbed," Cole added. "John insisted on meeting with Becca, but we weren't going to allow that when we didn't know enough about him, so Cade went in her place only he never showed up."

"Because he was too busy organizing to have me and Essie taken," Gabriella said softly.

"We knew he had to be involved somehow because he was in Cambodia with Becca," Connor said, wrapping an arm around his girl-friend's shoulder and tugging her against his side as they both likely realized just how much danger Becca had been in and hadn't even known it.

"But we didn't know that he was in this deep," Cooper said. "He had to be the one in charge, the one who orchestrated all of this because he wasn't involved in the actual abduction but turned up there."

"He was," Gabriella assured them, remembering his presence and the air of authority he gave out.

This revelation only left them with more questions than answers. Who was John? Was he really Cassandra's half-brother? How was he connected to Cade's mom's rape and murder? And where did he have Cade right now?

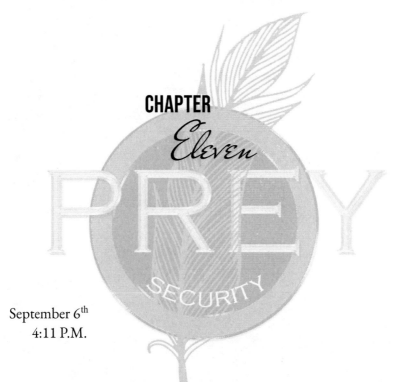

CHAPTER
Eleven

September 6th
4:11 P.M.

"You know I find this whole thing quite distasteful."

Cade fought the urge to roll his eyes at John's ridiculous statement.

They'd been going back and forth with this charade for the last couple of hours. John would ask for answers, wanting to know what Cade and his family knew, then when Cade wouldn't provide any answers, he'd instruct one of his men to slash at him.

When that didn't work, John would throw a huff and storm out of the basement, only to return a while later to start the process all over again.

Rivulets of blood covered most of his body. They'd cut his clothes off him, leaving him in just his boxers, and trails of blood marred his chest, his arms, and his legs. None of the cuts were particularly deep, just enough to slice through skin. Although Cade had no doubt that given enough time, the wounds inflicted would become deeper and deeper until eventually, they cut through an artery, and he bled out.

That would take time, though, which gave him time to play a little.

One thing he found himself torn between hoping for and against was that Gabriella had seen John while she was being held captive. If she'd seen his face, she would have passed that along to his brothers, who would know for certain that the man was involved. That would give them time to dig deeper into who exactly this man was because Cade would bet anything that John Jones was not his real name.

But if Gabriella had seen John, he had no doubt the man would have done something to hurt her, and that alone filled him with enough rage to keep him well and truly fueled even though he hadn't been given anything to eat in hours.

"Shedding blood like this is so barbaric," John continued, and this time Cade couldn't hold back the eyeroll.

"Sure," he scoffed. The man was very clearly enjoying every single second of this. While John might not enjoy getting his hands dirty and putting them directly on people, he absolutely did enjoy watching, knowing he was in control, that he got to play God and decide who lived and who died and what happened to them until he ordered their death.

Narrowing his eyes in irritation that Cade wasn't fawning all over him and giving him the adoration he was obviously used to receiving, John huffed. Whoever this man was he was definitely powerful enough to be the one who kept ordering teams to attack his family. But it was also clear to Cade that John didn't really know anything about how to formulate and follow through on a targeted attack. His attacks had been too random, attempting to discern and go after the weakest link. Despite his power, money, and being accustomed to being in charge, he was afraid of their family.

Finding out the names of the men who had raped their mother would bring John's world tumbling down around him and Cade found great satisfaction in knowing that.

Because it was happening.

Nothing John Jones could do short of killing them all would stop them from getting answers. And killing them would draw far too much attention to him, and besides, Prey would continue their quest.

These men weren't getting away with what they did, and if John had gotten involved in this mess by trying to help cover it up, he was going down with them.

As far as Cade was concerned, it had always been a foregone conclusion.

Deciding it was time to push John a little, anger him enough that he gave away his true identity, Cade cocked his head to the side and studied the man until he began to squirm a little. Despite his big talk and air of superiority, this wasn't a world John was used to. He had rich, spoiled, entitled brat written all over him.

"You know, Becca would never have gone out with a man like you," Cade told the other man, smirking when anger painted John's cheeks red. Becca was like a little sister to him, and even if she and Connor hadn't been able to work through their issues, there was no way Becca would have been attracted to a man like John. He had no heart, no soul, and she was one of the most loving, giving, caring people Cade had ever met.

"If your brother hadn't come back, she would have," John insisted in a huffy tone that only served to prove Cade's point. Becca didn't go for men like this, who were arrogant and cocky and thought they were way better than they really were.

"Nah, man, she doesn't go for rich guys who can't even hack it in the jungle," Cade taunted.

"I was hacking it," John gritted out. If looks could kill, Cade would be dead already.

"Not what Becca said. When you called her the other day, she told us how you creeped her out, that she thought it was odd you didn't seem to care about the people or want to be there."

"I never creeped her out," John insisted.

"If you say so." Cade shrugged as best as he could with his arms chained to the chair. It did the job though, because John was fuming.

"All women like me."

"If you say so."

"I do say so," John snapped, sounding more like a petulant child than a fully grown man talking to his prisoner.

"Sure, bud." Growing up with three younger brothers and a baby sister, he'd well and truly learned the art of provoking others. Just because he'd had to grow up quickly when he was fifteen and his dad had died, and then his mom had been arrested and "committed suicide" didn't mean that he hadn't been a regular kid before that. Given the fact that the boys were all fairly close in age, they'd driven one another crazy while at the same time being close friends, not just brothers.

Now he was using that finely honed childhood skill to his advantage.

"What's not to like?" John exploded. "I'm richer than you could ever hope to be, I'm well respected, I have a job where I can make connections with people who are going to be industry leaders in every field you could possibly imagine. I have everything any woman could ever want."

"And yet Becca rejected you. I'm guessing she's not the first woman to turn you down. With an ego like that, you're pushing away any woman who wants more than an accessory and a meal ticket," he taunted.

"You have no idea who I am and what I can offer a woman," John roared. "I'm the principal of the most exclusive school in the country. Politicians' kids, ambassadors' kids, celebrities' kids. I have connections to almost every wealthy, powerful businessman in the country, as well as connections in the government and the military."

As though realizing what he'd just blurted out in anger when he registered the smug smile on Cade's face, all the air left his sails, and John Jones deflated right in front of him, regret marring his features.

With that information, it finally clicked, and Cade knew exactly who John Jones really was.

"John Gaccione," he said slowly, looking the man up and down. No wonder he looked familiar. He was the principal of the most exclusive private school in the country, following in his father's footsteps. His father, Richard, would have known Tarek Mahmoud, and could definitely be one of the rapists. Richard might even have had contacts who helped him take out a Delta Team and then set up someone to take the fall.

"I only found out what he did on his deathbed," John said wearily. "He confessed, told me everything. Your family was asking questions, and I convinced Tarek to take the fall. Told him if he didn't, I'd make sure he suffered the consequences. I had to pull in every single favor I'd ever earned from a family by giving their kid a place at the school or writing them a reference that got them into an Ivy League college or a job. But I did it. I targeted Susanna thinking it would work. I went to Cambodia to be close to Becca when I learned who she was. But you just wouldn't back off."

"Did your father really believe he was also Cassandra's father?"

"He wasn't sure. It wasn't Tarek, which meant there were only three other possibilities. One of the other men involved was of Asian descent, so it wasn't him. Apparently, he had a heart attack not long after Cassandra was born. That only left two possible candidates, one of which was my father. It was too risky to go after her so they hoped that everything would die down, but you and your brothers are relentless," John told him.

"But we are Cassandra's brothers. How can you come after us knowing we might share a sister? Especially given you weren't even involved."

"My father was a monster. The things he did to my mother ... let's just say your mother should have considered herself lucky he didn't kill her. But he left me a legacy, one that I didn't want to lose. If the truth about him came out, I would be ruined. He's done enough to me, I'm not losing anything else. I deserve the money, the prestige, the power. It's my payment for everything I endured at his hand. I won't lose it because of him. Which means I can't ever let you go. I was weak when it came to your daughter, I should have killed her and the nanny. If they tell about me then I might lose everything anyway."

John looked right at him, and there was actually a small sliver of regret in his dark eyes.

But regret or not, they both knew how this ended.

"I can't let you live," John said aloud.

Then, with a nod at one of his men, he turned and walked away, not watching as the man plunged a knife deep into Cade's flesh.

~

September 7th

7:57 A.M.

"What if I got it wrong?" Gabriella whispered her biggest fear into the quiet car.

Despite trying to call several times yesterday to set up a time to meet with the man who called himself John Jones and claimed to be Cassandra's half-brother, all those calls had gone unanswered.

They were taking a big risk going there.

Last time someone had set up a meeting with John it had been Cade, and the meeting had merely been a ruse to keep all the brothers occupied and focused on the wrong thing so that someone could go after her and Essie.

That someone had to be John.

He had to be involved.

They were all in agreement on that, but they didn't know if he was the man in charge or if he was aware of what was happening and had tried to reach out to them to issue some kind of warning.

Most likely it was the former. It could not possibly be construed as a coincidence that one night Becca gets a call from a man who had worked with her in Cambodia claiming to be another brother to Cassandra when it wasn't common knowledge how Cassandra had been conceived, and then the very next morning she and Essie were abducted.

Prey was running the image she'd made with the sketch artist through facial recognition software, and she knew that it would eventually get a hit, and they'd learn his true identity, but it hadn't yet. Without that hit, she was worried that she'd messed up somehow with the drawing and was setting everybody up with false hope.

"You didn't get it wrong, Gabs," Connor assured her, reaching over Becca, who was sitting in the backseat between them, to squeeze her knee.

No one had wanted her to come along this morning, but she couldn't sit at home and do nothing any longer. If she tried, she was going to lose her mind. Despite none of Becca's calls being answered, and none of the messages she'd left being returned, Becca had told John that she was going to be at the original meeting place this morning if he wanted to meet with her.

The original instructions had been that Becca would meet with him alone, but the guys had rejected that. Now they felt they had no choice but to make it look like they were complying.

Not that they were.

Well, not one hundred percent anyway.

Becca would go alone to the mall entrance, but Connor and Cooper would be with her, and Cole would stay in the car with her. Gabriella had convinced them to let her come by saying she could confirm that she'd been right if she saw his face in person. Although she was the only one who seemed to have doubts, even her doubts were more fear than actually doubting she'd gotten the face correct.

"All right, Becca, time to call one last time," Connor said, and Becca gave a somewhat shaky nod.

Even though she hadn't known Becca for more than a couple of weeks, she'd known since she first started working for Cade that there was a woman from Connor's past that he wasn't over. She was so glad they'd gotten this second chance and were back together again where they belonged, but she hated that this cloud was hanging over all of them.

This family was full of good, honorable men and women and none deserved this.

Praying this worked, Gabriella watched as Becca easily slid her hand into Connor's, gaining support from him. She could imagine how Becca felt knowing she'd been watched and in danger, and hadn't even known about it. Talk about something that makes you feel completely vulnerable.

"Oh, John," Becca said a moment after bringing the phone to her ear after calling back the number he'd used to contact her.

None of them had expected him to answer, and now that he had, Becca's gaze darted to Connor's, silently pleading for help with what to say.

Connor just gave her a confident nod and lifted the hand he was holding to his lips, touching a soft kiss to the inside of Becca's wrist.

Since they could only hear Becca's side of the conversation and didn't want to risk having her put it on speakerphone so they could listen in case they gave away the fact that she wasn't alone, there was nothing the guys could offer to coach her on.

"I didn't expect you to answer since you haven't taken any of my other calls," Becca said.

That she was nervous was portrayed in her tone, but there was no way for John to know exactly why she was nervous. For all he knew, it was just because of the bombshell he'd dropped on her the other day that he believed himself to be Cassandra's brother.

"I'm sorry I couldn't meet with you the other morning, I hope you weren't left waiting long," Becca continued after a pause. "Something happened to Connor's family. His little niece and her nanny were kidnapped."

Since John hadn't outright said that he was involved in the plot to silence the Charleston Holloway family, it was smart of Becca not to let on that they knew who had taken her and Essie and why.

"Yes, they're both okay. We were able to get them back, but only because Essie's father, Cade, offered himself in their place."

Her chest tightened at those words.

They sucked the breath right out of her.

If Gabriella hated one thing it was that Cade had traded himself for her.

For Essie that would have been okay, but the little girl needed her daddy now more than ever. Cade was the only parent Essie had left and there was no way that Gabriella could fill his shoes.

While she'd told Cade when she first interviewed for the job that she was looking to do something different with her life after her failed marriage, she'd never told him why her marriage had failed.

Never admitted to him that the universe didn't think she had what it took to be a mom. That was the only reason in her mind she kept having miscarriage after miscarriage.

Part of her was afraid that if he found out, Cade would fire her, and she'd lose him and Essie. They might not really be hers, but she couldn't love them more if they were.

Which was why she wished Cade had just negotiated for his daughter's release and left her behind. What if she failed Essie the same way she'd failed her own babies?

As though sensing her growing distress, Cole shifted in his seat and reached around it to hold up his hand, offering it to her. There was no hesitation as she reached out to grab it, allowing the feel of his firm grip to ground her. It wasn't the same as having Cade with her, but it was better than nothing. All of these men and their partners had gone out of their way to reassure her of her place in this family over the last couple of days, and it only made her love them even more.

"I'm here if you're able to meet with me. As you can imagine, Connor's family is even more interested in finding out whatever you know about your dad and why you think he's Cassandra's father as well. If you can't meet now, just let me know a time that works for you and I'll be there."

A second later, Becca's dark blue eyes lit up and she nodded, grinning at all of them to let them know that John must have agreed to the meeting.

"Yeah, I'll wait for you. I'll be by the door, the same place you wanted to meet last time," Becca said, then after one more nod, ended the call and shot them all another grin. "He said he'll be here in fifteen minutes. If he's with Cade, then we know the search area has to be within that radius."

"You did amazing, moonlight," Connor said, leaning in to brush a quick kiss to Becca's lips.

Before anyone else could say anything, Cooper suddenly looked up from his phone, his gray eyes wide with surprise.

"What?" Gabriella asked, fearing the worst. Had Cade's body been found? If it had, how would she ever break the news to Essie that her daddy was never coming home?

"That was Prey, we got a hit on the facial recognition software," Cooper informed them.

"And?" Cole prodded when Cooper didn't immediately spit out a name.

"And you're never going to believe who John Jones really is," Cooper replied. "His real name is John Gaccione."

Gabriella gasped, knowing exactly who that was. John Gaccione was the principal of the most exclusive private school in the country. When she'd found out she was pregnant the first time, they'd spoken on the phone with him even though she was only a couple of weeks along because that's how early you had to get your kid's name down if you wanted a chance at a placement at the school.

The list of powerful people who attended the school was endless, and she already knew that to get your kid in you had to agree to repay a favor of John's choosing whenever he wanted to call in the maker.

There was no doubt a man with that many powerful people in his pocket could do whatever he pleased without consequence. And that was the man who had Cade.

CHAPTER

Twelve

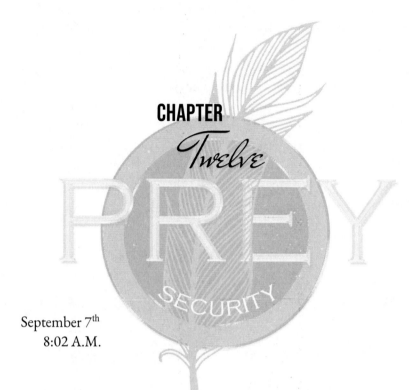

September 7th
8:02 A.M.

"Who could that have been do you think?" John asked as he lowered the phone from his ear.

Never in all his years as an adult had Cade rolled his eyes so many times at another person. Sure, when he was a kid, he might have rolled his eyes at his brothers, his parents, his teachers, his football coach, it was what kids did. But as an adult, he'd never really had cause because most people weren't as ridiculous as the man standing before him.

Despite delivering what could have been a life-ending knife wound the day before, the man who had delivered it hadn't angled the blade correctly to hit his femoral artery. So instead of bleeding out in a matter of minutes, Cade was still alive more than twelve hours later. The wound on his thigh was a bloody mess, but it had already clotted and formed a scab, he wasn't going to bleed out from it.

Infection was another story.

If he didn't receive treatment for the deep gash, there was the possibility that infection would set into the wound, and if left long enough, could wind up killing him.

But that was a worry for another day.

Right now, he'd just been given something to eat and drink and he already felt his strength returning. He was ready to make a move and had a plan in place.

"It was Becca asking to meet up with me," John informed him since he hadn't done the obvious and asked who had been on the other end of the phone.

If his brothers had okayed Becca attempting to arrange a meeting with John, that had to mean they knew something. If they didn't know who John Jones really was, then at the very least, Gabriella had been able to give a description of the men who had taken her and they knew that John had been part of it.

Perfect.

Time to make his move as soon as John left.

"Give my regards to the woman who turned you down multiple times and called you creepy," he shot back.

"How about I do better than that." John lifted the phone and snapped a photo of him, then turned and walked back up the stairs out of the basement.

When he reached the top of the stairs John paused. When he turned around his expression said he was clearly conflicted. The man was a walking contradiction. In some ways, he seemed to actually care about other people, but in other ways, he was quite obviously a narcissist.

"Letting the woman and child go was a mistake. I knew that when I agreed to the terms of your deal. But ... the way she protected the girl ... reminded me of how my mother would do her best to protect me from my father's rages. So I can't regret my decision. I can call in enough favors and have any description she gave of me wiped out, have her painted as suffering from PTSD and labeled as not a reliable witness. Anything she says won't destroy me, but I can't risk you getting away. I'm sure you understand." Turning to his men, he said, "If I don't contact you within the hour, kill him. He's outlived his usefulness."

Those words probably should have instilled fear in him, but instead, they resolved his determination that it was the right time to make his move.

With a last look that conveyed a slight measure of regret, John turned and headed out the door, leaving him alone with two of John's men.

He had to give it to John Gaccione, the man certainly had confidence.

Stupid confidence if he really thought that with all of Prey's resources and connections, he was going to be able to undo Gabriella's claims that he was one of the men who had been part of abducting her and holding her and Essie against their will.

Cade knew he owed a massive thanks to John's deceased mother. Because if it wasn't for her instilling some humanity in her son and doing her best to protect him from his abusive father, there was no way Gabriella and Essie would be alive right now.

He owed a massive thanks to Gabriella as well.

Because if she hadn't fought for his daughter, reminding John of the mother he'd obviously loved,there was no way either she or Essie would be alive.

Shoving all thoughts of his daughter and the woman who had woken up the heart he believed had died along with his wife, Cade focused on what he had to do if he even wanted to stand a chance at getting home to his girls.

There was no way his brothers weren't planning on being there for that meeting. Once they got their hands on John, he had no doubt they would do whatever they had to in order to make him talk.

But they didn't know they had less than an hour to get John some-place secure, get him talking, and then get there to wherever he was being held, otherwise he'd be dead.

If he wanted to live, wanted to go home to his girls, then his fate was in his own hands.

With their boss out of the way, the two remaining men in the room headed over to the small table they'd set up and sat down, picking up the card game they'd abandoned when their boss showed up. While he'd been left alone before John arrived, ever since the man had made sure he had at least two guards in the room at all times. Seemed John wasn't big on trust and did realize how great a threat he was even if the men he'd hired didn't.

Before it annoyed him, hampered his ability to act while being constantly watched, but now he was grateful for their presence.

For his new plan, he needed them close by.

One shot.

That was all he was going to have.

If he didn't get it right the first time, there would be no do-overs. If he wanted to live and figure out what came next for him and Gabriella, he had to get this right. If he wanted to ensure that his daughter didn't lose the only parent she had left, he had to succeed.

With the pressure weighing heavily against him, Cade focused. This was the most important mission of his life.

There was literally zero room for error.

Dragging in a deep breath he got himself in the zone. He had a plan, all he had to do was follow it through step by step and he should make it out alive.

Knowing he could have his little girl and Gabriella in his arms in just a few hours was all the motivation he needed.

Gagging, he fought against his body's natural instincts to not throw up and instead expelled everything he had in his stomach. At the same time, he ordered his body to jerk uncontrollably like he was having a seizure, one that sent him and the chair he was still chained to crashing to the floor.

He barely felt the pain as his already battered body hit the hard concrete because the two men were hurrying over.

"What's wrong with him?" one asked.

"Looks like he's having a seizure. Could be because of the wound? How long does it take for infection to get in?"

"No clue. What even are the symptoms of infection? I didn't think they were seizures."

"Does it matter? Something's wrong with him."

"Maybe we should just let nature take its course. We're supposed to kill him anyway in an hour if we don't hear from the boss."

"You want to risk not following orders to a T?" the other asked incredulously. "He said kill him in an hour if we don't hear from him.

It's been like thirty minutes. If we do hear from the boss, he might not want him dead at all. We should try to help him."

"Fine," the other said with a long-suffering sigh. "Unchain him from the chair."

Success.

Exactly what he'd been after.

"Leave the other chains on. Boss said he's dangerous," the man who'd advocated for him said.

That was fine. He could work with that. It should still be easy enough to take these two out even if his wrists were chained together.

Knowing he'd have to take them both out almost simultaneously, Cade waited until he felt himself slump away from the chair, then the two men laid him out flat on the concrete. Keeping his body limp and unresponsive, when he felt them both close by, he sprang into action.

Hooking his legs around the neck of one of them, he used the cuffs binding his wrists to his advantage and swung his bound hands up and around the other man's head. Using his legs to snap the neck of one man, he squeezed tight around the other's neck.

The first was dead before he realized what was happening, the second took a little longer, but soon his attempts at fighting back died down and then stopped altogether.

Sighing in relief, he let go of both dead bodies and quickly shifted so he was on his knees. Finding the keyring with the keys he needed to unlock himself, Cade freed himself from the last of his chains and shoved to his feet.

A wave of light-headedness reminded him that he wasn't in optimum condition. Not that it mattered. He had to get out of there quickly before the remaining guards came to check on their friends.

Claiming both weapons, he ignored the burning pain in his thigh and took the stairs two at a time to reach the top.

Only just as he was swinging the door open, he came face to face with the barrel of a weapon.

Just like that, his one chance at living went up like a puff of smoke.

~

September 7th
    8:26 A.M.

This was crazy.

Never in her life had Gabriella been this close to anything this dangerous.

Growing up in foster care, she'd spent some time around kids who were lost and alone and searching for a place to belong and found it in all the wrong places. Some of those kids were into dangerous things, drugs, gangs, and fighting, sometimes with knives or guns as weapons.

But nothing to this level.

The anger rolling off the Charleston brothers was off the charts. They were furious that John Gaccione had been targeting their family and were ready to do something about it. It helped a little to know that part of their anger stemmed from what had happened to her and Essie, and she knew she was in no danger from them, none of them would ever lay a hand on her, but she was thinking maybe she should have stayed home with Essie, Jake, and Jax.

Too late to back out now.

Becca was already standing by the mall doors.

Connor and Cooper were hovering nearby but out of sight.

Cole was sitting in the car with her.

The wheels had already been set in motion, there was no stopping what was about to happen. While they all waited to see if John was actually going to show his face, Prey was running through every piece of information they could gather about the man including a list of properties where he might be holding Cade.

Please let us find him soon.

For some reason, Gabriella felt like time was running out. It was probably just because things were about to get serious, but she had this horrible feeling in her stomach just like she'd had the morning before she was beaten that said something bad was going to happen.

"Incoming," Cole suddenly said into his comms, and she followed his line of sight to see a vehicle driving past them taking a parking spot a couple down from where they were, closer to the door.

From where she was, she got a perfect look at the driver and it was indeed John Gaccione.

Maybe she should have recognized him right away when she'd first seen him in that room, but honestly, she'd been too scared to focus on anything else. Still, her delay in identifying him could have cost Cade his life, and if it did she would never forgive herself.

Since she'd declined wearing a comms unit because she didn't really want to be involved in the actual takedown, she didn't know what the guys were saying, or what was happening.

Seconds ticked by.

Cole didn't say anything, but she could feel the tension rolling off him and knew he wished he was out there with the others instead of sitting with her.

Just as she was about to tell him she'd be okay on her own so he could go out there and do ... whatever the guys had planned, she saw them.

John being walked between Connor and Cooper toward their vehicle. If you didn't know any better, you'd just see three men walking side by side through a busy mall parking lot, but she did know better and could see the bulges of the weapons the twins were wearing. She could tell how they were angled toward John even as they were hidden from anyone not specifically looking for them.

To his credit, John didn't look to be concerned, in fact, he almost had what she would consider to be a smug grin on his face.

That feeling she'd been having intensified a hundredfold.

Something was wrong.

Why wasn't John more worried? Why wasn't he even a little bit worried? He had to know he was likely walking into a trap because he knew he'd let her and Essie go and that she'd seen him and would tell people. Yet he'd come anyway. He had to have a plan, some reason he thought he was going to walk out of this alive.

Did he not realize how dangerous these brothers could be?

Mess with their family and they would do everything in their power to take you down. Cade and his brothers also had the entire might of Eagle Oswald and Prey Security at their back. While it was true that John had a lot of contacts through his job, it still wasn't comparable to

Eagle's contacts. She'd met the revered former SEAL a handful of times and Eagle was an intimidating figure, oozing confidence and charm, who was always so sure of himself and his decisions. She wouldn't want to be on the man's bad side, yet John didn't seem to worry about it at all.

When their gazes connected, Gabriella couldn't help but shrink away from the window. The intensity of John's gaze brought back all those memories she didn't have time to deal with right now.

But stuffing them away was so much harder when one of the men who'd made her get on her knees before him so he could roughly take her mouth was too much.

She wasn't even aware she was whimpering until Cole reached around to shoot her a worried look.

"You okay, Gabs?" he asked.

Unable to speak she just nodded.

There was no time for her to have a meltdown.

Whether she was okay or not—and most definitely was not—the priority was getting Cade home to his daughter.

That was what mattered.

Once the two were reunited then she could fall apart.

Maybe.

Unless they needed her.

"Gabriella and I are going to take an Uber home," Cole told the others when Cooper reached out and opened the back door of the SUV.

"No," she said, still shrinking away from John's approach, but confident she wanted to be there. "I'm okay. I just ..." she trailed off because she still hadn't told the others what had happened to her when she was being held captive. They knew about the kiss because it was on the video that had been sent, but they didn't know about the oral sex she'd been forced to give, or about the bite on her breast that burned with pain, but she was steadfastly ignoring it.

"Yes, yes, of course she is," John said as he was shoved into the back of the SUV behind where she was sitting.

"Don't talk to her," Connor snarled as he climbed into the backseat beside her. Cooper joined him and Becca took the front passenger seat.

"Of course," John agreed amicably. "Was just trying to make conversation. I understand why you're all so on edge. It's why I felt like I must reach out to Becca and let her know that I might be related to the woman I assumed would one day be her sister-in-law. I was just trying to do the right thing, Becca, you know that. You know me."

"Shut up," Cooper ordered, and John gave an agreeable nod.

They rode in silence until they got to the building she knew was where Cade and his team planned their ops and ran training drills. Prey's main office was in Manhattan, but since that was several hours away, they had their own office building close to home. There were plenty of times that they had to go into the main office, but most of the time, Eagle allowed his teams the autonomy of working independently so long as they ran things by him.

She'd only been there a handful of times over the years, but never like this.

Never with a prisoner in tow.

Since she knew Prey always did things in a way that there would be no blowback to them, she had to assume they had already alerted authorities to the fact that John Gaccione was involved in her and Essie's abduction and had permission to interrogate him.

Whatever John thought was going to happen was not.

Life as he knew it was already over.

This was all just a formality because they needed to know where Cade was being held.

Please be alive, please be alive, please don't let us be too late.

It felt like it was too late.

That's what she was thinking as the car drove into the underground parking lot and came to a stop.

As the guys pulled John out of the vehicle, she and Becca trailed behind as they all headed inside. Instead of taking the lift to the main floors, they took it down to a level she hadn't been to before.

Not that she needed an imagination to figure out what this level was for.

These were the interrogation rooms.

"Wait here, moonlight," Connor said, pausing to drop a kiss to Becca's lips. "You too, Gabriella."

That was fine with her. She didn't want to watch this even as she knew it was necessary.

Cade's life was hanging in the balance.

It didn't take long for the first scream to hit the air and all she could do was slump against the wall, wrapping her arms around Becca as they held onto each other and prayed for the answers they needed to save Cade's life.

CHAPTER

Thirteen

September 7th
8:49 A.M.

"What the—" The man with the gun was startled when he saw Cade standing before him.

There was no time to waste if he wanted to hold onto his chance of escaping. He didn't know how much of the hour was left, but he had to have waited a solid thirty minutes at least before enacting the first stage of his plan so he didn't have much time left to waste.

Because he was still hoping not to alert anyone remaining in the building that he was staging an escape attempt, instead of firing one of the weapons he'd taken from the guards he'd killed, Cade swung out using his claimed weapon more like a club to knock the man sideways and unbalance him. Then he reached out with one hand, grabbed the man's weapon with his free one, and yanked as hard as he could while sidestepping and tossing the man down the stairs.

Each thump he made as his body connected had Cade wincing.

Not because he cared if the man was hurting, but because each sound seemed so loud to his ears that he was sure it must be echoing through the entire building, a beacon calling in anyone within hearing distance.

But nobody came.

At the bottom of the stairs, the man lay still. Possibly not dead, but hopefully incapacitated enough that he wasn't going to be a problem.

Not wanting to waste precious seconds by running back down the stairs and checking on him, finishing him off if need be, Cade instead headed out through the door and then paused to close and lock it behind him. If the man was still alive this would at least keep him contained.

With the door safely locked, he took a second to rest his aching leg and check his surroundings. From what he could see, he was in some sort of small office building. The basement wasn't big enough to be an underground parking lot or anything, but he was standing at the bottom of a stairwell like one you'd find in an office building.

This had to be the ground floor because he'd just come up from the basement, so he moved carefully, ignoring the throbbing in his leg, and moved so he could see how many flights of stairs went up above him.

It looked like five which meant this building wasn't anything too large.

What he cared more about, though, was how many people were currently still inside and where it was located.

It couldn't be overly remote given that most office buildings were in central locations, but he needed to be sure. Given how badly his leg was hurting, he couldn't hike a huge distance to get himself back to civilization.

Then a picture of his daughter's smiling face and Gabriella's tinkling laugh flitted through his mind and Cade knew he would absolutely walk a thousand miles if that was what it took to get home to his girls.

Heading for the door that would lead out of the stairwell, Cade inched it open just enough to peer through and saw a large lobby area with several doors leading to other rooms.

There was also a door leading outside.

Since he could not know if any of the other rooms were occupied, he would have to risk making a run for it. There was no cover out there. As soon as he stepped through this door, he'd be an easy target, but it wasn't like just staying there was an option.

Three of the five men he knew had abducted him were either dead or contained in the basement, but that still left two others.

Even injured, he wouldn't hesitate to take them on and do whatever it took to win.

Fighting wasn't the issue, it was being shot in the back while he made a run for freedom that had his heart knocking on his chest.

He and Gretel had gotten together while he was in training, so even from the very beginning of his career he'd always had every reason in the world to make it home alive. It meant he'd long since developed the skills of being careful in any situation, no matter how dangerous it might be.

Never had the stakes felt so high.

Dying now would leave his daughter an orphan, and he had a feeling Gabriella had done so much more than any of them realized to protect his daughter. They both needed him and the thought of failing them left him barely able to breathe.

The longer he waited the higher the chance that someone was going to see him.

Sooner or later one or both of the remaining men would come to check on him and their colleagues. If nothing else, he was sure they had been informed of John's orders that if they hadn't heard from him in an hour, they were to kill their prisoner.

That hour had to be close to being up, and if they found him lurking around, they would likely open fire. They'd be both following their boss' orders and eliminating him as a threat.

Still, there wasn't any other option.

He was going to have to risk crossing the open space and pray for the best.

Focusing his energy, he did his best to convince himself this was no different than any other op he'd ever been on but was failing miserably.

As he edged open the door he debated his three options. He could either go slow, stick to the walls, or get down low and crawl on his stomach to the door, trying to remain as inconspicuous as possible. Or he could just go for it and run. The first option might be the safer but it was also slower, and he wanted to get the hell out of there.

Deciding he had to play it safe no matter how badly he wanted to get out, get to a phone, and call his brothers, Cade slipped through the door and immediately down to his stomach.

Better to be safe than sorry.

Dragging his injured leg behind him, he slithered along like a snake toward the door, the weapons clutched in one hand.

"Hey!"

Damn.

Halfway to the door he'd gotten caught.

Knowing that he had a limited amount of time if he wanted to get the odds back in his favor, he rolled onto his knees, his thigh burning with the sudden movement, and the weapon in his hands aimed in the direction the voice had come from.

It was one of the remaining two guards, and the man was pointing a weapon directly at his head.

But he was doing the same.

Which left them at an impasse.

For now, it was one against one, but those odds could change in a heartbeat if the guy summoned his partner.

Taking perhaps the biggest risk of his life, Cade acted because he knew if he didn't, it was already over for him.

This at least gave him a chance.

Ignoring the weapon aimed at his head, he lunged toward the man. Tackling him around the legs, he took him down and they both hit the ground.

Cade swung his weapon, connected with the man's head, and was rewarded with a grunt of pain. The man was down but not out, and he kicked out, one of his feet connecting with the wound on Cade's leg and he bit back a howl of pain.

For a second the world spun around him.

Realizing he'd scored a direct hit the man brought back his foot and slammed it out harder this time.

White dots danced in front of his eyes, and Cade swayed and then toppled sideways as the pain in his leg soared until it consumed him in a fiery ball of red-hot agony.

Kicking him one last time, the man broke free of Cade's weakening hold and shoved back to his feet, reclaiming his weapon and staring down at him with a triumphant smile.

He'd won and Cade had lost.

Only the loss wasn't just his life, it was also everything the people he loved would suffer as well. His daughter would lose her only remaining parent, Gabriella would lose what could have been between them if he hadn't been such a coward and just admitted he had feelings for her, and his brothers would lose another family member.

Too much loss, too much death, too much suffering and grief.

If he could change it, he would.

But there was nothing he could do to change the fact that he was looking down the barrel of a weapon.

Shifting his gaze, he met the eyes of the man holding that weapon. If he was going to die, he was going to do it facing his death head-on. No hiding, no cowering, he'd done that enough the last few years and it wasn't how he wanted to spend his final moments on earth.

I'm sorry, Essie. Never forget that your daddy loves you.

I'm sorry, Gabriella. I should have given you—us—a chance.

～

September 7th
9:36 A.M.

The waiting was killing her.

Gabriella was going to lose her mind if they didn't hear from Cooper or Cole soon.

This was too much.

The pressure, the anxiety, the gut-curdling fear.

There was no way she could keep going on like this.

How had Cade survived when it was his own child who'd been taken from him?

Well, she supposed he hadn't.

That's why he was the one currently being held hostage.

The guys had gotten an address from John Gaccione. She had no idea how, nor did she want to know, but she would be forever grateful to them for whatever they'd done in that room that had elicited those blood-chilling screams and got them an address.

Connor had stayed with her and Becca at the Prey building while Cooper and Cole had gone after Cade. She'd wanted to insist that Connor go with them. They weren't sure what they were walking into, and the more of them against John's men the better. But Becca had clearly needed Connor close by as the reality of what could have happened to her while she was vulnerable in Cambodia truly sank in.

The three of them were upstairs, sitting in an office she knew was Cade's because of the photos of Essie on the desk and her artwork hanging on the walls. She wasn't sure if Connor had chosen this room at random since it was the closest office to the lobby, or because he knew she needed to feel close to Cade right now.

While the others sat on the couch in one corner of Cade's office, she paced about, unable to be still, needing a way to work out the terror-fueled energy buzzing inside her. Fears about how she would tell Essie if the worst happened, and how she would raise the girl on her own at least served the purpose of numbing her pain. She was still a mottled mess of bruises, and the bite mark on her breast hurt just from the feel of the material of her sweater brushing against it.

When Connor's phone rang, she froze.

Good news or bad?

Was her life about to irrevocably change?

Becca squeezed Connor's free hand as he answered the call, and they locked their gazes on her.

Reading Connor's expression was impossible. Was it Cooper or Cole? Had they found Cade? Had they been able to rescue him? Was he dead or alive?

Connor didn't say much and what he did speak was mostly drowned out by the thudding of her pulse echoing in her ears. As much as she needed to know what had happened, Gabriella was also aware that these might be the last few seconds where she had hope.

Once she heard the news there would be no going back.

"Wh-what did they s-say?" she stammered as soon as Connor lowered the phone.

Seconds felt like years as he stood and crossed to stand before her. It was bad news. Had to be. Tremors wracked her body. She wanted to know, but at the same time she didn't.

Then his face broke into a smile. "He's alive, Gabriella. Cade is alive and safe."

Relief hit her so hard her knees buckled, and she would have hit the floor if Connor hadn't whipped out an arm and wrapped it around her waist to hold her up.

"He's a-alive?" she repeated, the words not fully sinking in yet. What if this was just a dream, and she was going to wake up to find that Cade was still missing or worse, dead?

"Alive," Connor confirmed.

Tears blurred her vision. "Is he okay?"

His smile dipped a little but didn't disappear altogether. "He's got a nasty wound on his leg, and he's lost a bit of blood. Coop said he's also got lots of bruises and some smaller cuts, but he's not going to die."

"Can I speak to him?" Knowing he was alive wasn't the same thing as hearing his voice, hearing him tell her himself, maybe then she could actually believe it.

"He's unconscious at the moment, but they have an ambulance on the way, and we can meet up with them at the hospital," Connor told her.

Unconscious.

So not that okay after all.

The tremors wracking her body increased, and she saw concern in Connor's gray eyes. They all knew, her included, that she wasn't okay. Just like they all knew she'd been pretending that she was both for Essie's benefit and so that everybody's focus could remain on searching for Cade. She wasn't eating or sleeping, she was running on fear and adrenalin, and it wasn't sustainable.

Sooner or later, she was going to crash.

But not today.

Today was a day for celebrating.

"Yes, I want to go to the hospital. I'll call Essie on the way and tell her that her daddy is coming home, but I won't tell her he's hurt. I don't want her to worry until she can see him for herself."

"Cole called Jake while Cooper called me, so they'll know and be waiting for you to tell Essie. They'll keep her occupied, and once Cade is awake, they can bring her to the hospital."

Together the three of them rushed through the building and into Connor's car. As soon as they were on the way Gabriella pulled out her phone. She knew how worried Essie was about her daddy, and she didn't want the child to worry a second longer than she had to.

Since Cole had called Jake, she called Jax just in case Jake was still on the phone. He picked up almost immediately.

"Hey, Gabs, you calling to tell Essie the good news?"

"Yeah. Is she okay?" Leaving the little girl this morning hadn't been easy, but she knew it was the right thing to do. She couldn't help but feel the whole kidnapping was her fault. After all, she was the one who had insisted on keeping Essie's routine as normal as possible. So she had a duty to do whatever she could to help find Cade and bring him home.

"She's fine. Beating the socks off us at Mario Kart," Jax replied.

That made her chuckle. "She's four, the only reason she's beating you and Jake is because you're amazing uncles who like to build her confidence by letting her win."

"Kid's got lots of natural talent, she could definitely be a race car driver when she grows up."

"Cade would just love that." Actually, he wouldn't care what Essie wanted to do with her life so long as she was happy. He was a good dad who would support his daughter in anything she wanted to do. How different her own life might have turned out if either of her parents had been like Cade.

Jax chuckled. "He'd be the proudest dad around. I'll get messy Essie for you."

"I'm not messy, Uncle Jax." Essie huffed in the background, making Gabriella smile.

"Hey, cuddle bug," she said a moment later.

"Gabby, I miss you, I want you to come home," Essie said.

"I miss you, too, sweetie. So much, but I have the very best news to tell you."

"Daddy is coming home?" the little girl asked hopefully.

"Yep, he is! I'm just going to see him right now, and then in a bit, Uncle Jake and Uncle Jax will bring you to see him."

"I want to go now."

"I know you do, cuddle bug. But remember how after we got away from the bad men we had to have a doctor check us out? Well, that's what daddy has to do, too. The hospital is so boring so it's better for you to stay home and play until Daddy is ready to see you," she explained.

"Okay," Essie reluctantly agreed.

"I'll talk to you soon, sweetie. I love you."

"Love you, Gabby."

After hanging up she wriggled in her seat, desperate to get to Cade. The drive didn't take more than fifteen minutes, but it felt like a lifetime.

As soon as they parked and went through the emergency room doors, they were met by Cole who led them through to the small room where Cade was lying on a bed.

The first thing that hit her when she finally laid eyes on him was that he looked uncharacteristically vulnerable. His big body was so still and there were bruises on his pale skin. With his eyes closed he looked like he was sleeping but not peacefully. Even unconscious, he couldn't seem to fully relax.

"We'll be right outside," Cole told her gently, and she was vaguely aware of the others moving outside the little curtained-off room, but most of her attention remained fixated on the man lying in bed.

Slowly, she moved toward him. When she reached the bed, Gabriella moved a hand to cover one of his but stopped before making contact. Things had always been weird between them because she liked him as more than a boss and yet knew her feelings would never be reciprocated.

But now they were even weirder.

She was at least partially responsible for his daughter being kidnapped, but he'd saved them both, been using her old ragdoll as a security item, and given her custody of his daughter. She didn't know what that meant but she did know that her love for this man had only grown over these last several hellish days.

A surge of pent-up emotion had all the feelings she'd been keeping bottled up exploding out in a flood of tears, and she snatched up Cade's limp hand and brought it to her face, rubbing her wet cheek on it, feeling like her whole world was hanging in the balance. Only she didn't know if she was going to find everything she'd ever wanted or once again be left alone out in the cold.

CHAPTER

Fourteen

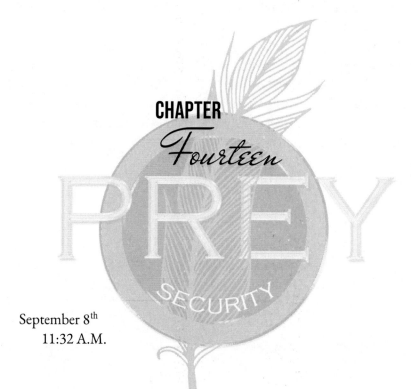

September 8th
    11:32 A.M.

He couldn't take his eyes off them.

Either of them.

They were both so beautiful, so precious, so important to him.

It meant he had some hard decisions to make over the coming hours, but for now, Cade couldn't allow himself to think about that.

All he could focus on was how grateful he was that his plan had gotten Essie and Gabriella out of that hell alive.

Although not unscathed.

Essie was particularly clingy, totally to be expected, but still hard to watch as his usually confident and outgoing little girl made sure she was always within touching distance of him or Gabriella. More Gabriella than him, and while he wanted his daughter to seek comfort in his arms, he knew how lucky he'd been when he decided to hire Gabby.

No one else outside himself and his family would have protected her the way she had.

Which brought him to the nanny.

While she had a permanent smile on her face, there was something haunted in her eyes that he hated and wanted to get rid of. Maybe no one else was picking up on it, although he couldn't imagine how since it seemed so blatantly obvious, but he was, and it killed him.

Like his daughter, Gabriella was confident and outgoing, she loved hard and wasn't shy about sharing how much she cared for the people in her life. She was always thinking of others, wanting them to be included and never feel left out, but who was there for her making sure she knew that she was a vital piece of this family?

"All right you ready to get out of here?" Jax asked, appearing at his hospital room door with a wheelchair.

Cade growled at it. So his leg was a little messed up, so what? It didn't mean he had to be taken through the hospital halls in a wheelchair.

When his brothers had shown up and saved his life, he'd passed out. He had no memory of being brought to the hospital or being examined. His memories started up again after he woke up from surgery to clean and stitch his leg to find Gabriella sitting in a chair beside his bed, holding his hand. The relief in her green eyes when she saw him wake up would stay with him forever. If he had ever had any doubt about how deep her feelings for him ran that had eliminated them.

"More than ready," he said, shoving off the bed and ignoring the crutches Gabriella held out to him.

"You're coming home, Daddy?" Essie asked, hovering by his side, an anxious look on her normally calm and happy little face.

They'd already gone over that several times, but his daughter needed a lot of reassurance, and he was more than happy to give it to her. He knew how lucky they were to be alive and, relatively speaking, unscathed.

"We're all going home, little one," he assured her.

"Gabby and I made ice cream, can we have it for lunch?" his devious little munchkin asked, showing that even though she was struggling after her ordeal, inside his precious little daughter still existed.

"Sure we can," he agreed.

"Cade," Gabriella rebuked. "You know the rules, treats are for dessert and afternoon snacks if we do some baking."

"Rules were meant to be broken," Cade said simply.

"Okay, who are you and what did you do to my brother?" Cole teased.

Shrugging, he hobbled toward the door. What did rules matter when he and his daughter were alive? If it made her happy, Essie could eat ice cream for breakfast, lunch, and dinner for the rest of her life.

Automatically, he reached out and took his daughter's hand, but he didn't realize he'd also taken Gabriella's until he reached the door and Jax blocked his path. Reaching for her seemed so necessary, a vital part of his recovery, and hers too. Not just their recovery but their lives, too.

Just because he'd never told her didn't mean she hadn't been the glue holding him, his daughter, and his life together these last four years.

"Uh, dude, it's hospital policy," Jax told him when he tried to maneuver past the wheelchair.

"Essie, you want to ride on Daddy's lap as we go downstairs?" Gabriella asked, effectively cutting off any protest he could make.

When he shot her a frown she simply smiled—a smile that didn't reach her eyes—and he rolled his eyes. At least some things never changed.

"Yay!" Essie bounced up and down in excitement and he knew he'd definitely been outplayed by his girls.

Taking a seat, he reached down and picked his daughter up, settling her on his lap but careful to avoid his wound. It was going to keep him out of action for a little while, but he didn't care, his focus was on his daughter right now anyway. Between helping Essie heal from her trauma and continuing to look into the other men who had been involved in the rape he'd have more than enough to keep him busy.

It didn't take long for them to reach the car, and again it was only when he went to stand that he realized somewhere along the way he'd taken hold of Gabriella's hand again. Cade wasn't just consumed with a need to keep his daughter close but Gabriella as well.

Even if he had a million years, he could never repay her for the sacrifices she'd made to protect Essie. Taking that beating and allowing that man to kiss her had saved his daughter from suffering the same fate, and he was eternally grateful.

The three of them piled into the back of his car since it had Essie's car seat installed, and Cole drove them home. The ride was short, Essie babbled away about how she'd beaten Jake and Jax in Mario Kart the day before, and Gabriella just sat there watching him.

As much as he couldn't tear his gaze away from her and Essie, she seemed to be in the same boat. Her eyes had been on him constantly, even when she was focused on Essie, he could feel a thread of her attention on him.

Something had changed between them. Her abduction had forced him to confront feelings he had previously been content to ignore.

The problem was, he still wasn't sure he could do anything about it.

The danger against his family would only grow now that John Gaccione was in custody. They knew that Tarek Mahmoud was deceased, and according to John, his father and one of the other men were as well, but John claimed not to know the other man's name.

"We're home," Essie announced as they pulled into the driveway.

Home.

Without his daughter and Gabriella, it hadn't felt like home, just an empty house. It was the same feeling he'd had when he first walked into it after Gretel had died. The heart that turned a house into a home was missing. It had only returned when he hired Gabriella and she moved in.

"We're going to take turns watching the house," Cole informed him. "So you guys can enjoy some time together, but we're going to have to talk about a better plan from here on out. These men are too dangerous and we're getting closer. You know how cornered animals react."

That was true.

And it was what had a heavy ball of regret sitting heavily in his stomach.

He knew what he had to do, he just didn't like it one little bit.

While Gabriella rounded the car and helped Essie out of her car seat, he swung his bad leg out and carefully placed his weight on it. The wound wasn't bad enough that he couldn't use the leg, but it did throb annoyingly. A constant reminder of how close he'd come to losing his life.

Watching Essie skip down the path toward the door, Gabriella rifling through her bag looking for the keys, was so normal that tears actually blurred his vision for a second. These little moments of everyday life had always just slipped by unnoticed. Sometimes it wasn't until you came so close to losing something that you realized how important those regular moments really were.

Before Gabriella could unlock the door, it opened, and Cooper shot them a grin.

"House is clear, coffee is made, and there might be some donuts on the counter," Cooper told Essie.

"Donuts!" she squealed, taking off at a run for the kitchen.

"Just one, if you want some ice cream," Gabriella called, hurrying after her.

"You guys going to be okay? I can hang around if you want," Cooper offered.

"We're okay. Appreciate everything you did for me and for them," he said gruffly, pulling his brother in for a somewhat awkward one-armed hug.

"Course, brother. We're family. All of us." Cooper gave him a look that wasn't hard to decipher. He meant that Gabriella was part of them too.

Cade wasn't disagreeing.

This was her family. She'd proven that time and time again, in how deeply she loved Essie, in everything she'd done to protect her.

It was what made what he was going to have to do so hard. It was the equivalent of amputating a part of himself, and there were no guarantees he'd ever heal from the wound.

∼

September 8th
    8:08 P.M.

"I didn't think she'd fall asleep so easily," Gabriella whispered as Cade eased closed the door to Essie's bedroom. "I guess having her daddy back home helped."

She knew it was going to help her.

Tonight she might actually be able to sleep for more than a handful of minutes at a time. Cade would be in the house and that meant she'd be safe. No one else could make her feel as safe as he could. Having his brothers watching the house was a bonus, but knowing he was asleep in his room down the hall would allow her to actually relax enough to fall asleep.

As she turned to head down the hall for the stairs, Cade captured her hand.

He'd been doing that a lot since he woke up yesterday afternoon, not that she was complaining. She loved the way his large hand covered hers, his strong fingers twinning with hers, holding just tight enough to make her feel like she was cared about.

Did he care?

In more than a she was Essie's nanny way?

Or had she allowed herself to get her hopes up these last few days?

There had been no time for them to talk since he was rescued. They hadn't been alone, and his focus had been on Essie, as it absolutely should be. But they were going to need to have a conversation at some point. She had to understand what it meant that he'd been carrying around her old doll and that he'd given her custody of his daughter and possession of his house.

The pad of his thumb brushed across the inside of her wrist making her shiver as she turned to face him. He was so much taller than her own five foot two frame and she had to tilt her head back to look up at him.

There was something indecipherable in his brown eyes, but he gave her a small smile that she could read easily.

Gratefulness.

Her stomach sank a little.

Was that the only reason for the doll and the legal paperwork? Gratefulness because she'd done her job and protected the little girl she loved?

"Thank you," he whispered. "For everything. I can never repay you." Leaning down he touched a tender kiss to her forehead.

A kiss that brought tears to her eyes.

She didn't want his thanks. Of course, she did what she could to protect Essie. What she wanted was ... something she was pretty sure she could never have. She wanted his love.

Stupid of her.

A woman already owned Cade Charleston's heart, and it wasn't her. Would never be her.

"You don't have to thank me, Cade," she said wearily, trying to tug her hand free from his grip. They needed to talk, but she couldn't handle that kind of emotionally intense conversation right now. It would have to wait until the morning.

The hand around hers tightened, just enough to maintain his hold on her. "Don't go. Please," he whispered, his voice raw with a thousand different emotions.

Spinning around to look back up at him, her eyes widened, confused but hopeful. "Why?"

"Because I need you close right now," he answered truthfully.

"I don't ... what does that mean exactly?" There was no way she was going to make any assumptions. Her poor battered heart couldn't take it. She was in love with this man, had been for a long time, and she wasn't sure he quite got that he had the power to crush her if he so chose.

"It means come to bed with me," he said bluntly, and whatever expression was on her face must have been funny because her gruff guy chuckled, his face breaking out into one of those rare breathtaking smiles of his usually only reserved for his daughter. "Please."

"G-go to bed with y-you?" she stammered, wondering if she was hallucinating. The Cade she knew would never take her to bed.

"Yes."

"You mean for like ... s-sex?"

Another chuckle. "Unless it's not what you want."

"It is," she said in a rush. It was everything she'd craved but told herself she could never have for years.

"Then come, please." He tugged her gently toward his bedroom and she allowed him to pull her along with him.

"So polite tonight," she teased. It felt like a giant weight had been lifted off her chest. Finally, the man she'd pined for was showing her that he had feelings for her in return. She'd always understood that part of his heart would always belong to his wife, that wasn't something she wanted to change, after all, Gretel would always be Essie's mother. All she wanted was a little sliver of his heart to call her own. He and his daughter already owned hers.

"I think I'm about to change your mind on that, sweetheart," he told her as he tugged harder on her wrist as they entered his bedroom, bring her body flush up against his. "On a scale of one to ten, how sore are you? And don't even think of lying to me," he warned.

Pain had been a constant friend to her these last few days, but right now, she barely even felt it, there were too many other emotions and feelings taking its place. "Maybe a five," she said, deciding that was the safest answer.

"You'll tell me if that changes." An order not a question, and she squeaked as he shifted his arms so he could pick her up and carry her the remaining distance to the bed.

"Cade, you're bruises, your cuts, your leg," she reminded him.

"Don't care about my leg, sweetheart. All I care about is this."

Laying her out on the mattress that smelled so deliciously like him, she drew in a deep breath to fill her lungs with the scent, he grabbed the waistband of her leggings and panties and drew them down her legs as he moved to the bottom of the bed.

"Do you know how long I've been waiting to do this?" he asked as he buried his face between her legs and dragged in a long breath that ended on a moan. "So sweet."

Gabriella gasped at the first swipe of his tongue. Her ex hadn't been very adventurous in the bedroom, and any time she'd asked him for oral sex he'd complained and done it only under sufferance. She'd never gotten off from it, and in the end, she'd stopped asking since it was easier than the humiliation of knowing her husband didn't enjoy bringing her pleasure.

This was nothing like that had been.

Each swipe of his tongue, each time he teased her entrance, each time he circled his lips around her bud and suckled it sent little electrical currents of pleasure blasting through her body.

Slipping a finger inside her, and then another, he stretched her open, and his tongue plunged deep inside her, bringing her hips off the bed.

Eyes falling closed, head tipping back on the pillow, she began to writhe as he built her higher and higher.

"Come for me now, sweetheart," he ordered as his fingers stayed inside her, pumping in and out and grazing that special spot with each movement as his mouth moved to cover her bundle of nerves. He sucked hard, his tongue flicking over her bud over and over again until there was no way she couldn't obey his command.

She shattered into a thousand pieces as her orgasm rushed through her. White light flashed behind her closed lids, and her body thrashed as intense pleasure claimed her.

By the time she felt him moving back up her body she was panting, her cheeks were wet, and she was trembling from the intensity of the orgasm.

That was nothing like she had ever experienced before. She'd known orgasms could be powerful, but she'd never known they could be like that. So all-consuming that she hardly maintained the ability to think, move, or do anything but feel.

"I can't carry a pregnancy to term," she admitted when he went to rip open a condom, averting her gaze so she didn't see the pity in his eyes.

Taking her chin between his forefinger and thumb he nudged and waited patiently until she met his gaze again. "I'm sorry." He touched a tender kiss to her forehead and her heart swelled until it felt far too big for her chest.

"I haven't been with anyone since my husband," she told him.

"I haven't been with anyone since my wife. At first, I was too busy grieving, too busy wondering how I was going to handle being a single parent, and then ..."

"Then what?"

"Then a fiery redhead exploded into my life, and I couldn't think about touching another woman." As he said the words, he lined up and buried himself inside her in one smooth thrust of his hips.

There was a moment of pain as her body stretched and adjusted to his size, but it quickly morphed into pleasure as he began to move.

Lifting her legs she hooked them around his hips, drawing him deeper. Her hands landed on his shoulders, again bringing him closer, and her lips sought his. For so long she'd dreamed of this, been convinced it was never going to happen, that he would never see her as anything other than Essie's nanny.

But now ...

Now she had hope.

It wasn't like she was expecting a ring and a proposal any time soon, but she wanted a chance to see if she and Cade could work as partners, if they could truly fall in love and build a life together.

His mouth devoured hers in a hungry kiss as he picked up the pace, thrusting into her with an urgency that echoed inside her.

Faint flutters built low in her belly, they quickly grew until she felt them shimmering throughout her body. When Cade reached between them and tweaked her bundle of nerves once again, she combusted in an orgasm that ripped through her body, tearing its way into her soul and lodging there.

This man owned her.

He had from the first time she'd seen him interact with his daughter. He was everything a father should be, and she knew he would be everything a husband should be as well.

Tugging on him, she urged him to allow some of his body weight to rest against her, needing to feel cocooned in his embrace, surrounded by not just his body but his feelings for her as well.

For the first time in her life, Gabriella felt a sense of belonging.

This was where she was supposed to be.

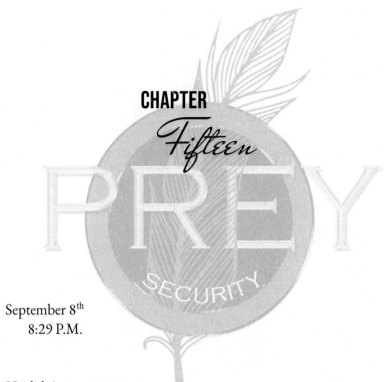

CHAPTER *Fifteen*

September 8th
8:29 P.M.

He didn't want to move.

Didn't want this moment to end.

Because when it did, he would have to break the heart of the beautiful woman holding him close.

A woman who looked at him like he hung the moon, who cared for his daughter as though she were her own, who fit into his family like she was made to, and who had brought his dead heart back to life.

"Mmm," she moaned happily, pressing her face to his neck and nuzzling it. "You're so warm and snuggly, who knew you could be such a great cuddler," she teased.

A lot of things he'd done in his life had felt impossible, insurmountable mountains he could never overcome. Losing his wife, being a single dad, missions he'd gone on with his team, watching his daughter get abducted.

In this moment this felt like it topped the list.

All of those things he'd never had a choice in. They'd been things he was forced to face whether he wanted to or not.

Unlike this.

This was a decision he'd made on his own, after weighing the pros and cons and knowing that he had no other options. Well, he did, but they were ones he couldn't stomach.

So it had to be this.

All he could do was pray that Gabriella wasn't going to hate him and that maybe when they finally had the names of the other men involved in his mother's rape and subsequent murder, she might be willing to allow him a second chance.

Who was he kidding?

There would be no second chance.

Once he did this it was done. For good. There would be no going back.

"Cade?" Gabriella asked as he slowly lifted his body off hers and pulled out of her.

She looked so sweet all sex rumpled. Her wild red curls framed her face, her cheeks were tinted pink, and her lips had that well-kissed look that begged him to claim them all over again.

But it was the bruises that stole his focus.

A reminder of what she'd sacrificed for him and his daughter. A reminder of what she would sacrifice again if those men got their hands on her. A reminder of why he was doing this.

"Hold on," he told her, there was no way he could have this conversation with her while she was lying in his bed looking so delicious he wanted to bury his face between her legs all over again and then keep her right where she was and never let her go.

But that wouldn't be fair to her.

This wasn't Gabriella's fight, and keeping her in the line of fire was selfish. It wasn't what you did for people you cared about.

And he cared about Gabriella Sadler.

More than he'd ever allowed himself to realize.

Going into his bathroom, he took a moment to compose himself, then grabbed a washcloth, ran it under warm water, and returned to the bedroom. Sitting on the side of the bed he carefully wiped her down, doing his best not to let Gabriella's soft smile influence him.

"I always knew you'd be sweet and tender like this," she told him as her fingers lifted and began to play with his hair.

Unable to stop a small rumble from vibrating through his chest, he leaned into her touch before he could stop himself.

No.

Don't change your mind.

You're doing this for her even if she won't understand that.

Be strong.

Capturing her wrist, he gently tugged her hand away from his hair and then stood, needing to put a little distance between them if he was going to do this.

Confusion and hurt warred on Gabriella's pretty face but he hardened his heart to it. He didn't want to do this, but it was something he had to do. For her.

Better to just say it and get it over and done with.

"I think you should go," he told her.

Her mouth dropped open, but then understanding flooded her eyes. "Of course. I don't want Essie to get the wrong idea if she wakes up and comes in here. Which she probably will. We were both sleeping in here while you were gone. We can take things slow, I don't want to confuse her. Once we get to know each other as a couple, we can let her know we're dating."

Damn.

She was making this so hard.

His chest was literally aching, and he realized he was rubbing at it with the hand still holding the washcloth he'd used to clean her up.

"That's not what I meant," he told her.

"What did you mean?"

"I think you should go. As in go. Leave the house."

For a second she just lay there, shocked, as she stared up at him like he'd just spoken to her in another language, and she was having trouble comprehending his words.

"I ... I don't ... understand ..." she said helplessly.

"You're fired, Gabriella."

Her sharp gasp of pain would echo in his mind for the rest of eternity, as would the horrified look on her face.

Why did this have to happen?

Why did these people who had messed with his mom's life and created a ripple effect none of them could have ever predicted have to keep hurting him?

This wasn't what he wanted.

He wanted to be in his bed, his body curled around Gabriella's, reassured by her warm presence that she hadn't lost her life protecting his child.

"F-fired?"

"I think you need to focus on yourself and your healing," he told her.

"No! Essie is more important. She needs me." Angry fire raged to life in her big green eyes as she scrambled up onto her knees.

"You let me worry about my daughter."

She flinched at his words as though he'd physically struck her. "I love Essie as though she were my own."

"But she's not yours. She's mine." The words tasted filthy coming out of his mouth, and the way her entire being seemed to cave in on itself made them that much worse. He hadn't known that she couldn't carry a baby to term, and he hated that for her because she was a natural when it came to kids. Worst of all, he didn't believe what he'd just said. Essie was every bit as much Gabriella's as she was his even if she wasn't biologically related to the little girl.

"What was this?" she asked, waving her hand at his bedroom and her half naked body.

"It was sex."

"You didn't just decide to fire me and kick me out when you walked into the bathroom. You knew you were going to do this in the hall, probably knew it all day. Why would you ask me to have sex with you if you were about to throw me out of your life?"

Because he was selfish.

Because he wanted one taste of her before he had to set her free.

The pink of her cheeks turned bright red as rage took over. "Was this thank you sex? Gabriella, you're not good enough for my daughter to stick around and help her heal from her ordeal, but thanks for allowing yourself to be beaten to protect her?"

"No!" He whisper yelled the word only because his daughter was asleep in the next room and he didn't want to wake her. "I wanted you. I have for a long time."

"I don't believe you," she said as she scrambled off the bed and scanned the room, searching for the rest of her clothes.

Fair enough.

After this, she had no reason to ever believe him again.

It didn't matter that the truth was he was doing this because he couldn't stand the thought of her ever being in danger because of him again. He was doing this to protect and keep her safe, because he cared deeply for her. Deeper than he'd realized until she was snatched away from him.

But why would Gabriella believe that?

"I can't believe you would do this to me, Cade. I can't believe you would rip me away from the only people I have when I'm at my most vulnerable. I can't believe you would take me away from Essie when she needs me. I can't believe you would use me for sex and then throw me away like trash."

"You are not trash," he growled as he stalked toward her, but she scuttled away from him like she was afraid of him, and he froze, his chest sliced open, his heart tumbling right out of it. He'd done that. Taken her feelings for him and soured them to the point that she was now scared of him and couldn't stand to be near him.

"Of course I'm trash. I've always been thrown away like I didn't matter. By my father, by my mother, by all the foster families I lived with, by my ex, and now by you. Of all of them, you were the one person I thought would never hurt me. I thought you were the one person that actually saw me. I thought I'd finally found a place where I belonged, where I was wanted, where I was supposed to be."

Her tear-filled words destroyed his soul, and he knew without a shadow of a doubt that he'd just lost one of the best things to ever happen to him.

~

September 8th
    8:42 P.M.

How could this be happening?

Never in her life had she felt so incredibly stupid.

Not just stupid but naïve and gullible as well.

How else could you explain why she had ever believed that Cade could truly want her?

Even her own parents hadn't wanted her, and none of the foster families she'd lived with had ever cared about her beyond the money they got for having her live with them. Her husband had dumped her when she couldn't give him the heir he craved, and now Cade was throwing her away because she was no longer useful to him.

What was wrong with her?

Why didn't anyone ever stick around?

Was she truly that unlovable?

"Look, Gabriella, I ..."

Against her will her gaze darted to Cade when he spoke. He was agitated, his hands raking almost compulsively through his short dark hair. She got it. He felt somewhat bad about kicking her out, but she didn't want to hear anything else he had to say.

Any feelings she had for him died when he told her she was fired.

Damn that word hurt.

Mainly because it made her feel like she had only ever truly been the nanny, nothing more. Anything else she'd thought she'd seen or felt when it came to him and his family had clearly been nothing more than her overactive imagination and deeply ingrained desire to be loved and belong somewhere.

It was pretty clear this wasn't where she belonged though.

With no care or thought about what she was going through, what she'd suffered, he was kicking her out in the middle of the night and leaving her to fend for herself.

Feeling hollow, she snatched up her leggings and panties and quickly yanked them on then hurried down the hall to her room. She was vaguely aware that Cade had followed her and was standing in the doorway watching as she yanked out a suitcase from the back of her closet and threw clothes in it.

Growing up in foster care she'd learned how to pack quickly. She also learned that having too many sentimental belongings wasn't worth it because those could too easily be left behind if someone else did the packing for her.

Neither of them spoke as she filled the suitcase with as many clothes as she could fit into it. Whatever she couldn't fit, she'd leave behind. She had more than enough money to buy herself a thousand new wardrobes so she didn't mind the loss.

Anything to get away from there and cut contact as quickly as possible.

This wasn't fair to her, and it wasn't fair to Essie.

Regardless of what Cade said or thought, that little girl loved her and needed her. They'd endured that ordeal together and needed one another to get through the next few weeks and months.

At least he could have given them both some time before firing her.

Giving the room a scan, she didn't see anything else she needed other than her purse and cell phone, which were downstairs in the kitchen. Since her car had been the one they were driving the day of the abduction, she didn't have a vehicle. She'd have to call an Uber and have it take her to a hotel. She didn't have a house since she'd moved in with Cade, so a hotel was her only option. She'd also have to hire some body-guards, just in case the people after Cade's family mistakenly thought she was a useful tool to get to them.

Affording both the hotel and the bodyguards wasn't the problem, she was a millionaire after all, but it left her feeling so empty and so alone that it physically hurt.

When her gaze landed on the ragdoll sitting back in its place on the bed she shuddered. That damn doll had made her think something was going on between her and Cade, which had led her to believe he had feelings for her.

She hated that doll.

Never wanted to see it again.

She should never have kept it in the first place. Her mother hadn't cared about her and neither did Cade.

Grabbing the suitcase handle, she headed for the door and was forced to stop a foot away from it because Cade was still standing there.

Unable to look at him, she kept her gaze firmly on the floor and waited.

Eventually, with a deep rumbly sigh, he stepped back and allowed her past.

"Let me take that," he said, reaching for the suitcase as she got to the top of the stairs.

Jerking it away so quickly she almost stumbled and fell, his hands darted out to grab her shoulders, stopping her from tumbling down the stairs.

Only his touch felt like a million frozen spears jabbing into her skin, and once again, she jerked away. "Don't touch me," she shrieked, somewhat hysterically. Unlike just minutes ago when his touch had grounded her, making her feel safe and protected, now it did nothing but remind her of the feel of those men's hands on her body.

"Gabriella—"

"Don't, Cade," she ordered as she dragged the suitcase down the stairs.

She thought he hadn't followed, but when she found her purse and shoved her cell phone inside it, deciding she'd order an Uber once she was out of the house, she found him waiting for her by the front door, the ragdoll in his hands.

"You forgot this," he said, holding it out to her.

Shrinking away from the doll, she shook her head. "I don't want it. Throw it in the trash. Donate the rest of my clothes. I don't want any of them," she ordered as she edged around him to open the front door.

A wave of relief hit her as she stepped out of the house she'd loved, the first house she'd lived in that had felt like a home, and hurried down the path.

When she reached the sidewalk, she saw someone hurrying toward her. Since she recognized the figure as Jake she didn't flinch, merely ignored him and pulled out her cell phone.

"Gabriella? What's going on?" Jake asked, coming to a stop beside her.

"Cade fired me and kicked me out. I'm calling an Uber and going to a hotel. I'll organize my own security," she rambled in a monotone that scared her. It felt like she was shutting down, like every ounce of emotion had bled out of her on the floor of Cade's bedroom, and there was simply nothing left.

"What the hell? Why would he do that?"

"Don't know, don't care," she intoned, setting her phone back in her purse, the Uber ordered.

"I'll take you to a hotel, honey. I'll stay and watch over you," he offered, but she shook her head wildly.

The last thing she needed was to be around this family she'd already begun to think of as hers.

A clean break, that's what she needed.

They both stood in silence as they waited for her Uber to arrive.

When it did, Jake forcefully took her suitcase for her and set it in the car's trunk. Then he placed his hands on her shoulders and leaned down so they were eye to eye.

"I don't know what's going on, honey, but I'll talk to Cade, I'll get this sorted out. He's probably just panicking after everything that's happened. If you need anything you have all our numbers, you call and we'll be there."

The kiss he touched on her forehead was brotherly, but she was already shutting down all her feelings for this family.

They weren't hers and they were never going to be hers.

The last thing she would ever do was call any one of them.

And she didn't want this to be sorted, she didn't want to hear from Cade again. If he could throw her away like she was used garbage when he knew she'd just lived through a horrific ordeal and had literally no family to be her support system, then he wasn't the man she'd thought he was.

He wasn't the man she needed.

Maybe there just really weren't any good men out there.

Or it was her.

Maybe she was the problem.

She was unlovable, she was trash, she wasn't worth anyone's time, effort, or attention. She was nothing.

The drive to the hotel passed in a blur and she barely remembered thanking the driver and lugging her suitcase inside. How many times had she done just this as a child? Walk away from the house she'd been living in with nothing more than a bag of clothes. Always alone.

Checking into a suite, she left her suitcase for a porter to bring up to her room and stumbled in a daze into a elevator. Aware of nothing happening around her, Gabriella just clutched her purse in one hand and the key card for her room in the other.

Finally, the elevator reached her floor, and she looked through blurry eyes to see which hall her room was down. Getting inside her room was a relief. She was out of sight now, she could fall apart if she wanted to.

And she did.

With a sob that seemed to cleave her chest right in two, she staggered through the bedroom and into the bathroom. There was a huge walk-in shower and she stripped out of her clothes, turned the water on as hot as she could bear, and stepped under it.

Under the pulsing hot spray, she allowed her tears to flood out. Crying for everything she'd never had, everything she'd lost, and everything that would never be hers.

Alone.

The word screamed through her head on a loop.

Caving under its pressure, she sank to her knees and curled up in a ball.

Alone.

Always alone.

Always going to be alone.

It was time to accept that fact and stop pretending that somewhere out there was a family that would be hers.

CHAPTER

Sixteen

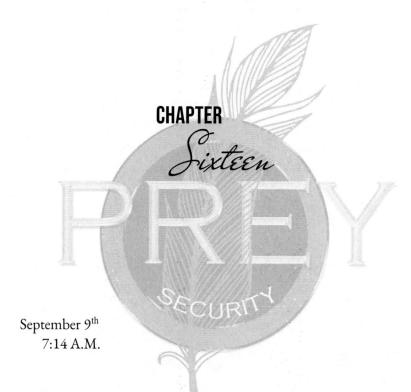

September 9th
  7:14 A.M.

"Where's Gabby?" Essie asked as they walked hand in hand down the stairs to the kitchen.

Because he was the lowest form of scum, he'd had Prey hack her credit card information so he knew which hotel she was staying in. It probably wasn't his smartest decision because knowing where she was only intensified his need to go to her, take back the words he'd said, and beg her to understand he was trying to keep her safe.

"Gabriella's not here, she had to leave," Cade told his daughter as he led her into the kitchen.

Essie's little face scrunched up in confusion. "Gabby wouldn't leave me."

The words were spoken with such confidence that his pain thudded through his body with each beat of his heart.

His daughter was right. Gabriella would never willingly leave Essie. She'd proven that in how she'd protected his child at great physical and psychological cost to herself. If he hadn't kicked her out, Gabriella would have prioritized his daughter's healing over her own, and it would have only made him fall harder for her.

What she needed was someone to make sure she was taken care of while she was busy worrying about others.

He could have been that person.

He could have her there with him right now, could have slept beside her all night. He wasn't really worried about what Essie would think about him and Gabriella being a couple, his daughter already loved her like a mother. Could have been sitting his girls down at the kitchen table and taking care of them, cooking them breakfast, making sure they had appointments to speak with a counsellor, making them laugh so they forgot for a moment the trauma they'd endured.

But he didn't have her there.

Right or wrong, he'd made his choices, and now they all had to live with the consequences, his daughter included.

"Gabriella isn't here," he repeated as he lifted Essie into her chair at the table. "Now what do you want for breakfast?"

"I want Gabby. Where is she? Why did she leave?" Essie asked, her big gray eyes growing watery and her bottom lip trembling.

Just because he had Gabriella there as a full-time, live-in nanny didn't mean he didn't parent his daughter as actively as he could. He was used to dealing with her occasional tantrum and soothing her tears when she was sad, hurt, or scared.

What he wasn't used to doing was explaining to his daughter that he was the reason she was hurting. It was easy enough to say no to her over little things, staying up too late, eating too much candy, and not buying her a treat at the store. But this was nothing like that.

His daughter was hurting because of him.

He was going to break her little heart.

It would be easy enough to lie and say that Gabriella had left because she needed to heal from what had happened and that she couldn't be there for that. But saying those words would make her daughter hate Gabriella, and there was no way she deserved that. He'd hurt her enough, he wasn't going to let her take the blame for his actions.

Pulling out the chair beside Essie, he took a seat and reached out to take his daughter's little hands in his. "I asked Gabriella to leave."

"Why?"

"Because I thought it was for the best." How could he explain to an almost five-year-old that neither she nor her beloved nanny were safe, and it was because he was consumed with a need to clear his dead mother's name? The last thing he wanted to do was scare Essie even more than she had already been. If she knew the danger she was in, his daughter would never feel safe again.

"Why?"

"Because you and Gabriella both got hurt and I don't want her to get hurt again."

"Am I gonna be hurted 'gain?" Essie asked, eyes wide with fear.

"No, princess. I'm going to make sure that no one ever hurts you again," he promised. There was nothing he wouldn't do to fulfill that vow.

"Then who's making sure that no one's hurting Gabby?" Essie asked.

Since he'd asked Prey to hack her credit card information, he knew she had contacted a security company early this morning and hired some bodyguards. It hurt to know she was out there alone with strangers watching over her when what she needed was him and his family, but he couldn't get over the fact that it was him and his family that had put her in danger in the first place.

How selfish would it be to keep her close knowing she wouldn't be safe?

With John Gaccione in prison and Gabriella out of his house, it should be clear enough to this remaining rapist that going after her was pointless, she wasn't family and she wasn't a useful tool.

"Gabriella is safe, I promise," he assured his daughter.

"But I want her to come home," Essie said, pouting.

"She's not coming back." As badly as it hurt to say the words aloud, and as much as he knew he was hurting his daughter by saying them, they were the truth, and they all needed to adjust to their new normal.

"But I want her!" Essie yelled, pushing him away. "I want her here, and what 'bout my birthday? I'm going to be five years old, and Gabby said we're going to put up balloons and streamers and make cupcakes. And she's going to get me a unicorn cake."

"I can do all those things," he told her.

"No! I want Gabby. Gabby has to do them. She promised she wouldn't leave me."

"She didn't want to leave you." This was hell. How had he thought he could do this? Sending Gabriella away had about killed him, but watching his daughter's reaction to learning she was gone was crushing the final pieces left of his heart.

"Then why did she leave?"

"Because I told her she had to. It was for the best."

"It's not best. Gabby is best, I want her to come home," Essie wailed, tears tumbling down her round little cheeks.

When he reached out to pick her up and hold her, she shimmied backward out of his reach, and the gravity of what he'd done sunk in.

Gabriella was alone and hated him.

His daughter was there but hated him.

And he hated himself more than the two of them combined.

"It's going to be okay, Essie," he assured her. Somehow, he had to make things okay. "I'm here. And you have all your uncles, and Willow, and Susanna, and Becca. You have lots of people who love you and are here for you. Lots of people who will make sure you have the best birthday in the world."

"I want Gabby," the little girl howled. "Gabby plays with me, reads to me, cooks with me, and tucks me in. I don't want my birthday without Gabby. I want to stay four forever."

With that, Essie climbed off her chair and ran back up the stairs. A moment later he heard her bedroom door being slammed.

Normally he wouldn't allow tantrums like that, and certainly not the slamming of doors, but how could he begrudge his daughter's reactions when he'd ripped her away from the person who was always there for her?

Cade had never doubted how much his daughter loved him. He had to travel for work sometimes and might be away for a few days, a few weeks, or a few months. Even when he was home, he often had to work long hours. But he always knew that Essie was in safe hands with

Gabriella, and in the time he spent with his daughter he was one hundred percent with her. They played any games she wanted, nothing was off the table, he'd dress up like a fairy, do makeup parties, anything his little girl's heart desired.

This was the first time he felt he had made a decision that didn't have his child's best interest at heart. He'd panicked about Gabriella's safety because he could sense the toll her ordeal had taken on her even if she was doing her best to pretend that she was handling everything just fine.

So, he'd tried to push her out of the danger zone.

Instead, he'd done something that might have tainted his relationship with his daughter beyond repair. He'd broken Essie's trust in him.

What was best for her was always his first consideration, but this time he hadn't stopped to fully consider the ramifications of ripping Gabriella out of Essie's life at a time when both of his girls were so emotionally vulnerable. He hadn't realized just how deeply the two needed to be together to start their journey of healing because all he'd been able to see was that Gabriella was in danger, and he couldn't risk losing another woman he loved.

There was no doubt in his mind that he loved Gabriella and knew he'd pushed her away with the best intentions.

But that didn't undo the damage it caused.

It didn't change the fact that Gabriella was alone in a hotel room, and Essie was alone in her bedroom, when if he hadn't interfered, the two could be together. Instead, he'd ruined everything, lost Gabriella's love, lost his daughter's trust, none of which he was certain he could regain.

What had he done?

~

September 10th
  2:37 P.M.

. . .

Staring at the ceiling of her room, Gabriella wondered how her life had come to this.

To many people looking in from the outside, it would seem like she had taken a terrible childhood and turned it into something amazing. She'd overcome having an absent dad and an addict mom, survived foster care, and built a name for herself, designing something that made the world a little bit safer and made her a millionaire.

She was young, smart, and rich, she should have the world at her fingertips.

Yet, she was lying alone in a hotel room, staring at the ceiling, unable to come up with enough motivation to do anything other than stay on the bed where she'd been most of the last eighteen hours or so.

Sleep was still off the table no matter how exhausted she was, so after she'd checked in and cried herself out, she'd looked up private security firms and picked one. It would be so much easier to go with Prey, she knew they were the best of the best, but they were Cade's, and she wasn't part of his life anymore, so she didn't want to have to call them and ask to hire them.

So, she'd gone with her gut, picked another company, and hired round-the-clock security. The two men who had shown up within the hour of her paying the bill seemed nice enough, and she felt a little better knowing they were standing outside her hotel suite, but she didn't feel safe.

Not really safe.

All she felt was a crushing loneliness that was slowly smothering her to death.

When her phone dinged with a text, it was purely automatic to reach out and pick it up. She didn't really care who was texting her or why.

Susanna's name was on the screen, and the text said she was downstairs and on her way up.

How did Susanna even know where she was staying?

Had one of the Charleston Holloway brothers hacked her phone to get her location, or her credit card to find out where she was staying? If they knew she was there, all they'd have to do was flash their Prey ID at the front desk and she was sure they'd get her room number.

Which meant she couldn't avoid this meeting even though she wanted to.

Badly.

The last thing she wanted was to see anyone from Cade's family. It was just a reminder of what could never be hers.

Still, Susanna was nice, and she felt a connection to the woman because they'd both grown up unwanted by their families.

It took almost more effort than she had, but Gabriella shoved herself off the bed and stripped out of the clothes she'd been wearing since leaving Cade's house. Unable to summon enough energy to bother changing, she'd just thrown them back on after her shower when she first arrived at the hotel.

Knowing they must smell by now, she opened her suitcase, rummaged through it, found a pair of soft leggings and an oversized sweater, and carried them to the bathroom. Pale beneath the bruises that littered her body, her gaze was drawn to the bite mark on her left breast. It was an angry red, and the edges of the teeth-shaped wounds were puckered and puffy. There were some pussy areas to it as well, it was clearly infected, but she honestly just didn't care.

What was the point in caring?

It didn't change anything, it didn't help her in any way.

Splashing a little water on her face, she dried it on the towel, then shimmied into the clothes. They seemed to hang off her, and she wasn't surprised she'd lost weight over the last week and a half. She still had zero appetite, and now that it was just her, even pretending to be taking care of herself seemed pointless.

Just as she finished running a comb through her tangled red curls, she heard a knock on her door.

"Ms. Sadler, a group of people are here to see you. They claim you know them," one of her bodyguards called out.

With a weary sigh, she dragged her heavy body through the bedroom, out into the small sitting area, and over to the door. Removing the chain, she opened it and offered Travis a small smile.

"Yes, thank you, I do know them, and they texted to say they were coming," she assured him. Images of Gavin and Dave's dead bodies flashed in her mind, and she made a determination not to get attached in any way to these bodyguards. They were her employees for the fore-seeable future, not her friends.

Maybe if she'd taken that advice to heart when she took the job as Essie's nanny, she wouldn't be in this position right now.

"Come in," she muttered to Susanna and moved away from the door, crossing the room and dropping down in one of the armchairs around a small table.

"We brought breakfast," Susanna told her, holding up a brown paper bag.

"Not hungry," she said, fighting the urge to press a hand to her stomach as it churned at the very thought of eating.

"Gabs, you have to take care of yourself," Cole told her, and as she looked over, she started in surprise. It wasn't just Susanna and Cole who had come, it was the entire Charleston Holloway family, minus Cade and Essie, of course.

Her heart ached with how badly she missed them.

Missing Essie was fine, she loved that little girl every bit as much as she would have if she'd given birth to her. But missing Cade was stupid. He'd shattered her heart into a million pieces, how could she possibly miss him? Yet she did, and it majorly sucked.

Having all these people here was hard.

Too hard.

She'd allowed herself to believe that she was a part of their family, allowed their words that they thought of her as part of the family to make it a reality.

Only it wasn't reality.

Reality was that she was nothing to them now that Cade had fired her. She wasn't part of the family, she wasn't an employee of the family, and trying to be friends with them was too hard, it only reminded her of what she'd missed out on.

Still, there was one thing she needed to know.

"Is Essie okay?" she asked.

"She misses you so much," Connor told her.

"Doesn't stop asking for you," Cooper added, making the ache in her heart grow.

Her little girl needed her, and she wasn't there. She was failing Essie the same way she'd failed her babies when her body couldn't carry their pregnancy to term.

"Did she go to school?" Gabriella asked. She hadn't gotten around to discussing with Cade what he wanted to do about Essie and school. It was probably safer for the little girl to stay home, but starting school was such a big thing and she hated the thought of the child missing out. Knowing she might have missed Essie's first day of school hurt more than she would have guessed.

"No, Cade thinks it's too dangerous. He's considering sending her off to Delta Team to be with them and Cassandra," Jax explained, and she nodded. That would probably be for the best, Essie had to be safe, and she and Cade had already discussed that possibility when Connor and Becca returned from Cambodia.

"Does he know you're here?" she asked, resting her head against the chair. "He fired me, I doubt he'd like you going behind his back and telling me things about his daughter."

"Look, Gabs, Cade knows that he made a mistake but he's too proud to do anything about it," Jake told her.

The words washed over her and she was pleased to find that she'd numbed herself enough that they didn't hurt too badly.

Truth was, nothing Cade had said was untrue. She was just the nanny, he was the father, if he felt like she was no longer the right person to care for his child, it was his right to terminate her employment. With him back, the guardianship papers were voided, and she had no claim on Essie, and even if she still had a legal right to his house, she didn't want it.

Money and things were nothing to her, it was people that she craved. A family of her own, people who loved her, people who would never leave her or throw her away when they were bored with her, that's all she'd ever wanted.

It had been a mistake to think she could have that with Essie and Cade.

"We'll keep talking to him, keep trying to get him to see sense," Connor said.

"And in the meantime, we are one hundred percent here for you. If you want to talk, all you have to do is call me and I'll come," Susanna promised.

Offering a weak smile because it was a lovely offer from a woman who was still struggling to deal with her own trauma from these same men determined to keep a decades-old secret safe, Gabriella shook her head.

This was too much.

She couldn't do it.

"Just leave him alone. Essie is his daughter, and he doesn't want me around her. That's his prerogative," she reminded them.

"It's wrong when she needs you," Cooper growled.

"Wrong when you need her, too," Cole added.

"Don't give up hope just yet," Jax said.

They were all too nice to get it. Or maybe they were just so used to having a family that they couldn't understand.

"Look, I appreciate all you're trying to do, but this isn't what I want. Cade made his choice and I'm accepting it. Please, don't make this harder than it has to be, okay? Just put your focus on supporting Essie, she needs you all so much."

"You need us, too," Jake said harshly.

"I'm used to being on my own, I'll be fine, I'll figure it out like I always do. I have a place to stay, I have security, and when I'm ready I'll find a therapist, but this is too hard. Seeing you all and knowing I'm not a part of your family anymore is too much. I can't do it. It's making everything worse. So please, don't come around again. Don't call or text. It's not that I'm not grateful for what you're trying to do its just ... I can't do it. It's just too hard," her voice wavered on that last word, but she was pleased that she'd managed to get it all out without breaking down in tears.

A clean break was what she needed. She had to figure out a way to move on, and there was zero percent chance she could do that if Cade's family—however well-intentioned—kept trying to insert themselves in her life.

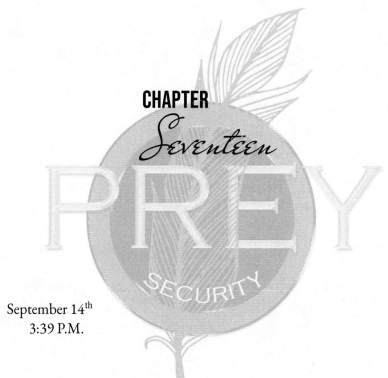

CHAPTER
Seventeen

September 14th
  3:39 P.M.

"Do you want some ice cream?"

"No."

The sullen look on Essie's face told him exactly what she thought he could do with his ice cream in four-year-old language.

Cade sighed.

It had been this way for the last week. Essie was grumpy, agitated, cried a lot, was scared of everything, and didn't want to do anything. She wasn't sleeping, was extra picky about her food, and was generally miserable.

She also asked about Gabriella a lot.

More than he'd thought she would.

Not that he thought his daughter wouldn't be devastated about the only mother figure she remembered suddenly being ripped out of her life on the heels of a massive trauma, he'd just thought his explanation would settle things.

Only it hadn't.

Essie asked about her several times a day, probably at least once an hour. It got worse at mealtimes and bedtime. He was an okay cook, but Gabriella managed to take simple things and make them a million times tastier and that was not a skill he possessed. At bedtime, he read to his daughter, but she cried that she wanted Gabriella to sing her to sleep. If he tried to sing, she complained that he was doing it all wrong.

Now she wouldn't even eat ice cream.

"Are you sure? There's still some of the ice cream you and Gabriella made together."

Tears filled his daughter's big gray eyes. "I don't want to eat it cos Gabby isn't here to make me more," she wailed.

Why the hell had he thought this was a good idea?

His daughter was miserable, he was miserable, and he had no doubt that Gabriella was especially miserable.

Now that his emotions had had a chance to settle down, he could admit that maybe this wasn't his brightest idea. He still agreed with his reasoning, but maybe he should have gone about things differently.

Too late to do anything about it now, though.

Forty-eight hours after kicking her out, Cade had caved and texted Gabriella, asking if she was okay.

She'd promptly blocked him.

If that sting of rejection was only a tenth of what she'd felt when he told her she was fired and needed to leave, then he didn't know how she'd managed to survive it.

The doorbell rang before he could attempt to comfort his child, and Essie jumped off her seat and ran for the door.

"Gabby!" she cried out, flinging it open only to sigh in disappointment. "Oh."

"Sorry, messy Essie, it's just us," Cole said.

Without her usual complaint that she wasn't messy, Essie turned and trudged back to the living room, climbed onto the couch, clutched her teddy bear, and resumed watching TV.

Cade also sighed.

When were things going to start getting better?

"She's still missing Gabriella I see," Connor said as his siblings trailed inside his house.

"More each day," he admitted. The same was true for him. Without Gabriella's presence his house felt so empty, no longer the warm, inviting home it had been ever since she moved in with them. It was definitely true, sometimes you didn't know what you had until it was gone.

"So, when are you going to call her and fix this?" Cooper asked like it was actually that simple.

Sighing again, he dropped onto a couch in the lounge room rather than returning to the family room where Essie was, not wanting his daughter's little ears to hear this. "I tried texting, and she blocked me," he admitted.

"Then go to the hotel," Jake said. His stepbrother had been furious with him since Gabriella had stormed out of his house and refused to let Jake take her to a hotel. It wasn't just that he'd fired her it was when he'd done it and how he'd done it. Cade could agree kicking her out at night wasn't ideal, but if he'd done it during the day, Essie would have seen.

"It's not that simple," he snapped. Did they think he liked imploding his life, his daughter's life, and Gabriella's life all in one fell swoop?

"Why the hell not?" Jake demanded.

"Bro." Jax punched him lightly in the shoulder then dropped onto the other end of the sofa from where Cade was sitting. "Do you not have feelings for her?"

Throwing a glare Jax's way a low growl rumbled through him.

They all knew the answer to that.

In fact, his brothers had known he'd fallen for the nanny long before he realized it for himself.

He didn't know exactly when it happened, but somewhere along the way, things had shifted, and Gabriella changed from being Essie's nanny to also being the woman who had him tied up in knots.

Still in love with his wife, he hadn't known what to do with those feelings, so he'd done nothing.

Ignored them.

Pretended they didn't exist.

But there was no getting rid of them.

Every time he saw her cuddling his daughter, or teaching her things, playing with her, and making her laugh, every time he saw Essie smile at her, looking at her with love and adoration, listening to her, and learning from her, his feelings grew.

Grew until he couldn't ignore them anymore.

Couldn't pretend they didn't exist.

Knowing that she had been abducted purely because he hired her to be his daughter's nanny was tearing him to shreds inside.

She hadn't opened up to him about what she'd gone through, but he knew it was worse than what he'd seen, what he knew about. Thinking that she might be subjected to more horrors because of him wasn't something he could handle.

Shoving her out of his life was the only way to keep her safe even if it killed him.

Which it felt like it was doing.

"You know the answer to that," he grumbled, annoyed he had to justify himself to his brothers. Mainly because in attempting to do so he was realizing how utterly unjustifiable his actions had been.

"Do we?" Connor asked. "Because you've never admitted anything."

"To look at you it seems like you barely tolerate her when she's clearly in love with you," Cooper added.

"What do you expect me to do?" he demanded in a muted roar so he didn't disturb his daughter. "Do you expect me to have her stay here knowing we're in danger? Do you expect me to send her away with Essie so she's locked up somewhere with Delta Team? Do you expect me to hand her over to be assaulted and beaten all over again?"

"Why is it all or nothing?" Cole asked. "Gabriella is a big girl and didn't want to leave even knowing the risks."

"I'm the cause of the risks. I'm the oldest. I'm the one who always insisted we had to make it up to Mom for treating her so badly those last few months by finding the truth. You're all in this mess because of me."

"Is that what you really think?" Cooper asked.

"Of course. I'm the oldest, it's on me. And I wouldn't shut up about it because I felt guilty. I made it our entire life purpose, and because of that, Susanna was hurt, Becca was targeted, and all of you have been in danger. I can't live with myself if Gabriella is hurt again because of me."

"Can you live without her?" Becca asked quietly.

That was the million-dollar question.

When he'd lost Gretel, he'd been convinced he would never be able to get over her, and while she would always hold a piece of his heart and she'd left a piece of hers behind in Essie, Gabriella now also held a significant piece of his heart. Living without her presence was nothing other than hell, but he couldn't risk losing her too.

It was better to shove her away of his own volition than risk witnessing her death.

"Gabriella has been part of this family for a long time," Conner reminded him. "Longer than Willow and longer than Susanna. Yet we're protecting both of them, Becca too, and Essie, and Cassandra. We put precautions in place, they failed, but we can adjust, tighten things up, and keep our family safe."

"You're trying to play God, Cade," Susanna said gently. "Trying to control everything. I get you're the oldest, and you take responsibility for all your brothers and your sister, for Willow, Becca, and me too, and of course for your daughter. But you're not God and not responsible for all of us. You're allowed to make decisions that are best for you."

"Even if it costs Gabriella her life?"

"You can't control the future. You protected your wife and still lost her anyway. Life sometimes just happens," Susanna said softly. "You can't stop it, but you can enjoy it. You can grab hold of the happy moments and not let them go. I know that's what I'm doing with Cole, it's what he taught me." She gifted her boyfriend a bright smile and he felt the love pulsing between them.

The same love that flowed between Connor and Becca, and Cooper and Willow.

The same love that he could have with Gabriella if he could get over his fear of being selfish and potentially costing her her life.

Which he wasn't sure he could do.

Because he'd barely survived losing Gretel, losing Gabriella too would finish him off.

∼

September 18th
    5:53 P.M.

Her entire body ached.

The kind of throbbing pain that was hard to ignore.

Although Gabriella was giving it her best shot.

She was embarrassed to admit, even to herself, but she'd just kind of ... given up.

All her life she'd been fighting to survive, keep going, and find her place in the world. After believing she'd found it with Cade, Essie, and the Charleston Holloway family then losing it, she just didn't care anymore.

What was the point of searching for something that didn't exist?

At first, she'd thought she had to find a way to keep going, to figure out what her next step was, work through her pain, and come out the other side stronger than ever. But the more she thought about it the more she wondered why.

Why did she have to keep going?

Why did she have to figure out her next step?

Why did there even need to be a next step?

Why did it matter if she got stronger or weaker?

As far as she was concerned, nothing mattered and it made zero difference if she just lay there and did nothing for the rest of her life.

Technically, she could if she wanted to. She had enough money that she didn't have to work again if she didn't want to. Had enough money to do anything she wanted, including giving up and staying in this hotel room.

When her phone, which was lying somewhere on the large king-size bed, dinged with a message, she considered ignoring it. After their visit the other day she blocked every one of the Charleston Holloway brothers and their girlfriends. Well, all except Susanna.

For some reason, she couldn't make herself do that to a woman who, even though she had a family, had spent most of her life alone. It felt too unfair, and she didn't want to hurt Susanna, she'd already been through enough.

Or maybe it was her way of keeping a fingerhold on the world.

It wasn't that Gabriella wanted to die, not exactly anyway. She was just tired of living.

Tired.

Exhausted more like it.

With a sigh, she pushed herself up into a sitting position, fighting through a sickening wave of dizziness that made it feel like her brain had taken a ride on one of those horrible amusement park rides that tossed you up and down and side to side without her permission.

Finding the phone, she managed to lift it up and see a text from Susanna.

The woman had taken to checking in a couple of times a day. Usually in the morning, around midday, and then again in the evening. It felt like maybe it was because Susanna, a trained psychologist, was checking up on her because she was worried.

If she was honest with herself, Gabriella agreed that the woman had a reason to worry.

While it wasn't like she was actively going to take her own life, it also wasn't like she'd been doing much of anything to take care of herself these last several days.

The opposite in fact.

She still had pretty much zero appetite and wasn't eating anything more than the occasional piece of fruit that the bodyguards dropped off for her each morning. Sleep seemed like it had just evaporated from her life given how little of it she'd managed to get. Every time she closed her eyes, she was either back in that tiny room being forced to take beatings or perform sexual favors to keep Essie safe, or she was in Cade's bedroom reliving the moment he'd told her she was fired.

There had only been one time she'd dreamed anything pleasant, and that was sex with Cade. But after waking up to remember how he'd thrown her out of his and Essie's life, leaving her lost and alone, she'd sobbed so hard she couldn't breathe.

Normally, she'd reply to Susanna's text with an emoji or maybe a word or two, but today she just didn't have the energy.

No food or sleep were draining her bit by bit, and she wondered what happened when her energy finally ran out, leaving her completely empty.

Would her bodyguards come in one day to find her dead body lying in the bed?

Or maybe she'd last long enough for Cade and his family to find the final person involved in their mom's rape and she wouldn't need any bodyguards. Then it would be some poor housekeeping employee who would find her dead body.

It was becoming harder and harder to see herself having any sort of future. Happy or not.

Tossing the phone back onto the bed as a wave of heat crashed over her making it feel like she was burning from the inside out, Gabriella groaned and shoved the covers off her body, kicking them away so she was left lying in nothing but her panties and a tank top.

Too much.

Too much clothing.

It felt heavy against her skin, and she realized she was covered in a thin sheen of sweat.

Staggering to her feet, she wobbled wildly and had to throw out a hand to grab the headboard of the bed to remain standing.

Passing much too slowly, when the dizziness subsided enough that she could stand unassisted, she stumbled across the bedroom and into the bathroom.

Too hot.

She needed to cool herself down and a shower was the perfect way.

Turning the faucet until the water came out one step up from freezing cold, she stripped out of her panties.

When she went to remove the tank top, she found that the thin material was stuck to her body.

"What the heck?" she mumbled as she moved so she was looking at herself in the bathroom mirror.

Her eyes widened when she saw that the left side of the tank top was a mixture of red and brown. That kind of yellow-brown of puss.

The bite wound.

It had been looking red and enflamed for days, and she'd known it was infected, just hadn't cared to do anything about it. The pain from the wound helped to dull the pain in her heart from Cade's betrayal.

Anything was better than that.

Although as she tugged the material away from where it was stuck to her puss-filled wound, wincing as it ripped and tore her enflamed flesh, Gabriella realized that was probably a mistake.

She should have done something about the bite mark earlier.

Honestly, she didn't remember if a doctor had looked at it while she'd been in the hospital after being rescued. Considering she'd been covered in bruises and they'd known she'd been beaten, she assumed that they had, but she couldn't remember if they'd warned her about infection, or given her cream to put on it.

That whole day was a blur because she'd been too worried about Cade and him trading himself for her.

By the time she'd managed to pry away the material from the wound, tears were streaming down her cheeks, and blood was dribbling down her chest.

Tossing the ruined top onto the floor she flinched at the sight of the wound. The entire left side of her chest was swollen and bright red. An angry red. Kind of like how she was sure her face had looked after the shock of Cade's words had dulled a little and the anger had come roaring in.

There was no question about it, she definitely should have attended to this wound earlier.

Too late now.

It was a major note to how far her mental state had deteriorated and how deep into depression she was sinking that there was almost a bit of glee as she looked at her ruined flesh.

Infection was settling into not just the wound but her body as a whole. It was evident in the fiery feeling of her skin and the glassy look of her eyes. There was zero doubt she was running a fever, she was sick, and there was a little part of her that actually hoped she was getting sick enough to die.

That would solve all her problems.

She wouldn't have to think about what John Gaccione and those men had done to her, and she wouldn't have to live with this gaping Cade and Essie-sized hole in her heart.

Maybe it was for the best, Gabriella thought as she stepped under the shower spray and moaned in pleasure as the cool water danced across her overheated skin.

No one would miss her if she was gone. She was already out of Essie's life, and Cade had never loved her. His whole family would quickly adjust to her not being part of them anymore, even more so when he hired a new nanny for his daughter.

The thought of someone else cooking Essie breakfast, driving her to school, playing games with her, and tucking her in at night sent such a shaft of pain through her chest that Gabriella dropped to her knees.

Cade would fall in love one day too.

A woman would share his bed and his life and be a mother to his daughter.

Just not her.

Never her.

No one ever wanted her.

Curling up in a ball on the shower floor, Gabriella sobbed until she passed out.

CHAPTER
Eighteen

September 20th
10:22 A.M.

"What is this place?" Essie asked, curiosity in her voice, and since it was so nice to hear something other than anger or fear, Cade relaxed for the first time since he'd broken all three of their hearts by firing Gabriella and kicking her out.

"It's a cemetery," he answered as he parked the car in the small lot and turned off the engine, shifting in his seat so he faced his daughter.

Essie's little face scrunched up in confusion. "What's a semirary?"

Chuckling, he felt another little piece of peace slip back into his life. The more he made decisions about his future and what he wanted it to look like, the more he felt the panic tightening his chest begin to ease.

"Not semirary, cemetery," he said slowly.

"Cemetery," Essie repeated.

"Perfect. A cemetery is a place where people's bodies get placed after they die," he explained. Even though Essie had lost her mother when she was a baby, they didn't talk about it much and he'd never brought her to visit Gretel's grave.

Maybe it was something he should have done long before now.

There just hadn't seemed to be any point. Essie was so little, and she didn't remember her mom, she wasn't old enough to truly understand what death was, and he hadn't wanted to try to explain it, mess up, and freak her out instead.

Now it was time.

If he wanted to have any chance at reclaiming the future he'd probably already ruined beyond repair, he had to do this.

"Dead peoples are here?" Essie asked, eyes wide as she looked back out the window at the rows of graves they could see from the parking lot.

"Yes. When someone dies the people who love them, their family and friends, have a special service called a funeral, and then after that they bring the person's body and bury it in the ground."

Essie's eyes widened further as she absorbed this new information. "They puts peoples under the ground?"

"They do, but the person doesn't know it because they're dead. It's just their body, they can't think anymore, can't see or hear anything, can't speak or do anything," he said, praying he was explaining this in a way that a four-year-old could understand.

"How do they get dead?"

"Well sometimes they get very sick, or sometimes they get very hurt, or sometimes they just get very old. And then they die."

"Does everybody die?"

"Yes, eventually everybody will die."

"Like my mommy died," Essie said somberly.

"That's right. Your mommy got very sick, and she died when you were just a baby."

"Is her body under the ground here?"

"It is. I thought maybe we could visit her grave together and leave some flowers."

Essie's brow furrowed in confusion. "If dead peoples can't hear and they can't speak and they can't do nothing, then why do we bring Mommy flowers?"

"You know what? I don't really know. It's just what people do.

Maybe it's just a way to tell everyone that we haven't forgotten them and we loved them very much."

"Did you love Mommy lots and lots?"

"I did."

"Do you still love Mommy even though she's been gone a real long time?"

"I'll always love your mommy," he told his daughter truthfully. How could he not? Gretel and the sacrifice that she'd made was the only reason he had his precious little girl.

"Does that mean I won't ever have another Mommy?"

"What do you mean?"

"If you still love Mommy then you won't get married 'gain, and if you don't get married 'gain then I won't ever have a new Mommy."

When he'd lost his wife, Cade had been absolutely positive that he would never get married again. The possibility of risking his heart only to wind up going through the same soul-crushing pain all over again was too much.

But time did dull wounds even if it didn't heal them.

And maybe ... he was ready to take that risk.

"I wish Gabby was my mommy," Essie said with a wistful sigh.

His chest tightened at his daughter's innocent declaration. A part of him wanted to ask her to take her words back and tell her that she had a mother who loved her enough to delay possibly lifesaving medical treatment so that Essie could grow inside her and be born healthy. But the other part, the bigger part, knew that Gretel would be thrilled that Essie had a mother figure who loved her the same way she would have if she'd lived.

"That's another reason I brought you here today. I thought we could put some flowers on your mom's grave, but I also wanted to talk to you about Gabriella."

Essie gasped. Looking at him with horror. "Is Gabby dead? Is she under the ground, too? Like Mommy?"

"No, sweetie," he quickly soothed. "Gabriella isn't dead."

"Are you sure?" Essie asked, not looking convinced. "You said people can be dead because they getted hurt, and the bad men hurted Gabby."

"They did," he agreed. "But they didn't hurt her badly enough for her to die."

"You made Gabby go away," Essie accused, and he sighed, unable to refute her.

"I thought I was doing the right thing, but now ..." Now he was pretty sure he hadn't done the right thing at all. The opposite in fact. He'd done the wrong thing and hurt all of them in the process. "Let me come get you out and we can talk more as we walk to your mom's grave."

Climbing out of the car, he helped Essie out, then grabbed the bouquet of colorful flowers they'd gotten from the florist on the way there. Then Cade took his daughter's hand and they headed through the quiet cemetery toward Gretel's grave. One he hadn't visited as much as he should have over the years.

"I need to apologize to you," he told his daughter.

Essie gasped and looked up at him. "That means say sorry. Why do you need to say sorry to me, Daddy? Did you do something bad?" Essie sounded absolutely scandalized by the idea.

Cade chuckled. "I didn't do something bad, I was actually trying to do the right thing, but I did make a mistake. I shouldn't have asked Gabriella to leave. That hurt you and it hurt her, and I'm sorry."

Tugging her hand free from his, Essie wrapped her arms around his leg, hugging him with all the strength in her little body. "I forgive you, Daddy. Gabby says everyone makes mistakes, and if you make one you have to say sorry and try to fix it. You saided sorry, so nows all you got to do is fix it."

That's what he intended to do.

Or at least try.

There was no guarantee Gabriella would want anything to do with him, and he couldn't fault her if that's how she felt. What he'd done was unforgivable even if he had truly been trying to protect her.

"I'm going to try to fix it," he promised. "I want Gabriella to come back home to us, but I don't want it to be the way it was before."

"You want it to be different? What kind of different?"

"I'd like to ask Gabriella on a date, and then hopefully, one day, I'll ask her to marry me, and she'll say yes."

"Then she can be my mommy!" Essie squealed, clapping her hands and jumping up and down excitedly. "That was what I was going to wish for my birthday when I blew out my candles. I wished it last year, too."

He was pretty sure it was his daughter's constant wish that Gabriella would become her mother and never have to leave her. While he'd love nothing more than to promise her he'd make her dreams a reality, he couldn't.

Because, in the end, he didn't have the final say.

Gabriella did, and while she loved Essie, he was sure that right now she hated his guts.

"Daddy, when you go see Gabby, you have to say to her that you're sorry and you maded a mistake," Essie said, so serious that he smiled and ruffled her hair.

"I'll do that. Now go lay out the flowers for your mom, that's her grave right there," he said, pointing to the one they'd stopped beside. "Then tell her about you. Tell her all the things you like and all the things that you don't like, what makes you laugh and what makes you sad."

"Can I tell her about Gabby?" Essie asked uncertainly.

"Of course you can. Your mom would love Gabriella and be so happy that you have someone in your life who loves you so much."

As Essie took the bouquet and skipped over to the headstone, chattering away, sounding more like herself than she had since she was abducted, he followed her to Gretel's grave and began to talk. Cade told Gretel how grateful he was to have been loved by her, and that she gave him the most precious gift. He told her all about Gabriella and how much he liked her, how he'd fought his feelings for so long but couldn't fight them a second longer.

And he asked for any magical otherworldly help Gretel could give him to at least secure a chance at convincing Gabriella to forgive him.

~

September 20th
12:31 P.M.

. . .

It felt like she was burning up from the inside out.

Nothing helped anymore.

Gabriella didn't think she'd put on clothing in days. The feel of anything against her skin hurt, even the lightest fabrics. The pain, added to the pain already thrumming through her body from her injuries, and especially the bite mark, was too much.

Nausea was her constant companion.

It never left her alone.

Not even when she was sleeping.

Well, dozing more than sleeping because she still couldn't seem to shut her mind off adequately enough to properly sleep.

Because she was still too afraid.

It was like she'd never be able to feel safe again.

Worse than just feeling nauseous was that it reminded her of the five pregnancies she'd lost. Even though she'd lost all of them before the five-week mark, she'd been pregnant with each baby long enough to suffer morning sickness.

So now not only was she terrified to close her eyes because of fear that those men who had hurt her would come back for her, or other men would come and do worse to her, but she was mourning the loss of her babies all over again.

No doubt that was triggered by losing access to Essie because whether it was ever a conscious decision on her part or not, she'd begun to think of the little girl as hers. Which was stupid because she'd always known the job had an expiration date. After all, Essie wasn't going to stay little forever.

But she'd thought that expiration date would be Essie growing up, and she'd thought that Cade would likely be okay with her staying in touch with the girl so she would always be part of her life.

This was hell.

Losing that little girl when she was already so vulnerable was slowly killing her.

As much as Gabriella didn't want to admit that she was vulnerable, she liked to pretend that she always had it together and nothing could break her, the reality of her current situation forced her to accept facts.

She hadn't handled the abduction well.

Refusing to tell anyone everything she'd gone through was proof of that, as was her lack of appetite and inability to sleep.

Pretending she was okay for Essie's sake hadn't helped her.

The final blow had been Cade's rejection, and it had lodged like a bullet in both her heart and her mind, poisoning her bit by bit as she wasted away.

It was like his words had broken something inside her.

That part of her that had always been so determined to fight for herself, to find what she craved and not stop searching for it until she did.

Looking back, Gabriella could acknowledge that falling for Cade had been a mistake. He was emotionally unavailable, and she never should have put her entire life on hold because she'd stupidly fallen in love with him.

Her entire life had been built around Cade and Essie, and without them, nothing would stop her from withering away.

Which as she glanced down at her naked body, laid out against the cool white tiles of the bathroom floor, was exactly what she was doing.

Over the last few weeks, she'd lost a dramatic amount of weight. Enough that it was noticeable when you looked at her. Her hip bones poked out, and since she was lying flat on her back, she could feel her shoulder blades digging into the unyielding tiles. You could even make out some of her ribs.

There were times in her life as a child when she'd been in foster care that she'd barely been fed, her foster parents preferring to spend the money they got for her care on themselves rather than food for her, but she'd never been this thin.

Dangerously thin.

Especially with infection attacking her body.

The wound on her chest was so ugly, red and enflamed, oozing puss, that she couldn't bear to look at it anymore.

A fine sheen of sweat coated her skin, and she was alternating between burning up so badly she literally prayed for death and then chills so bad that she prayed for a fire she could throw herself into for warmth.

Fanning out around her head, Gabriella knew her hair was a tangled mess of red curls, she'd be lucky if she could untangle them without having to chop off half her hair.

Which was a silly thing to worry about.

Because it didn't really matter.

Was she even going to be alive long enough to have to worry about it?

Death was circling ever closer and although there was a tiny voice calling out at the back of her mind, urging her not to give up, to fight like she always did, to start over and build a new life, she was slipping ever further away.

She didn't want a new life.

She wanted her old life back.

If it helped her keep Essie and Cade in her life, she'd take back sex with Cade. As phenomenal as it had been it wasn't worth losing them.

Part of her hated Cade for what he'd done to her. Throwing her away like she was nothing, the same way everybody else in her life had, she couldn't just turn off her feelings for him. They weren't a switch and she'd loved him for most of the last four years.

More than the hatred was pain.

It hurt that he could do that to her.

Treat her like she didn't matter.

It wasn't like she was asking to be placed above his child she just wanted to be there for Essie. They'd both been through a trauma, and they'd lived it together, she knew without a shadow of a doubt that Essie needed her right now. And being there for the little girl would give her something to focus on even if she wasn't ready to face her own issues yet.

But Cade had torn them apart and now she couldn't seem to find any will to live to hold onto.

Without it, it was already only a matter of time.

If she didn't want to live, there was no way her body was going to heal.

She should care.

She should want to live.

But truth was, she was just too tired of fighting. It was one thing to fight if you had someone by your side, fighting along with you. It was quite another when you had to do it alone.

Always alone.

Death had terrified her when she and Essie were being held captive. The possibility of dying and leaving Essie all alone had gripped her with an icy claw leading her to do whatever she could to protect her little charge.

Now, she had no such external motivation and death felt more like a warm embrace than an icy terror to be feared.

It was time.

Time to just let go.

Release the last tiny thread binding her to this world.

Not wanting to die in the bathroom, Gabriella forced her limbs to obey her command and rolled over onto her stomach.

For a relatively small wound, the bite mark hurt so badly.

Badly enough that tears streamed down her cheeks.

Fighting off a round of chills, the tears felt like tiny ice blocks against her skin.

With a moan, she managed to push up onto all fours and somehow she managed to get to her feet.

For a second she swayed precariously, sure she was going to go back down. If she did, she knew she wouldn't be getting up again.

But she remained standing and staggered into the bedroom. Once she got on the bed, she could close her eyes and just wait for nature to take its course.

Only she didn't make it to the bed.

Her legs gave out halfway there and she hit the floor with a groan. No longer able to control her body she slumped down. The rough carpet rubbed against her wound making it feel like a thousand needles stabbing at her torn flesh.

A wave of heat crashed over her and she cried out against it as nausea swelled. If there was anything in her stomach, it probably would have come back up, but she couldn't even remember the last time she'd eaten.

Sounds outside her hotel suite caught her attention. It sounded like raised voices arguing.

Confident her bodyguards would handle it, Gabriella blocked it out and stopped trying to fight against what her body was telling her.

It was time.

Her eyes slid closed, and she went completely limp.

For a second she was sure she heard footsteps getting closer.

Then someone called her name.

It sounded like Cade's voice, which confirmed what she already knew. There was no way Cade would be there so she was hallucinating. Her mind blessing her with one final thought of the man she loved before she drifted away.

CHAPTER
Nineteen

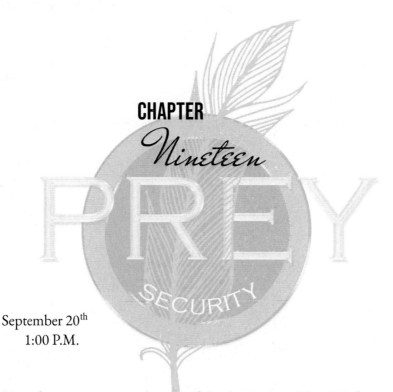

September 20th
1:00 P.M.

His palms were sweaty as he got off the elevator on Gabriella's floor.

Gabriella had always messed with his head but not like this.

Knowing she had feelings for him, although it had probably taken Cade longer to figure that out than it should have, meant he'd always felt a connection to her even if he hadn't done anything about his feelings for her.

But when he fired her and told her to leave, he severed that connection.

Now he felt off kilter.

Worse, he had a knot of anxiety in his gut that hadn't dissipated in the days since he'd last seen her.

As he strode down the hallway, he was at least pleased to see two men standing outside Gabriella's suite. Dressed professionally, they both shifted their stance when they saw him approaching.

Good.

They were doing their jobs and protecting his girl.

Shame filled him, though, because he knew *he* should be the one protecting Gabriella. If nothing else, he owed it to her for everything she'd done for Essie. But more than that, he cared about her, was on the way to falling in love with her, and he should always be there to stand at her back, her front, or her side, depending on what she needed from him in any given situation.

"I'm Cade Charleston, I work for Prey Security, and I'm Gabriella's former boss," he said as he strode toward them. Aware that with a huge bouquet in his hand, he didn't look like he was there in any official capacity, and while he had a twinge in his chest at calling himself her former employer it was true.

If he could convince Gabriella to come back to him it wouldn't be to work for him.

It would be as his partner and Essie's mother.

Recognition flared in their eyes.

"We were told this was connected to you and your family. Can we take it this is a social visit?" one asked.

"Yes. I would have brought my daughter, Gabriella was her nanny, but I didn't want to overwhelm her. Essie picked out the flowers herself." After they visited the cemetery, they stopped by the florist, then he'd dropped Essie off with his brothers. It wasn't really that he thought Essie would overwhelm Gabriella, in fact, he had no doubt she'd happily see his daughter rather than him. But he wanted to prove to her that he wanted her in his life for him not just for Essie.

"She didn't tell us she was expecting a visitor," one said as though there was any question he was getting into that room.

"I don't want to cause trouble, but I'm not leaving without seeing her," he informed them.

"Orders were not to let anyone in," the other spoke up.

"Again, I'm not leaving until Gabriella tells me that she doesn't want to see me," he said, attempting to keep his voice down but sure he was failing.

"I suppose since you know her it will be okay," the first finally agreed.

"Thank you." While he wouldn't have taken no for an answer, he was pleased he didn't have to call Eagle, beg for help, and have his boss reach out to the owner of the firm Gabriella had hired to have him cleared.

Anxiety pulsed through his system as one of the bodyguards used his room key to open the door to Gabriella's suite. For a second, he was afraid she would have put the chain on to deny them entrance because he had zero doubts she wouldn't have removed it to speak with him, that fear passed when the door swung open.

Something felt off when he stepped into the suite and closed the door behind him.

The room was too quiet.

Too still.

Maybe Gabriella was taking a nap? Or relaxing in a bubble bath? He knew she loved bubble baths and had spent more hours than he'd care to admit with a hard-on while he knew she was naked and luxuriating in the soapy water.

Now it wasn't pleasure he couldn't do anything about chasing that crashed through him, it was fear.

His gut said something was wrong.

The suite had a small living area where he stood, and there were no signs that Gabriella had been in it recently. There was a door on the opposite side of the room that he was sure led to the bedroom, and he hesitated barely a moment before heading to it.

"Gabriella?" he called out as he reached it, his hand hovering on the door handle. As much as he wanted to go barging in and bulldoze his way back into her life, he had to be respectful.

He was responsible for the distance between them.

He'd broken her trust.

He'd pushed her away.

It had to be up to her to decide if she could forgive and give him a chance. Not that he was giving up easily, but the least he owed her was respect.

"It's Cade," he called out again when there was no answer. "I came to check on you and see if maybe we could talk, and I could explain. I'm sorry, Gabriella. You deserved better than I gave you. I made a mistake and want to try to make it up to you."

There was no response to his words and his uneasiness grew.

Actually, it was already well past uneasiness and on its way to becoming full-blown terror.

"Gabriella, unless you tell me not to, I'm coming in," he warned. His gut told him something was wrong, and he wasn't hanging around in the living room if she needed him.

When once again there was no answer, he carefully eased the door open on the slim chance that she was just asleep and hadn't heard him or was in the bathroom.

As soon as he stepped into the bedroom his heart stopped beating.

She was there.

Lying on the floor.

So very still that for one horrifying moment, he wondered if he'd left coming to her too late.

The kind of too late that no number of apologies and hard work could fix.

Cade didn't remember dumping the flowers on the bed and rushing to her side. The next thing he knew, he was on his knees beside Gabriella's too-still body.

Gently brushing back her tangle of red curls, he noticed the flushed color of her face and the beads of sweat that dotted her brow. Her skin was warm to the touch as he pressed his fingertips to her neck, and when he felt it, her pulse was beating much too fast.

She was sick.

Why the hell hadn't she told anyone?

And why did the thought of the answer to that question leave his heart pounding painfully in his chest?

"Gabriella, I'm here, baby," he crooned softly as he carefully eased her over onto her back. As soon as he did, he gasped in shock as he saw her chest. Right over her left breast was a bite mark. The wound was clearly infected, and he knew without a shadow of a doubt that she'd gotten it while she was being held captive.

One of those monsters had bitten her.

On the breast.

And as far as he was aware she hadn't told anyone about it. She certainly hadn't told him, and when he'd asked about her condition and injuries his brothers hadn't mentioned it either.

She'd been hiding her pain and suffering because she was so focused on his daughter.

How had he ever let this woman go?

What the hell was wrong with him?

Shoving away his anger at himself because it wasn't what Gabriella needed right now, he smoothed a lock of hair off her sweat-dampened forehead. "Hold on, sweetheart, I'll get you help, you just fight for me. Don't give up, baby. Please."

The last was a tortured whisper as he yanked his cell phone from his back pocket and dialed 911. After asking for an ambulance to be sent to the hotel, he hung up, and focused his attention on his girl, lying so sick before him that he wanted to vomit.

This was his fault.

He knew that it was.

She hadn't asked for help or told anyone she was sick on purpose because ... he hated to consider the idea, but he couldn't not, considering how he'd found her and that she knew there were two men right outside who would organize a doctor if she'd just asked. Or she could have reached out to his family, they were all firmly team Gabriella.

But she hadn't done that.

Because she didn't want to.

She had made the conscious decision to lie there and allow the infection in the bite wound to slowly seep inside her body.

The only conclusion he could draw from that was that Gabriella didn't want to live anymore.

Leaving her side for even a second felt wrong, but he had to work on getting her temperature down while he waited for the EMTs to arrive. Running into the bathroom he turned on the bath, put in the plug, and then ran back to the bedroom. Scooping Gabriella's limp body into his arms, he carried her to the bath, toed off his shoes, and then stepped into the bath fully clothed.

As he sat, he settled Gabriella so her naked body was between his spread knees and rested her so she lay against his chest. Then he reached for a washcloth, dunked it in the cool water, and began to blot at her face.

After that, all he could do was beg.

Beg her not to give up.

Beg her to keep fighting.

Beg her to understand he'd been trying to protect her.

Beg her not to leave him like Gretel had.

Then, as he continued to smooth the wet cloth on her too-hot face, he did what he knew she would do for Essie if his daughter was sick and started to sing.

~

September 22nd

8:47 A.M.

Pain still pulsed through her body, but for the first time in weeks, it felt like maybe there was light at the end of the tunnel.

Gabriella knew she'd messed up.

She should never have allowed herself to get so sick that she just gave up.

As badly as she felt and as uncertain about her future as she was, she didn't really want to be dead.

All she wanted was to not be alone anymore.

Was that really too much to ask?

Everyone else seemed to have someone and she was so sick of always being left out in the cold.

Which only made her feel guilty because she knew she had lots of blessings, and she didn't like to wallow in self-pity when she had a lot more than so many others had. She just didn't want to face life alone anymore.

Sounds outside her hospital room had her turning her head on the pillow to look at the door. It had been almost forty-eight hours since she passed out and had been found unconscious on her hotel room floor. Those first hours were a complete blank. She didn't remember the ambulance ride to the hospital, didn't remember being examined in the ER. It wasn't until several hours later she woke up to find she was no longer in her hotel suite.

As well as the infection ravaging her body, she'd been severely dehydrated, and the fact that she hadn't been eating or sleeping had her so weak her body just couldn't compensate any longer.

With heavy-duty antibiotics being delivered via IV as well as fluids, she was slowly improving but still found the tiniest of movements a tremendous effort.

There had been a steady stream of visitors in and out of her room.

Apparently, Cade had found her and called in reinforcements. Other than when a doctor examined her, one of the Charleston Holloway brothers was with her.

It was odd, but not unpleasant.

And she didn't have the energy to figure out why Cade had been in her suite.

What possible reason could he have to come to the hotel to see her?

"I'll go check it out," Jake told her as he crossed the room and disappeared through the door.

A moment later, she heard the distinct excited squeal that could only come from Essie.

Her heart squeezed painfully. As badly as she wanted to see the little girl, there was no way that Essie was there without her dad, and she just wasn't ready to face Cade. A conversation was going to have to happen at some point because she needed to know why he'd gone to the hotel, but she wasn't up to it yet.

When Jake returned a minute or two later, he had a fierce expression that she recognized as his protective look. Jake could be similar to Cade. Both were gruff, could be intimidating, and didn't bother to mince their words. But both were also compassionate and loyal. They loved their family with everything they had, and right now, she knew that she was the focus of every one of Jake's protective instincts.

Even though she knew this wasn't the best thing for her long term to have Cade's family hovering around her. It was too easy to slip back into old ways of thinking and go back to considering them hers.

But they weren't hers.

Not really.

She didn't get to keep them.

So, it was better to maintain the clean break she'd initiated, but somehow, she couldn't seem to make herself do it. She was so weak, making her even more vulnerable, and she was lapping up their attention and care like she was starving. And she was, she wasn't denying it. A lifetime of having to be self-sufficient to survive meant she couldn't be anything but.

"It's Essie and Cade," Jake announced, somewhat unnecessarily as he crossed to the bed and curled his fingers around the guardrail.

"I figured, heard her voice and knew she wouldn't be here alone," she said. Since she hadn't had cause to speak out loud much when she was in her hotel suite it had been a shock to hear how weak she sounded.

Gabriella was pretty sure that the only thing holding back the Charleston Holloway brothers from reading her the riot act for shutting them out and not asking for help when she obviously needed it was the fact that she was so very weak. The last several weeks had taken a toll on her body and her mind, not just the abduction but her refusal to acknowledge what had happened to her, and her inability to take care of herself.

"They want to see you," Jake said.

"Today's the twenty-second, right?" She was pretty sure it was, but everything was a little hazy and she couldn't be sure.

"It is."

"So, it's Essie's birthday." Gabriella chewed on her bottom lip. There was no way she could say no to seeing her favorite person in the world on their fifth birthday, but she didn't want to see Cade.

Which meant she couldn't see Essie.

Because there was no way Cade would allow his daughter out of his sight.

"You don't have to see them, Gabs." Jake reached out and took her hand, giving it a gentle squeeze. "You've been through hell and deserve this time to rest and heal. I can tell them to go away."

"I want to see Essie, it's just ..." she trailed off not wanting to say it out loud even if it was true. After all, Cade was Jake's stepbrother, they were family, and she wasn't anything to any of them anymore.

"I'll tell him he can't come in here then," Jake said immediately.

"He won't let Essie come then."

"Oh, honey, he absolutely will. Essie has been begging to see you every single day since you left. There is no way Cade is going to deny his daughter anything, especially not today."

Before she could disagree, he headed back toward the door.

Since they were talking in hushed voices in the corridor, she couldn't hear what they were saying, and her entire body was tense as she waited. She so badly wanted to see Essie again, she'd missed that little girl something fierce. Nothing would help her heal faster than being around that precious child.

"Gabby!" Essie's squeal of delight had her breaking into the first smile she'd had in days and something inside her settled.

It didn't matter that she knew this wasn't going to last, that it would only make things worse when she had to say goodbye, she was going to soak up every second she got to spend with the little girl.

"Hey, cuddle bug," she said as the tiny tornado of energy scrambled up onto the bed, bypassing the guardrails by climbing up from the end of the bed. "Happy birthday, baby girl."

"I'm not a baby no more, Gabby. I'm five," Essie said excitedly, holding up her hand with all four fingers and her thumb sticking out straight.

"You're such a big girl."

Climbing over her legs, Essie snuggled against her, wrapping her little arms around Gabriella's neck and planting a kiss on her cheek. "I missed you so much, Gabby. I didn't want you to go."

"I didn't want to go either, cuddle bug." While she wouldn't talk badly about Cade in front of his daughter, she also didn't ever want Essie to think that she didn't love her. The last thing she would ever wish was for Essie to feel for one second that she wasn't wanted and adored.

"But you're coming back," Essie said so firmly that Gabriella didn't have the heart to break it to the child that this could be the last time they ever saw one another.

"Party time," Cole called out as he burst into the room with a handful of brightly colored balloons.

He wasn't alone.

Behind him came Susanna, Connor and Becca, Cooper and Willow, Jake and Jax. They all carried either more balloons or presents wrapped in cute unicorn wrapping paper, the exact paper she'd picked out a couple of months ago when she started preparing for Essie's birthday. Willow was even carrying one of the cakes in Essie's top three from the list she'd compiled.

It looked like they were planning to do Essie's birthday right there in her hospital room.

Why?

Cade wasn't even there. He hadn't come in with the others, apparently respecting her wishes that she didn't want to see him. Yet he'd allowed Essie to come in. More than that, he had to have been the one to gather together all the party paraphernalia and bring it to the hospital.

What did that mean?

And did she even want it to mean anything at all?

CHAPTER

Twenty

September 23rd
10:47 A.M.

Standing outside Gabriella's hospital room yesterday while his daughter and the rest of his family celebrated inside had been hell.

Not just because he wasn't there with them, but because Gabriella didn't want to see him.

Cade knew she was aware that he had been the one to find her unconscious in her room. He'd ridden with her in the ambulance, stayed by her side in the emergency room, it wasn't until she finally started to wake up that he'd reluctantly left.

It had been hard.

Certainly not what he wanted to do.

But his brothers had made too much sense telling him that he'd messed things up badly enough with Gabriella that the strong, fiery woman they'd always known had just given up. He shouldn't be the first thing she saw when she opened her eyes, even though there was nothing he'd wanted more than to get lost staring into those green depths of hers and prove to himself that he hadn't lost her.

That there was still hope.

It was time to put Gabriella first, so he'd left her room, listened from the hall as Jax had spoken softly to her in soothing tones, assuring her she was safe and being taken care of. He'd rallied the rest of his family, knowing he couldn't have the conversation he wanted with Gabriella until she was stronger. Until then, he didn't want her alone. Not even for a second.

He had a new mission in life, and it was ensuring that never again did Gabriella see herself as trash that was easily thrown away.

Yesterday he'd hung back and allowed Gabriella and his daughter to enjoy Essie's birthday together, like they should have all along. Sometimes admitting you made a mistake sucked, but sometimes it was a relief.

And right now, Cade felt relieved.

There was still a knot in his stomach because he knew he had a long road ahead of him to convince Gabriella to give him a second chance, but it was a relief to finally admit that he wanted her in his life. There was no more hiding from his feelings. No more pretending he wasn't aware of Gabriella's feelings.

It was freeing in a way but still terrifying.

Because his family was in danger and even though he acknowledged that sending Gabriella away to protect her hadn't been the right move it didn't change the facts. Losing her wasn't just some hypothetical he could lose her kind of worry, there was a very real possibility his entire family could be taken out.

With a deep breath, he knocked on the door to Gabriella's room once. She hadn't wanted to see him yesterday and while he'd been disappointed, he'd still wanted her and Essie to enjoy his daughter's birthday together, so he hadn't minded staying outside. He'd had plenty of time to enjoy Essie on her birthday and wanted to share his child with Gabriella.

But today he had to try to talk to her. Explain. Pray she was at least a little bit receptive to what he had to say.

There was no response to his knock and a tiny niggle of doubt tickled the back of his neck. Gabriella was improving slowly. Unfortunately, she'd completely run herself into the ground by not eating and was extremely weak, but she was improving with the help of antibiotics and fluids.

Just because she had been doing okay didn't mean she still was.

After all, no one had known she was even sick to begin with.

Shoving open the door, Cade stormed into the room and froze as he saw Gabriella walking out of the bathroom. She was wearing an oversized T-shirt he'd seen her sleep in plenty of times before, it was one of the things he'd packed in the bag he'd sent to the hospital with his brothers after he'd known Gabriella was stable. With her long red curls hanging free around her face, slightly less tangled than when he'd found her in the hotel, and her face free from makeup, she looked so young and vulnerable. Beautiful though, even the paleness of her skin, and the slight feverish splash of pink to her cheeks couldn't diminish that.

"Cade," she said, shocked that he was standing in her room.

On the other hand, he couldn't seem to say anything.

All he could do was stare at her and drink in the sight.

She was alive, still sick, still weak, but alive.

He hadn't lost her like he'd lost Gretel.

He still had a shot at convincing her he could be a good partner. One who would love and cherish her. Who would do anything to protect her. Who would make sure she never felt unworthy again.

It was a long shot but a shot nonetheless.

"What are you doing here?" she demanded as she continued walking toward the bed.

Her progress was so slow, and it looked like it was taking all the remaining strength she had left in her body just to walk across the six or so feet from the bathroom door to the bed.

When she wobbled precariously, he didn't think, just acted.

Cade was at her side before he even knew he'd moved, his arm around her waist, steadying her. Even though she felt so small in his hold, so very fragile, he soaked up the feel of her tiny body pressed against his.

There was every chance he could have stayed right where he was indefinitely, but Gabriella began to struggle in his hold, pushing away, so he reluctantly released his hold but remained close enough to catch her if she fell.

Shooting him an angry glare, she climbed onto the bed and pulled up the covers as though she needed a layer of protection.

It hurt to know that she felt like she needed to protect herself from him, but he couldn't fault her for it. After all, he had been the one to hurt her even if he'd done it for what he believed to be both logical and noble reasons at the time.

Slowly, the glare slipped off her face and she dropped her gaze to her hands, which she tangled together on her lap. "I should thank you for allowing me to see Essie on her birthday yesterday. I appreciated it." Drawing in a deep breath she lifted her face to meet his gaze. "Thank you."

"Don't thank me for that, Gabriella. Essie wanted to see you and I wanted you to see her, too." When he went to reach for her, he realized halfway there that she didn't want his touch, so he let his hands hang for a second before dropping to hang limply at his sides. Then almost immediately, he lifted them again to rake them through his hair. "Look, Gabriella, we need to talk. I—"

"No, Cade," she interrupted. "I don't want to talk now. I'm not ready."

"I get that. I do. I just need you to know how sorry I am for hurting you."

There was no anger left in her eyes as she met his gaze head on. More just sadness. A deep-rooted sadness he'd give anything to soothe away.

This mess might be one of his own creation, but that didn't make it any easier to deal with.

"I don't know if an apology is enough, Cade," she said softly. "I love Essie more than I love my own life. I thought you knew that. But you ripped her away from me when we needed each other the most. You th-threw me away like I was n-nothing," her voice began to waver, and tears flooded her eyes.

"No, baby. You're not nothing. You're everything," he growled. "Everything."

"I don't believe you, Cade," she said dully. "I could understand you not having feelings for me because you still love your wife. But I never thought you would be cruel. Never thought you would hurt me."

"I was trying to protect you. Trying to get you out of the danger my family is mired in so you didn't get hurt again." His gaze landed on her chest. He knew beneath the oversized T-shirt she wore was the bite wound. One of those men had bitten her deeply enough that it would leave scars. A permanent reminder of her ordeal.

Of what he'd put her through.

"But I did get hurt again, Cade. *You* hurt me."

"Please, sweetheart, I'm sorry, I'm so sor—"

"Just go, Cade. I can't do this with you right now. I just want you to go. It's too hard seeing you."

How could he make things better if she couldn't even stand to be in the same room as him?

"Gabs? You okay?" Connor asked, appearing in the room with a box of Gabriella's favorite donuts.

"I'm okay," she answered, even though they all knew it was a lie.

"Cade?" Connor turned to him. There was empathy on his face, Connor more than any of them knew all about messing things up with the woman you loved.

But Connor had made things right, gotten his happy ever after. Looked like the chances of the same happening for him were slim to none.

"He was just leaving," Gabriella answered for him.

"How do I fix this?" he asked desperately, not willing or able to just give up.

"I don't know, Cade." Gabriella sighed tiredly and rolled over onto her side, facing away from him. "I don't even know if you can."

∼

September 27th
4:56 P.M.

While her body and mind were getting stronger every day, Gabriella could feel her heart hurting worse.

Each day Cade brought Essie to the hospital to visit. The little girl still hadn't had her first day of school, Cade didn't want to take the risk of sending her somewhere that would be a security nightmare, so they spent a lot of their time together doing letters and numbers. While Gabriella had no formal childhood education training, Essie seemed to be learning so she must be doing something right.

It was so weird, as hurt and angry as she was with Cade, she was also grateful that he was no longer keeping Essie away from her.

But niggling at the back of her mind was the reminder that one day it would end.

Cade had fired her, and she didn't think she could go back to work for him again even if he unfired her. It was just asking to get hurt all over again. She still had feelings for him and there was no way she would allow herself to be in a position where he could break her heart again.

Once she was out of the hospital, she feared there would be no more daily visits, no more cuddles and giggling, no more snuggles and playing games.

When that happened, she worried that she would sink right back into that deep, dark place where she didn't care if she lived or died.

Resting back against the pillows, she fiddled with the scratchy blanket covering her. Cade had just left with Essie, and Connor, who had been playing babysitter, had walked them out.

While no one had outright yelled at her about allowing herself to become so sick when she could have picked up a phone and called any member of the Charleston Holloway family, or even a doctor, or an ambulance once she got bad enough, they'd all made their feelings known. They'd just done it in that way she'd heard parents did where instead of yelling they just talked and told you how disappointed they were. Not that any of them had used the word disappointed, they'd just told her they were sad that she hadn't been aware that they considered her family regardless of whether she was Cade's employee or not.

Those were words they'd all spoken to her, especially after the abduction when Cade was missing, but they hadn't sunk in.

Maybe now they were starting to.

After all, they might not have used that word disappointed, but she could tell that every single one of them was hurt she hadn't reached out when she'd needed help.

The door to her room swung open, and she turned, expecting to see Connor and maybe Becca, too, but instead, it was Cade standing there.

If there was one word you would use to describe Cade it was confident. He was always sure of himself, never cowered to anything, and guided his family with leadership skills that implied he was a whole lot more than a couple of years older than his brothers.

Only now he didn't look so confident anymore.

In fact, he looked the opposite.

So unsure of himself that she was actually the first one to speak.

"Hey," she whispered softly.

Surprise filled his brown eyes as his gaze darted to the bed. "Hey."

His gaze traveled her body, giving her an appraising once over like he hadn't just been in the room picking up his daughter five minutes ago.

Why was he back?

Something couldn't have happened with Essie.

Could it?

"Is Essie okay?" she blurted out as her pulse kicked into high gear.

A warm smile spread across his face, and she felt that smile down to her bones. It curled inside her, sending warmth spreading through her limbs. How many times over the last four years had she wished he would smile at her like that?

Had to be at least a hundred.

Maybe even a thousand.

All she'd wanted was for him to look at her like he cared, like she meant something to him and she mattered in a way that had nothing to do with her just providing a service for him.

It took everything she had to remind herself that she didn't matter.

Cade had kicked her out of his home and his daughter's life like he wasn't killing a part of her in the process. If he'd loved her, heck, if he'd even liked her, he wouldn't have done that to her. They'd spent so much time together over the years surely there was no way he couldn't have picked up on the fact that she was struggling even if she'd been doing her best to hide it. He had to have seen and just not cared.

Sure, he'd said he was trying to protect her by sending her away, but she wasn't sure she could believe that.

Did he think she should have done more to protect his daughter?

Did he blame her for the abduction?

Gabriella had to admit she wasn't sure she could be angry with him if he did. She blamed herself. He hadn't wanted her to go to the pool that day, but she'd insisted, saying it was important that they stifle Essie's life as little as possible so she didn't become aware that the danger surrounding her and her family was so great.

"Essie is fine, sweetheart," he assured her, taking a tentative step toward the bed.

"Are you sure?"

"Positive."

"Then why are you here? You should be with her. She needs you." Gabriella meant those words sincerely even as she felt a tiny twinge in her chest because she so desperately needed someone as well, there was just no one she could turn to. Well, there was the rest of Cade's family, but she felt weird about that, almost like she was making them choose between her and their brother.

"I think," Cade said, taking another step toward her, "that maybe you need me, too."

She shook her head even though his words were everything she'd once wanted to hear.

But it was too late for him to change his mind again. The damage was done, and it couldn't be undone. Could it?

"I'm not denying I messed up, Gabriella. Not at all. My motives were good, but my actions weren't. I should have been there for you the way you were there for my daughter."

Her heart sank.

Cade was only trying to be nice now because he felt guilty that she'd been so badly hurt while trying to shield Essie.

That wasn't what she wanted.

She wanted to be seen for her.

She wanted him to want her just because he had feelings for her, separate from anything to do with his child.

"I don't want your pity, your guilt, or whatever this is. Nor do I want payment for protecting Essie. I love her, what else would I do?"

"Which is exactly why I couldn't deny it any longer."

"Deny what?"

"I know you told me you weren't ready to talk yet, and I'm trying to respect you, trying to do the right thing, but I have something for you, and I can't wait any longer to give it to you."

"Something for me?"

"Mmhmm," he said as he nodded and pulled out a small red box from his pocket. "I was trying to think of a way to show you what you mean to me because I haven't done so well with my words."

Closing the distance between himself and the bed, he held out the box. Gabriella stared at it, not altogether sure that it wasn't a snake about to jump out and bite her. What game was he trying to play here? Was he trying to mess with her? Why was he suddenly being so sweet?

Very slowly she lifted a hand. It trembled and they both watched its progress as it reached out toward the velvet box. It felt smooth in her hand when her fingers closed around it and Cade watched her so closely as she opened the lid and looked inside.

Nestled on white satin sat a gold heart on a chain.

A heart?

The trembling in her fingers increased as she scooped it up, realizing it was a locket.

When her gaze snapped to Cade's he gave her an encouraging nod.

Opening the locket, she saw that the heart opened to become four hearts, making it look like a four-leaf clover. Three of the hearts had pictures in them. One was a photo of her, one was a photo of Essie, and one was a photo of Cade.

It almost looked like they were a family.

But they weren't.

"Cade," she said on a half sob as she shoved the necklace back toward him. How could she keep this knowing she could never have what she craved?

"I have one to give to Essie, too. We'll give it to her together when you're ready."

"When I'm ready?"

"It has a picture of her, her mom, me, and you inside her locket."

"Me?" she asked, voice wavering. What was he doing to her? He was dangling everything she'd ever wanted in front of her, but she couldn't reach out and take it, she was too afraid of being thrown away again.

"She loves you. You're the mom she knows, the mom she wants, and Gretel would want that, too."

"I don't want to be with someone who only wants me to be a stand-in mom to his child," she told him. That would never be what she wanted. She wanted to be loved for herself.

"No, sweetheart. That's not what I'm saying."

"Then what are you saying? I know you still love your wife."

"I'll always love Gretel. But that doesn't mean that I'm not falling in—"

"No. Don't say it," she begged. If he said it, she wasn't sure she'd believe it. Definitely wasn't sure she could trust it.

"I won't say it until you're ready to hear it, but it doesn't change how I feel or stop it from being true."

Her whole body shook. In shock, hope, or fear, she wasn't really sure, maybe a combination of all three.

"I need you to go," she whispered, afraid she was about to break down.

Clear disappointment was on his face, but he didn't argue. Just set the red, velvet box on the bed beside her and gave another warm smile that did funny things to her insides. "I'm not going anywhere, Gabriella. I'll leave for now, but I will fight for you. For us."

With that, he turned and walked out of the room leaving her staring after him and clutching the necklace he hadn't taken back.

Was he trying to tell her that he loved her?

Really?

As in, was actually in love with her?

She was so confused.

But she wasn't confused enough when the door to her room opened again, and her heart fluttered, excited to see Cade again even as she dreaded it because she couldn't trust him right now.

Only it wasn't Cade walking into her room.

It was a man dressed as a nurse, with a mask covering the bottom half of his face.

Not his eyes though.

And she recognized those eyes.

They belonged to one of the men who had held her and Essie captive.

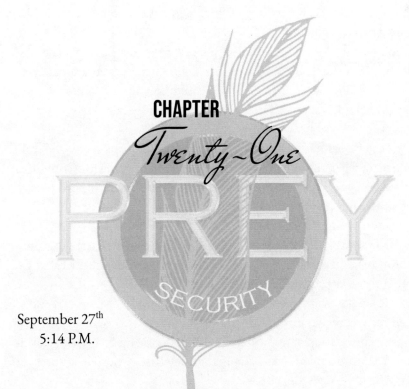

CHAPTER
Twenty-One

September 27th
5:14 P.M.

His phone rang as soon as he left Gabriella's room.

All things considered, it had gone better than he expected. Better than he could have hoped.

So far, she'd continued to tell him that she wasn't ready to talk to him yet, but not that she never wanted to see him again.

Was it unfair of him to keep bringing his daughter around to see her?

Cade guessed it probably could be considered such since he knew that Essie was a way to soften Gabriella toward him. But it wasn't the only reason he kept bringing his daughter to visit, it wasn't even the main reason.

Bottom line, Gabriella needed Essie, and Essie needed Gabriella.

From here on out, it couldn't be about weighing the needs of one of his girls against the other. Essie was his daughter and the most important person in his life, but Gabriella sat right alongside her because she was the woman he was falling in love with, the woman he wanted a future with.

Somewhat absently, he pulled his cell from his back pocket, still picturing the shock on Gabriella's face when she saw the locket. He hoped that one day the final heart would contain a picture of their biological child, but even if they never had kids together, Essie was every bit as much hers as she was his.

Cooper's name was on the screen, and he answered the call, wondering what was happening. Essie had gone home with Connor so he knew she was safe, and he sincerely hoped that one of his brothers or their girlfriends hadn't been targeted again.

He was getting sick of this.

Two more names, that was all they needed to put an end to this once and for all so he could finally put his guilt about how he'd treated his mother those last six months of her life to rest.

"Hey, what's up?" he asked as he accepted the call.

"Pretty sure we just IDed one of the other two men involved in Mom's rape," Cooper told him. There was excitement brewing in his brother's voice and it was catching. Immediately, he felt a surge of energy rush through his veins.

"Name?"

"Akio Yamamoto."

"Who is he?" The name didn't ring a bell.

"He was a famous, pioneering transplant surgeon."

"Was?"

"Died not long after Mom was raped."

"So he's not the remaining rapist?"

"Not Cassandra's father either. He's the Asian man you said John mentioned. Akio was Japanese, his parents immigrated when he was a couple of months old."

While he would have preferred to identify the living rapist first since he was the one who was a threat to the family and not a man who'd been dead for a quarter of a century, at least it was something. And the more intel they had the easier it would be to figure out who the remaining man was. They now had three of the four names so they could cross-reference all of them and come up with a list of potential suspects. From there, it would be a matter of obtaining DNA so they could test it against Cassandra's, and this would finally be over.

"There's more," Cooper continued. "Akio has a cousin who owned the stationary company, and he has a son who is former military."

"All the men we've been able to catch so far who have come after us have been former military."

"Right. So I looked into him a little more, and he matches the description and sketches both Gabriella and Essie did after they were rescued, and he matches the one who wasn't there when we rescued you."

They'd known one man had escaped, he wasn't amongst the ones Cade himself had killed, and he wasn't the man that had come seconds away from shooting him. They'd theorized that he'd gone with John Gaccione to the meeting but hung back so he wouldn't be spotted.

Knowing he was out there, another threat, had been adding to his stress, but now they had a name they could round him up, bring him in, and interrogate him. Chances of him knowing the name of the fourth rapist were slim, especially since John claimed he didn't and was yet to give in under intense interrogation, but it was worth a shot.

"Cade, there's more," Cooper continued, his voice tightening, and Cade's stomach tightened as he braced for bad news. "He works as a nurse. At the hospital."

Fear slithered up his spine. "What hospital."

"The one you're currently inside."

Already he was turning, hurrying back to Gabriella's room.

She wasn't safe.

And she was alone.

He'd been going to call Jax, who was next on the babysitting Gabriella roster, and have him come in, then pass the time in the waiting room down the hall where he'd have a clear view of the door to Gabriella's room. That way he could watch over her while still respecting her need for time and space.

But he'd had his back to the door while on the phone.

It couldn't have been more than a couple of minutes, but that was enough time for someone to sneak into her room.

Nobody would think twice about a nurse going into a patient's room. Particularly one who had official hospital identification.

Maybe Cooper continued to talk, Cade had no idea, his entire focus had shifted to getting back to his girl.

If he'd left her alone and she was hurt—or worse killed—because of him, he'd never forgive himself. As it was, he was having a hard enough time forgiving himself for firing her and he'd done that specifically because he was trying to protect her and get her out of the line of fire his family was sitting right in the middle of.

As soon as he reached the door, he knew something was wrong.

He could hear muffled sounds coming from inside and they weren't the sounds of Gabriella crying quietly to herself.

Flinging open the door hard enough that it slammed into the wall, red-hot rage clouded his vision as he took in the scene before him.

Gabriella was still on the bed where he'd left her, but instead of being curled up against the pillows looking so fragile and vulnerable all he'd wanted to do was drag her into his arms and hold her until the haunted look left her eyes, she was flat on her back. The blankets were tangled around her body, half on the bed and half on the floor.

And there was a pillow covering her face.

At the sound of the door opening, the man leaning over the edge of the bed pressing the pillow to Gabriella's face as she did her best to fight him off, lost his concentration.

That was all the advantage he needed.

If there was one thing you didn't do it was hurt the woman a man loved when that man was trained in a thousand different ways to kill someone, including many of those with his bare hands.

Any thought of keeping the man alive to try to get answers from him flew out of Cade's head as he launched himself at Gabriella's would-be killer.

Fury gave him extra strength and he picked up the man several inches shorter than him, weighed in at fifty pounds or so lighter, and threw him across the room.

Connecting with the wall with enough force to break through most of the plaster sending it flying everywhere, the man groaned as he slumped to the floor.

Apparently, he wasn't very bright because he staggered to his feet, swaying precariously, and attempted to charge at him.

Idiot.

Grabbing the man's head on both sides when he got within arms' reach, Cade leaned in close. "Never touch what's mine and try to take it away from me," he snarled, then with one simple twist of his hands it was done.

The man's neck snapped, and Cade tossed his now dead body on the ground and hurried back to the bed where Gabriella had pressed herself up against the headboard and was staring at him with wide eyes as she sucked in gasping breaths.

"I'm so sorry, sweetheart, I shouldn't have left your door until Jax got here. I just didn't think I could stay that close and not come back in here and haul you into my arms where I've wanted you for the last month."

Her whole body trembled, but something soft in her eyes hadn't been there when he'd left her room earlier. "Y-you called me y-yours," she stammered, her wide green eyes begging him for confirmation, to assure her that he'd meant what he said and it wasn't uttered in the heat of the moment.

Reaching out, Cade hesitantly brushed a stray curl off her cheek, smoothing it and tucking it behind her ear. "You are. It just took me a while to accept what I'd known from the second I laid eyes on you. I wasn't ready then, Gabriella, I was still grieving. I'm ready now. To make you mine, to build a life with you. When you're ready to make me yours. But make no mistake about it, you are already mine."

Tears leaked out of her eyes, and she shuddered, her breathing still uneven. Voices started to sound behind him and several sets of footsteps told him multiple people had entered the room.

Cade ignored them all.

Only one person needed his attention, and she was still staring up at him with wide eyes.

"Can I hold you, sweetheart?" he asked.

When she gave a tentative nod, he quickly scooped her into his arms, taking her spot on the bed and settling her on his lap.

Finally.

His girl was where she belonged and the weight of her small body nestled against him soothed everything inside him, giving him a peace he hadn't felt in decades.

~

September 28th
7:02 A.M.

For some reason, she couldn't take her eyes off the bite mark on her chest.

It had been almost a month since it was done, and because she hadn't cared for the wound it had gotten infected. Thanks to that decision, she would be left with a permanent reminder of that ordeal on her body that she would see every single day.

Her fault, nobody else's.

Yet she wished she could go back in time and make a different choice.

Despite the more than three weeks that had passed, the wound still looked angry and red, not at all like it could have. Still, it had improved over the week she'd been in the hospital. It no longer looked like it was full of puss, and while still red, it wasn't as enflamed as it had been.

It was healing, like the rest of her was.

Her cheeks were no longer stained bright red with fever and paper pale beneath, and she'd started to put a little weight back on although she still didn't have much appetite.

For the first time since she'd been abducted, she'd actually slept properly last night. Different than the sick, feverish sleep she'd had those first couple of nights in the hospital. That sleep hadn't been as deep or as restful, her body still in pain and suffering from her system swinging from too cold to too hot.

Last night was different.

Because Cade had been there.

Why did he have to be the only thing that made her feel safe enough to let go and sleep like her body so desperately needed?

Yesterday, he'd brought her that beautiful necklace, saved her life, and called her his. He was giving her all the signs and all the words that he wanted more from her than just being his daughter's nanny, but she was so afraid of letting herself believe it.

What if he yanked the ground from underneath her again?

"Gabriella? Are you okay? You've been in there for a while," Cade called out as he knocked on the bathroom door.

As much as she wanted to hide and put off the conversation she knew she and Cade needed to have, Gabriella also knew she couldn't do that forever.

It was time to put her big girl panties on and talk to him.

He'd been patient, given her time, but yesterday she'd agreed to let him hold her, and she'd been the one to ask him to stay with her, she had to do this.

"Gabriella?" The door to the bathroom opened and Cade stepped into the room.

Their eyes met in the reflection of the mirror, and after holding her gaze for a moment, his then dipped to her chest where the bite wound was exposed.

Of course, she knew that he'd already seen it, she knew he'd been the one to find her in the hotel after she passed out, and she'd been naked at the time. But this was the first time she was awake when anyone other than herself and the medical staff saw the wound, and shame flooded through her.

"Hey." Cade stepped up close, his thumb hooking beneath her chin and nudging until she reluctantly lifted her gaze to meet his again. "Do you know that I'm in awe of you?"

"In awe of me?" she repeated, totally confused. What on earth would he have to be in awe about? That she'd shut down to the point she'd stopped eating and sleeping and not gotten herself the medical help she'd known she needed?

"Awe," he said again. "You were so brave, sweetheart. You fought, and you protected my daughter at great personal cost to yourself. Tell me what they did to you, Gabriella. Get it out."

She shook her head as best as she could with his grip on her chin, but when she went to turn away from him, he tightened his hold slightly and brushed the pad of his thumb across her bottom lip.

"Tell me, baby. Please," he whispered. "Let me share your burden."

No one had ever been there to share her burdens.

Not even her ex-husband.

The only thing he'd cared about when she'd had miscarriage after miscarriage was that she was denying him an heir. Rather than offering comfort he'd given her anger, leaving her to grieve alone.

Could she trust that Cade would be there for her now?

Or if she trusted him, would he throw it back in her face and kick her out of his life again?

"I messed up, sweetheart." His thumb brushed across her lip again, pausing in the corner of her mouth before shifting his hand so his palm cradled her cheek. "I honestly thought I was keeping you safe by getting you away from me. It wasn't fair of me to ask you to take on my problems. You were abducted because of me, Gabriella. Hurt because of me."

His other hand shifted to brush with a featherlight touch across the bite mark on her breast. Leaning down, he rested his forehead against hers and circled his arms around her, pulling her flush against his body.

"I'm sorry, Gabriella. For letting my problems touch you and for pushing you away."

There was true regret and pain in his voice, sincere remorse, was it worth clinging to anger when he'd explained and apologized several times over?

"I forgive you, Cade," she said wearily.

A sigh shuddered through him, and when his lips touched the top of her head, she gave a sigh and let go, resting her entire weight against Cade, trusting him to hold her up. His strong arms tightened, and after giving her another squeeze he scooped her up and carried her back into the bedroom.

Climbing onto the bed, he settled her on his lap the same way he'd held her the day before after she'd almost died. His body was warm and strong against hers, and he locked his arms around her giving her the security she'd been so desperately craving. The steady beating of his heart soothed her as did the rhythmic rise and fall of his chest. When his hand smoothed down her hair she snuggled closer, soaking up his care and attention like the love starved woman she was.

"The first morning they made me get down on my knees and suck them all off," she said softly, hating saying the words out loud but Cade was right, she needed someone to help carry this burden. When she'd tried to carry it alone, hiding it from everyone, all she'd ended up doing was crushing herself. If Cade hadn't found her, she likely would have died, and as much as she wanted out from the pain and fear she didn't really want to be dead.

Cade's entire body stiffened, his hand stilling.

Gabriella waited for him to pull away, to reject her.

But he didn't.

Instead, he somehow seemed to pull her closer even though she was already tucked against his chest.

"I'm so sorry they did that to you, I'm glad they're all dead," he said softly, then he pressed a kiss to her temple. "But thank you for enduring that hell for Essie."

"How did you know I did it for her?"

"Because I know you. I feel you, inside my heart, like a warm light. You calm me, soothe me, remind me that there's so much good in the world. You love my daughter like she's your own and she loves you so much. I was afraid to let you in, afraid of falling in love with you and then losing you. Afraid I couldn't survive going through that again. Then you were taken from me, and I realized I could lose you anyway. I'm prepared to take things as slowly as you want, earn your trust back, and prove I can be more than the grumpy boss you've known for the last four years. But I want it all with you. I want to get married, for you to adopt Essie, and maybe have our own kids one day."

Of course he wanted more kids.

Kids she might never be able to give him.

"Cade ... I had five miscarriages when I was married. It was why my husband divorced me," she whispered, bracing herself once again for his rejection.

"I'm so sorry, sweetheart. I hate that you went through that. But I don't care if we don't have more kids. We can try and see what happens or not. Whatever you're comfortable with. I'm fine if we only ever have

Essie, or we can adopt or foster, anything you want. So long as I have my girls I'm happy."

"Why did you give me guardianship and the house when you could have asked one of your brothers?"

"Because you're Essie's mother in her mind. You were the right person to care for her if I hadn't made it out alive. Do I have a shot with you, Gabriella? Or did I mess things up beyond repair?"

Something warm unfurled inside her at his words.

Cade wanted her.

Forever.

As his partner and Essie's mother.

Tilting her head up, she warmed further at the softness in Cade's eyes as he looked down at her. For once his gaze wasn't shuttered when he looked at her. It wasn't just warmth in his brown eyes but love as well, or at least the beginnings of it.

"You have a shot, nothing is ever messed up beyond repair, not between the two of us," she told him, and it was true. She'd loved him for too long, and she loved his daughter with her whole heart. He'd hurt her, but he was sincerely sorry and wanted to make it up to her. Withholding her forgiveness and refusing to give them a chance was only going to hurt both of them and Essie too.

"I don't deserve you, sweetheart, but I'm going to do my best to live up to your view of me."

Then he leaned down and captured her lips in a kiss she'd been dreaming about for four long years, and it was even better than she could ever have hoped for.

CHAPTER
Twenty~Two

October 3rd
8:28 P.M.

"Mommy?" Essie's mostly asleep little voice mumbled.

"Yeah, my sweet cuddle bug?" Gabriella asked, running a hand over his daughter's silky soft hair.

"You'll be here when I wake up, right?" Essie asked. Even though she had already fallen half asleep there was still a thread of anxiousness in her voice.

It had been like this every night since Gabriella was released from the hospital five days ago. They'd had a discussion on whether or not she was going to come back home with him or stay in a hotel for a while. Cade would have done his best to accept her decision, but this was where he wanted her. At home with him and his daughter where he could keep her safe, take care of her, and make sure she didn't get sick again.

Thankfully, Gabriella had decided to come home, and it was perfect.

With her back where she belonged, things weren't just back to how they used to be, they were so much better. She wasn't there as Essie's nanny, his employee, she was there as his partner. She slept in his bed, and he wasn't holding back from being affectionate even though he wasn't usually that cuddly, snuggly, kissy guy. Essie was thrilled that he and Gabriella were dating and had already told both of them that she wanted to call Gabriella mom.

Gabriella had, of course, burst into tears at his daughter's proclamation, but while he had panicked, Essie had merely pulled Gabriella into an embrace and told her she loved her and had always been her mommy.

But as wonderful as things were, it didn't mean they hadn't all walked away from the ordeal with scars. Physical and psychological. One of Essie's scars was a fear that Gabriella wouldn't be there in the morning.

"I'll be right here, cuddle bug," Gabriella assured the little girl. "And you know if you wake up during the night and you're scared or sad, you can call out and your daddy and I will come, or you can come to our room and snuggle in the bed with us."

"Okay," Essie mumbled as she rolled over and drifted off, satisfied in her five-year-old way that everything would be okay so long as Gabriella was there in the morning.

Quietly they snuck out of Essie's room and into the hall. While Gabriella was recovering well and regaining her strength, she was still a little weak and they'd been heading to bed after tucking Essie in. Expecting to do the same tonight, he was heading for the stairs to go down and make sure everything was locked up and all the lights were out when Gabriella caught his hand, stopping him.

"Thank you," she said softly. "For letting me be here and for sharing her with me."

Because she'd said those same exact words every night for the last five nights, and he'd told her every time that she didn't need to thank him for that. That Essie had been half hers pretty much from the moment she started the job and loved his daughter with the same ferocity that he did, he used her hold on his hand to his advantage.

With a tug, she came plastered up against him and he pressed their joined hands over his heart, wondering how he'd managed to hold off from acknowledging his feelings for this amazing woman for so long.

Now that he was no longer holding back, Cade found that loving

Gabriella was so much easier than he'd thought it would be. There was no competition in his heart between Gretel and Gabriella, part of him would always love Gretel, but she was his past, and Gabriella was his future.

"You know," he said slowly, dipping his head so that his lips hovered above hers, Gabriella drifted closer as his breath puffed against her plump lips. "I've already told you several times to stop thanking me and you don't seem to be getting the message."

His free hand landed on her spine and trailed its way slowly down her back until it cupped her backside. She was still too thin but was putting back on the weight she'd lost and she had a perfect little bottom, one he'd stared at a thousand times before.

Stroking the small curves, he felt her moan and shudder against his touch, pressing closer where she could no doubt feel the evidence of his arousal pressing into her stomach.

"Maybe a punishment would be a more effective method of teaching you a lesson," he said huskily. Reading her body language, not wanting to do a single thing to trigger or upset her in any way, when all he got from her was need and an arousal echoing his own he lightly tapped his hand against her backside.

Another moan tumbled from her lips and the hand that was still entwined with his tightened its grip.

"Do. Not. Thank. Me. Again. For. Sharing. My. Daughter," he said, a light smack accompanying each word. "Is she mine or ours?"

"Ours," the word escaped on a breathy moan as she wriggled in his hold.

"That's right. Ours. Who does she call mommy?"

"Me."

"Who's going to marry me one day and adopt her, making it official?" Already he was starting to plan out the perfect proposal. When he was young and even less romantic than he was now, he'd asked Gretel to marry him when he'd gotten back from basic training, no fanfare, nothing, just a ring and a question on her doorstep. This time he was going to do it right.

"I am," Gabriella said, her voice hitching with emotion.

Bringing his hand down one more time, a little harder, he then grabbed her hips and lifted her. Immediately Gabriella wrapped her legs around his waist, pinning his hard length between them, and her arms around his shoulders.

Wanting to be certain she was okay with this, they'd talked in more depth about her time being held captive and he was sure she wasn't holding back any more secrets, but he didn't want the fact that she'd had sex with him before he fired her to mean she was okay with this now.

"Sweetheart, can I—"

"You better," she said before he could even get the question out and ground her hot center against his erection.

Chuckling, he quickly carried her down the hall to their bedroom, a room Gabriella was already beginning to make her own. Her clothes now hung in the walk-in wardrobe, and her bedding and curtains had replaced his. The ragdoll that he'd continued to cling to after throwing her out once again sat on the bed, only now it sat on their bed rather than hers.

Tossing her onto said bed, Gabriella landed with a bounce and a giggle, and his heart broke wide open at the carefree sound. This was the Gabriella he wanted back, the one who was open and confident, bright and bubbly, and lit up his world.

But he was aware it would take time for her to recover from her ordeal, so moments like this were ones to cherish.

"Hurry up, Cade. You're wearing too many clothes, and I'm wearing too many clothes, and I want you to hurry up and get inside me. I've missed you and dreamed about you being mine for so long."

Unable to deny her anything, especially pleasure when she deserved all the good things in the world, he stripped out of his clothes in what had to be record time and then climbed on the bed. Taking his time removing Gabriella's clothes, he enjoyed each brush of his fingertips against her petal-soft skin, each frustrated huff she made because he wasn't moving quickly enough for her liking.

By the time he had her naked and spread out before him, he licked his lips as he appreciated every inch of her body. Even the healing wound on her left breast because it spoke of her strength and bravery.

How could she ever think that she was garbage?

She was a treasure.

His treasure.

Leaning down, he touched his lips to the bite mark.

"Cade," she whispered, her voice wavering with emotion, and when he looked at her, he saw tears shimmering in her eyes, making them appear an almost ethereal shade of green.

"You're so strong, sweetheart, so brave. I'm so in awe of you and love you so much."

A half sob escaped and then she reached up and framed his face, pulling it down so their lips met. Both poured all their feelings into that kiss and he could feel them building, filling the room with their intensity.

Without breaking the kiss, he shifted so he was spread out above her, then balanced his weight on one hand and his knees which found their place between her spread legs and swirled the pad of a finger over her bundle of nerves. Her responsive body squirmed and writhed as he alternated between teasing her entrance and then her bud.

Somehow, their kiss only deepened the more it went on, and he couldn't believe how lucky he was to have this woman for his own. To belong to her in every way.

"Cade, hurry up and get inside me, I want us to come together," Gabriella said, her voice husky with arousal as she reached between them and grabbed his length, guiding it to her center.

One thrust was all it took to bury himself deep inside her. Hooking her ankles around his hips, she drew him deeper still, and then they both began to move together. He was close but she was, too, and when he touched her where their bodies joined, she came on a scream that was swallowed by his lips.

Her internal muscles clamped around him, setting off his orgasm, and it rushed through him like a tsunami, shoving away everything else in its path until all that was left was crystal clear love. Pure and complete. Perfect.

When all that was left were the last aftershocks of pleasure, he pulled out of her and headed for the bathroom. Returning with a warm washcloth, he cleaned Gabriella up, then lifted her so he could pull back the covers and lay her down again. Tossing the cloth into the sink, he climbed into the bed and curled himself around his girl, cocooning her in an embrace, making sure she knew she was safe.

Gabriella was his to love, protect, and cherish.

His to guard and ensure she never again felt like garbage that could be thrown away.

And he intended to spend the rest of his life doing just that.

～

October 9th
11:20 A.M.

"I don't see why I have to wear this," Cade grumbled. The pout on his face was so adorable and so unlike the old Cade that Gabriella couldn't not giggle as she looked up from the sewing machine she was running like crazy. She'd lost over a month so she had a whole lot of sewing to do if she was going to be ready in time.

"What else would you wear, Daddy?" Essie asked, looking at her father like he was crazy.

"Literally anything else," Cade answered as though it were obvious.

Essie just giggled indulgently. "Silly Daddy. You have to wear this."

"I honestly don't see that I do."

"Course you do. We gots to all match because we're a family." Essie said it like she dared either of them to disagree with her.

It wasn't really the reason they were wearing these costumes for Halloween. Alice in Wonderland was Essie's favorite book since she was three. For the last two years, she'd wanted them all to dress up as characters from the book, but both of those last two years Cade had been away for Halloween, so they'd scrapped the idea. The year Essie was three, they'd gone as Cruella de Vil and a Dalmatian puppy, then last year they'd gone trick or treating with her as a witch and Essie as a black cat.

Cade would be home this year, and they were making Essie's dreams come true.

She deserved it.

Which meant Cade wasn't getting out of wearing that costume.

"I could wear something else, there are other characters in Alice in Wonderland," Cade suggested, shooting her a look that was clearly asking for her help.

Gabriella just grinned back at him.

The sooner he accepted this as his fate the happier he'd be.

"Well, I'm being Alice," Essie said, planting her hands on her hips and going full sass mode. "Did you want to be Alice, Daddy?"

Reaching out, Cade plucked up his little girl and set her on his lap, tickling her until she squealed with delight and wriggled like a little worm. "No, my princess, I don't want to go as Alice."

"Did you want to go as the Queen of Hearts?" Essie continued, in full-on sass mode today. "Cos Mommy is being the Queen."

Like it did every time the little girl called her mommy, Gabriella's heart did a little flip in her chest. Honestly, she wasn't sure which was better, Essie calling her mommy or Cade telling her he loved her.

A tie.

Definitely a tie.

How could she feel like garbage that would one day be thrown away when she had these two loving on her every second?

It would take time, but they were healing her old wounds a little more each day.

"I think Daddy would make a great queen," she teased, making Cade roll his eyes. "Well, if you don't want to be Alice, and you don't want to be the Queen of Hearts, then pray tell us what you *do* want to be."

"Anything but the White Rabbit," Cade said with an exaggerated shudder that made both her and Essie laugh.

"I guess you could be one of the singing flowers?" Gabriella suggested, and the aghast look Cade shot her way made her laugh again. It felt so good to laugh. So freeing.

"I don't think so," Cade said firmly.

"What about the King of Hearts then?" she suggested, enjoying needling Cade in a way she wouldn't have when she was just the nanny. Not that she'd ever let him walk all over her, not that he ever would have done that either, but while she was always open and honest with him, she also did her best not to blur the lines between employer and employee too much. She'd been doing her best to protect her heart, thinking she could never have Cade.

Only now she did, and she didn't have to worry about her heart any longer. It was safe with Cade.

"Ha-ha, very funny," Cade said with a roll of his eyes.

"Daddy, you could be the caterpillar, or Tweedledee," Essie suggested.

"Or Tweedledum," Gabriella added with a smirk.

"Yeah, I'm not going as Tweedledee or Tweedledum." The look Cade shot her had her pressing her legs together, it was one that said she was going to pay for this teasing tonight, in bed, after they tucked Essie in.

And she couldn't wait.

Gabriella had had no idea that she would enjoy a little bit of light spanking, but each tap of Cade's hand against her backside had sent a jolt of heat straight to her core.

"You could go as *both*, Daddy," Essie offered with an excited squirm like she thought her idea was fabulous, making them both laugh.

"Tell us what you were thinking then," she told Cade.

"I could be the Mad Hatter or the Cheshire Cat," Cade said hopefully.

"But I like the White Rabbit better, Daddy," Essie said on an almost whine. "He leads Alice into Wonderland, and he's so cute and fluffy."

"Cute and fluffy. This is what my world has been reduced to?" he said with a dramatic sigh, but deep affection was in his eyes as he looked indulgently at his daughter. While Cade didn't spoil his only child, he would go to the ends of the earth to ensure she was happy and protected.

Their lives were still uncertain, one more rapist was out there who was still a threat to the entire Charleston Holloway family, and they didn't know when the next strike would come. Although they were making costumes, they wouldn't do the usual neighborhood trick-or-treat since Cade thought it was too dangerous. Instead, they were going to go to a local nursing home that was putting on an entire Halloween experience. It would be fun, and according to Cade and the guys, an easier security job.

Still, even though she hated living in constant danger, Gabriella would much prefer to be there with Cade and Essie than off on her own.

Security had been doubled at the house, and one more hint of a plot to go after them and Cade was sending her and Essie off to join Cassandra with Delta Team. So far, the pattern had been if targeting one of them didn't pan out these men moved onto the next member of the family, which suggested either Jake or Jax were going to be next.

"Daddy! Mommy!" Essie suddenly squealed, her voice dripping excitement.

"What, cuddle bug?"

"We could go as a wedding." Essie clapped her hands and bounced on her father's lap, overcome with enthusiasm for her new idea.

"A wedding?" Gabriella asked.

"You can be the bride and daddy can be the groom because you're going to gets married someday anyway. Daddy said you were going to bes my new mommy and you said I could call you mommy, so that means you're going to get married and we're going to be a family for reals," Essie challenged, daring them to disagree.

It was true. Cade had made his intentions about their future clear, and it wasn't like they had to get to know each other or find out if they could live together without tearing each other's hair out, they'd been doing that for the last four years. She just needed some time to heal, begin recovering from her ordeal, and for the sting of Cade's rejection to soothe away. Understanding why he'd done it, agreeing to forgive and move forward, didn't automatically erase all the pain.

There was still some lingering, but Gabriella knew it was only a matter of time until she was ready to give Essie the locket, which in her mind meant agreeing to marry Cade.

Whether that was days, weeks, or months away it didn't matter.

The two people sitting beside her, looking at her with such love and adoration were everything she had ever dreamed of, everything she had ever wished for, and everything she could ever want. They were already her family, and they would be her future.

Nothing could change that.

At least she hoped not.

Because she was keeping a secret.

One that could potentially tear Cade and Essie out of her life.

"Maybe we can be that next year," she suggested, hoping the thread of worry she felt inside didn't seep out into her voice. "After your daddy and I are married for real."

Shooting her a look that said he knew something was running through her mind, Cade gave his daughter a smile. "And what would you be, pumpkin?"

Essie thought for a moment. "I can be the mini-t."

"Mini-t?" Cade asked.

"You know the person that makes them married, that says you can now kiss the bride," Essie explained.

"You mean the minister," Cade said, pronouncing the word clearly.

His daughter just shrugged. "Okay. I for sure want to do that next year," she said with all the confidence of a five-year-old who couldn't imagine changing her mind a dozen times in the next twelve months.

"Alice in Wonderland it is, guess you better keep sewing that White Rabbit costume," Cade said with a pretend sigh, then tickled his daughter again, making her squeal in delight.

As she started up the sewing machine again and watched the happy father daughter duo, Gabriella sent up another prayer, begging not to have the future and the family she longed for snatched away from her all over again.

That was something she didn't think she could survive.

CHAPTER
Twenty-Three

October 13th
12:34 P.M.

Gabriella was hiding something from him.

Cade had been certain of it for days, but so far, all his attempts to encourage her to open up had failed.

Whatever it was, she was holding onto it tightly and he wasn't sure how he was supposed to proceed.

Given that he'd already messed up once before and was lucky Gabriella was even giving him the time of day let alone had forgiven him and agreed to date him, he didn't want to push her too hard. So far, she wasn't pulling away from him, if anything they continued to grow closer with each passing day. She reached out to him for comfort during the day and curled into his side in bed each night. She was affectionate and loving, they made love after tucking Essie in, kissed during the day, talked and laughed, and shared beautiful moments with his daughter.

Nothing had changed, well it had but only for the better, but he couldn't shake this feeling there was something she was afraid to tell him.

For the life of him Cade couldn't figure out what it could be.

The longer this went on the bigger the knot in his stomach grew. It didn't feel like she was having second thoughts, but what if she was? Although he was confident she loved him and his daughter it was a lot to ask of her to remain in a dangerous situation because of them.

Maybe giving her space was the wrong thing to do. After all, he'd spent years avoiding his feelings, which hadn't done either of them any good.

Mind made up, Cade captured Gabriella's wrist as she walked past him in the kitchen, packing up after lunch. Her gaze shifted to meet his and her eyes went from curious to concerned in a heartbreaking second.

"Can we talk, sweetheart?" he asked, his tone low and soothing, attempting to show her that this didn't have to be a big deal. Whatever she was worrying about, she could just tell him and he would move heaven and earth to make it better for her.

"Yes," she whispered, allowing her gaze to drop and he felt helplessness flowing off her in waves. Whatever this was about, she'd no doubt worked it up in her head to be bigger than it actually was.

"Essie, Mom and I are just going into the other room to talk for a bit, you okay in here?" he asked his daughter who had Lego spread out all over the family room floor.

"'Kay," Essie answered vaguely, too engrossed in her game to worry about what the grownups were doing.

Keeping hold of Gabriella's hand, because he felt she might flee the second he let go, Cade guided her into the living room and onto the couch. Sitting beside her, Cade maintained his hold on her hands and brushed his thumbs across the inside of her wrists, hoping to soothe her.

"Talk to me, baby," he urged. "Something is wrong."

Her gaze met his, then skittered away, only to return again. He could sense her gathering her courage and wondered what could be so upsetting to her that she felt she needed courage to tell him about it.

After dragging in a long breath, Gabriella tugged her hands free and stood up. "Wait here for a moment, please?"

"Of course."

With a nod, she turned and hurried up the stairs. His anxiety grew, but when she returned less than a minute later, she looked like she had composed herself a little.

"I was going to give this to you tonight, but since you brought it up, here." She crossed to him and held out a small rectangle of paper.

As soon as he took it in his hand, he knew what it was. His mouth dropped open in shock and his gaze landed on her flat stomach where her hands were absently stroking.

"You're ..."

"I am. For now at least," Gabriella said in a small voice.

Right then it all clicked.

She'd told him about the miscarriages she'd had, how angry her ex would get, that she had to grieve those losses alone, and how her inability to carry to term was why her ex had divorced her.

Surely, she had to know that he would never do that to her.

Already he'd told her that he didn't care if they never had more kids, if they had biological kids, or adopted or fostered. He already had Gabriella and Essie, and they would always be enough for him.

"Come here." Grabbing hold of her wrist, he tugged her down into his lap, then placed his hands over hers, wondering at the tiny life growing inside her. He'd missed a lot of Gretel's pregnancy because of his job but he would try to be there for as much of this pregnancy as he could. "I'm guessing it was that first night before I messed up."

"Yeah. I don't know how this little one survived me being so sick, but somehow the little peanut managed it."

"Strong like his or her momma."

"I wasn't trying to keep it from you, Cade. I swear. I found out in the hospital, but I didn't think there was any future for us. If I didn't wind up losing the baby, I would have told you. Even if we weren't together, we would have figured something out. I swear I wouldn't keep your child from you because I was hurt and angry."

"Never entered my mind that you would," he assured her, dropping a kiss to her forehead.

"I didn't expect it to last, that's why I didn't say anything," she explained. "But today it's five weeks, that's as far along as I've ever gotten. I know it's not really very far, all things considered, but it felt important. Like a milestone. So I was going to give you the sonogram picture tonight after we put Essie to bed, then after we talked I thought tomorrow we could have given her the locket."

Cade froze.

Was she saying what he thought she was saying?

When they'd finally talked in the hospital, Gabriella had said they could give Essie the locket when she was ready to make things official and allow him to propose.

A slow smile slid over his face. "You sure?"

"If you are."

"Why the hell wouldn't I be? I think I've wasted enough time as it is."

"Because, Cade ... you know there's a good chance I'll miscarry ... right?"

Anxiety rolled off her again, and he pulled her against him and locked his arms around her. "Then we'll grieve together but it doesn't mean I won't want you. We're already a family, sweetheart. This." He brushed his fingertips over her stomach. "Is an addition to our family, not the glue that will hold us together. I want to be with you, I love you. This is just a little something extra that is going to turn all our lives upside down in the best way possible."

Finally, she relaxed and snuggled into him. "I really hope that winds up happening."

"Me too, sweetheart, but if it doesn't, we'll be there for one another, it won't be something you have to go through alone."

"Thank you, that means a lot to me."

Shifting his hand to trace it over the curve of her bottom, he stroked it for a moment. "I thought you already learned your lesson about not having to say thank you for the most basic things."

She giggled and nuzzled her face against his neck. "Maybe I need another lesson."

"Maybe you do, sassy girl." The enormity of the coming changes in his life filled him with an uncharacteristic excitement. "I can't believe I get to start planning the perfect proposal."

"Cade," she said seriously, taking his face between her hands. "There's no such thing. My ex flew me to Paris and proposed at the top of the Eiffel Tower. At the time, I thought it was so romantic but it was only for show. He didn't love me. It's not about trying to do it perfectly, it's about us loving each other and wanting to be together forever."

Gabriella was right. It was a gorgeous fall day, and the backyard was already a riot of autumnal color. They could go build a fire in the fire pit, make S'mores, and he could propose to Gabriella, and they could both give Essie the locket.

What could be more perfect than being with his girls, in their home, doing something they loved?

"You're right, sweetheart. Go grab your coat, and get Essie to put hers on too, then meet me outside in fifteen minutes." That should be plenty of time to get prepared.

"You don't mean you're going to—"

"I most certainly do," he assured her. Her face was so soft as she looked at him, and there was so much love, tenderness, and affection in her eyes, that his heart squeezed in his chest. He was one lucky guy.

"I love you, Cade."

"Love you back, sweetheart."

After sharing a kiss, Gabriella headed off for the family room, and he headed upstairs to retrieve the ring he'd ordered while Gabriella was in the hospital. Just as he retrieved it from where he'd hidden it in his nightstand drawer, his phone rang. Almost absently he answered it when he saw Jake's number.

"What's up?" he asked.

"My gym just got set on fire, and my best friend and I are trapped inside."

A threat to his best friend changes everything for Jake Holloway in the fifth book in the action packed and emotionally charged Prey Security: Charlie Team series!

Corrupted Lies (Prey Security: Charlie Team #5)

Also by Jane Blythe

Detective Parker Bell Series

A SECRET TO THE GRAVE

WINTER WONDERLAND

DEAD OR ALIVE

LITTLE GIRL LOST

FORGOTTEN

Count to Ten Series

ONE

TWO

THREE

FOUR

FIVE

SIX

BURNING SECRETS

SEVEN

EIGHT

NINE

TEN

Broken Gems Series

CRACKED SAPPHIRE

CRUSHED RUBY

FRACTURED DIAMOND

SHATTERED AMETHYST

SPLINTERED EMERALD

SALVAGING MARIGOLD

COCKY SAVIOR

SOME REGRETS ARE FOREVER

SOME FEARS CAN CONTROL YOU

SOME LIES WILL HAUNT YOU

SOME QUESTIONS HAVE NO ANSWERS

SOME TRUTH CAN BE DISTORTED

SOME TRUST CAN BE REBUILT

SOME MISTAKES ARE UNFORGIVABLE

LITTLE DOLLS

LITTLE HEARTS

LITTLE BALLERINA

NURSERY RHYME KILLER

FAIRYTALE KILLER

FABLE KILLER

IVORY'S FIGHT

PEARL'S FIGHT

LACEY'S FIGHT

OPAL'S FIGHT

Prey Security: Bravo Team Series

VICIOUS SCARS

RUTHLESS SCARS

BRUTAL SCARS

CRUEL SCARS

BURIED SCARS

WICKED SCARS

Prey Security: Athena Team Series

FIGHTING FOR SCARLETT

FIGHTING FOR LUCY

FIGHTING FOR CASSIDY

FIGHTING FOR ELLA

Prey Security: Charlie Team Series

DECEPTIVE LIES

SHADOWED LIES

TACTICAL LIES

VENGEFUL LIES

CORRUPTED LIES

Prey Security: Cyber Team Series

RESCUING NATHANIEL

Christmas Romantic Suspense Series

THE DIAMOND STAR

CHRISTMAS HOSTAGE

CHRISTMAS CAPTIVE

CHRISTMAS VICTIM

YULETIDE PROTECTOR

YULETIDE GUARD

YULETIDE HERO

HOLIDAY GRIEF

HOLIDAY LOSS

HOLIDAY SORROW

Conquering Fear Series (Co-written with Amanda Siegrist)

DROWNING IN YOU

OUT OF THE DARKNESS

CLOSING IN

About the Author

USA Today bestselling author Jane Blythe writes action-packed romantic suspense and military romance featuring protective heroes and heroines who are survivors. One of Jane's most popular series includes Prey Security, part of Susan Stoker's OPERATION ALPHA world! Writing in that world alongside authors such as Janie Crouch and Riley Edwards has been a blast, and she looks forward to bringing more books to this genre, both within and outside of Stoker's world. When Jane isn't binge-reading she's counting down to Christmas and adding to her 200+ teddy bear collection!

To connect and keep up to date please visit any of the following

Made in United States
Cleveland, OH
08 April 2025

15914795R00141